Where the Rhythm Takes You

Where the Rhythm Takes You

SARAH DASS

BALZER + BRAY
An Imprint of HarperCollins*Publishers*

Balzer + Bray is an imprint of HarperCollins Publishers.

Where the Rhythm Takes You
Copyright © 2021 by Sarah Dass
All rights reserved. Printed in the United States of America.
No part of this book may be used or reproduced in any manner whatsoever without
written permission except in the case of brief quotations embodied in critical articles
and reviews. For information address HarperCollins Children's Books, a division of
HarperCollins Publishers, 195 Broadway, New York, NY 10007.
www.epicreads.com

Library of Congress Control Number: 2020951734
ISBN 978-0-06-301852-5

Typography by Jessie Gang
21 22 23 24 25   PC/LSCH   10 9 8 7 6 5 4 3 2 1

First Edition

For Mummy,
Who bought all the books
Who listened to all the stories
Who always believed

In loving memory of my father.
I wish you could have seen how all the bedtime stories led to this.

Where the Rhythm Takes You

Tabanca. /taˈbaŋka/ *noun*

A West Indian term that refers to a deep, yearning desire
   that consumes a person's mind and spirit and leaves
   them a lost, aching shell of their former self.

An insatiable longing. A need for a particular person who
   does not or no longer feels the same.

Unrequited love.

The worst.

ONE

When I was younger, the holidays promised freedom. No school. No early mornings. Nothing but heat, the beach, sunburned lips, sweat-soaked clothes, and sea-scented hair. There were lazy morning lie-ins with nowhere to go, nothing to be done, the hours of the day allowed to unravel without aim or urgency.

When I was younger, it also meant music. And where there was music, there was Him.

> *The first night I see she cross the room*
> *The type of gyal that know jus' what to do*
> *Meh eyes stick, cyah look away*
> *The way she move make me want to stay*

I tried to ignore the song, and the prickle of annoyance it inspired, as I skirted around the edge of the hotel's pool. My shoes skidded a little, even as I avoided the worst of the puddle and the

Caution: Wet Floor sign. I glanced around the deck. A few loud twentysomethings clustered around the bar, but my father wasn't there.

Where was he?

My phone vibrated in my pocket. I didn't have to look to know it was my best friend, Olivia. I didn't answer. She'd already messaged seven times that morning. I didn't know what else to do to make her understand I was busy.

And the girls say
Let me make your day
Make my day
Make every day a holiday

"Hey, Jerald." I approached the barman. He had an empty glass in hand, a checkered rag tossed over his shoulder. In his late forties, he had a broad build and full cheeks that gave him a boyish appearance. "Have you seen my father?"

He spun toward me. "Not since this morning."

The days alive, nights are wild
I know you'll never forget
If you think this is real bacchanal
You ain't seen nothing yet

"Can we skip this one?" I pointed toward the speaker.

"You en like the song, Boss Lady?"

I rolled my eyes at my unofficial title. *Boss Lady.* The staff at the Plumeria Hotel seemed to find it hilarious. I'd been hearing it for as long as I could remember, probably dating back to my days in diapers. The irony was that they never called Mummy—the real Boss Lady—that. Now that she was gone, the name only reminded me how little I measured up.

Jerald laughed. "I thought this was what all the young people listening to."

"Not me." I reached over the bar and snatched a maraschino cherry out of the open container in front of him.

"Ay!" He yanked the rag off his shoulder and swatted at me.

I'd already retreated out of reach, laughing as I popped the fruit between my teeth.

No rhyme, no reason
No hesitation, no fear
Jus' leggo, jus' listen
Let de rhythm take you there

Once again, I wondered if I could get away with banning DJ Bacchanal songs from the property. The only thing that stopped me from trying was that I knew I'd have to explain why, and as far as I was concerned, that can of worms could stay shut.

I tossed the cherry stem into a bin behind the bar and returned to my most pressing problem—my father.

The steps from the deck led onto the main lawn. Out here, the scent of earlier rain still clung to the air. I trudged across the freshly mown grass, the earth soft and damp beneath my feet.

Finally, I spotted Daddy fishing at the lookout point—a low-lying seaside cliff suspended about ten feet above the water. Overhead, the midmorning sky held clear. The Caribbean water below burned a rich sapphire blue. The tide had rolled back just enough to reveal the full arc of the bay on our right, the horizon stretched out on our left.

Daddy wore a button-down shirt printed with a riot of parrots, their multicolored wings raised in midflight. Unfortunately, this was far from the most embarrassing outfit he owned. In fact, I'd long suspected he'd amassed the most horrible wardrobe on earth on purpose. It was the only explanation I accepted.

Daddy held a wiggling fish. Its silvery scales glimmered in the sunlight. The species was beautiful but inedible. He threw it back into the ocean.

I jumped straight to the point.

"Daddy, please explain to me why there's a booking for the villa? For three weeks? Under *your* name?"

Daddy smiled. His dark-brown fingers carefully baited the hook before casting it out. He held the fishing line between his thumb and forefinger, giving it just enough length before pinching it tightly. The ancient, rusted metal reel hung around his arm. No matter how many new, expensive fishing rods people gave him over the years, he seemed determined to use the steel relic. He said it was something about the feel and pull of the line.

"Calm y'self, Reyna," he said. "Is a favor for Jake."

"Jake?" Why did my brother-in-law want to rent the most

expensive accommodation at the hotel? He and my half sister, Pam, had a whole house of their own.

"He asked me to do it for his sisters," Daddy said. "Don't worry, they the ones paying. They jus' thought is better the booking not under their name."

I opened my mouth, then shut it. The wind, which seemed refreshing seconds earlier, now felt strong enough to blow me over. "Daddy!"

My father startled, whipping around to look at me. "What?"

"Are you saying the booking is for Jake's sisters? As in Eliza and Hailee Musgrove? Those sisters?"

"He has other sisters?" he asked slowly, though we both knew Jake did not.

"This is a big deal! How could you not tell me?"

Hailee Musgrove was a supermodel, and Eliza (from what I could tell) an influencer on Instagram and YouTube. Neither profession inspired any more than indifference from me, but for millions of people, they were undoubtedly a Big Deal. I was supposed to meet them for the first time at Pam and Jake's wedding a year ago, but in typical Pam and Jake fashion, the couple canceled everything at the last second and eloped without warning.

"I didn't realize you were a fan," Daddy said.

I snorted. "Not particularly." But I didn't need to be a fan to know this would be great for the hotel.

"Be nice nah," Daddy warned.

I folded my arms and sniffed. "I am always nice."

Daddy didn't say anything, but he looked doubtful. "Is just

going to be Jake's sisters and a few of their friends staying at the villa. No reason to make a fuss."

I checked the time on my phone. There was much to do. So much fuss to make. "You should've told me before." Like the very second Jake asked for the booking.

"You're doing too much as it is." Daddy waved a hand. "I'm sure William took care of it—it is his job."

I gritted my teeth.

William. The new reservations manager.

I highly doubted that whatever *William* did to prepare was enough. For one thing, he definitely hadn't followed Mummy's checklists for preparing the villa, or her protocols for hosting high-profile guests. I knew that because I hadn't had a chance to show him yet.

"Actually, Pumpkin." Daddy started to pull up the fishing line. "Is a good t'ing you remind me. Their plane must be here by now. We should get ready to greet them."

My stomach dropped. "They're here already? The booking is for tonight."

Daddy eyed me warily, probably noticing the rising alarm in my voice, on my face. "They . . . called yesterday to ask for an early check-in."

"Daddy!"

"Is just a few hours early. Is not like someone else staying in the villa."

I spun around and sprinted toward the main building. "That is not the problem!"

TWO

I made it to the lobby in record time. Speeding past the front desk, I ignored William—the traitor—when he called out to me, and barged into Daddy's office. During her last days at the hotel, Mummy made tons of helpful notes. She'd thought Daddy and I would need them when we took over. As far as I knew, Daddy hadn't given them more than a quick read, whereas I'd studied them like a bible. Most I could recite by heart, but it was so rare for someone to stay at the villa, much less a celebrity, I couldn't remember the ones I needed today very well.

My phone buzzed. I checked it quickly and saw it was Olivia again.

Buy you lunch? I miss your face

As much as I appreciated her attempt to bribe, flatter, and induce guilt in so few words, I really couldn't. Sorry. Busy

Her reply was quick. U always busy :(

I set the phone on the desk and logged on to the computer. I'd just pulled up the documents I needed when William marched in.

"Didn't you hear me calling you?" He stopped on the other side of the desk, a clipboard tucked under his arm. He set a hand on his hip, his bright-yellow shirt popping against his dark-blue Plumeria blazer. "What happened to you? You look *terrible*."

I glared at him over the top of the computer. I didn't need to check to know the wind at the lookout point had caused my curls to break free of my hair tie. Instead of charmingly wind-swept, I probably looked as frantic as I felt.

"Did you finish preparing the villa?" I asked.

"Do you know what happened to the contractors I hired this morning?" he countered without missing a beat.

I straightened up. "You mean the contractors you hired *behind my back*?"

"Answer the question."

"You answer mine first."

I folded my arms, and so did he.

Twenty-four-year-old William had joined the Plumeria staff about four months ago. He came into his job hot, pitching a hundred ideas for improvements and upgrades. Months later he still hadn't given up on his plans. He didn't seem to understand that things around here were done a certain way, and had been since Mummy ran the place. It was getting to the point where he'd surpassed being an Annoyance and edged into Pain-in-the-Butt territory.

"Of course I got the villa ready." He rolled his eyes, breaking first. "I had it cleaned and aired out since Tuesday."

"What about the light bulbs? You always forget—"

"Had them checked and replaced where necessary. Now tell me what you did."

I shrugged. "I don't know what you're talking about."

"Don't try that. Your father signed off on those contractors. The job was already paid for."

I took in that news with a pinch of irritation. Daddy and I were going to have a chat later.

"Now the workmen have all disappeared," William said. "And the company's not taking my calls. I know you did something."

I tried not to smile. It wasn't easy. "I simply explained to them that we no longer needed their services."

And that there was no one named William Ellison working for us.

A little extreme, I know. But he'd been trying to tear down the gazebo—*my gazebo*. The small hexagonal structure where my parents had been married. The one where I'd held three birthday parties, won two Easter egg hunts, and had my first kiss. The place I used to hide when I needed a break from the guests, the staff, Daddy—everyone.

Okay, so maybe the structure of the gazebo wasn't technically "stable" or whatever. It was still mine. William had no right to look in its direction, much less break it down.

"The gazebo is a lost cause," William said. "The foundation is weak. The ground can't support it. There's no point in sinking money into something that's literally sinking. One way or another, that thing's coming down."

"If that's what you want to think, fine." I waved my hand in a circular *wrap it up* motion. We didn't have time for this. "We've had this argument already. You never win. Stop pouting."

William's jaw ticked. "I do not pout."

"Sure you don't." I checked the time on my computer. "For now, let's run through this checklist for preparing the villa. I need to make sure you didn't miss anything."

"There's no time for that." He frowned, then crossed the room to the window that overlooked the main entrance. "They'll be here any moment."

"Just sit down, please. We'll make use of whatever time we've got. It may be a lot, if they got stuck in customs."

"Actually, you've got two minutes." He pulled two slats of the blinds apart. "Or less. They're pulling into the driveway now."

I ran for the door, then circled back to the computer. I'd send a copy of the list to my phone, then check the villa on my own. "Can you stall them?" I asked William. "Take them on a tour of the grounds, show them the path to the beach—"

"What the hell?"

I startled, surprised by his tone.

William pulled the blinds farther apart. His nose pressed against the glass as if ready to push right through. "Is this some kind of joke?"

"What?" I asked, confused.

"Is that Hailee Musgrove? What would Hailee Musgrove be doing here?"

Oh. That. I rolled my eyes. "The same reason everyone comes

here, I'd imagine." I uploaded the files to the cloud.

"This is crazy," he said.

"Isn't it?" Part of me wanted to hang around just to watch the stuffy reservations manager completely unravel, but I had no time for that. I headed for the door. "Can you distract them for me or what?"

"And . . . there's Eliza Musgrove," he said, ignoring or not hearing me. He sounded like he was in pain. "I can't believe this. And Leonardo Vale too? DJ Bacchanal!"

Wait. What?

I joined him at the window. At the entrance to the hotel, two black SUVs idled on the roundabout. Three of the porters were removing and stacking several pieces of designer luggage from the trunk. I recognized Hailee easily, her long, lithe frame towering over everyone. She wore ripped jeans and a T-shirt with a logo too faded to be read. As I watched, she tossed her inky-black shoulder-length hair and locked arms with someone, pulling him into view.

No. Way.

My hands shook as I pried the blinds farther apart. William was right. It *was* Leonardo Vale. The front man for DJ Bacchanal stood in front of my hotel, smiling at Hailee Musgrove. And they weren't alone.

I also spotted Fish—obviously not his real name. The mystery of why he'd chosen to call himself that eluded even the most dedicated fans. At that moment, Fish was at the entrance to my hotel, precariously sitting on one of the larger suitcases, his silver-blue hair falling over his eyes. He was sleepily slumped over the raised handle until Eliza Musgrove poked him on the forehead, startling him upright.

Unlike the rest of the group, Eliza didn't look like she'd spent hours on multiple planes, but like she'd jumped right off a magazine page. She seemed to be one of the few people who could pull off a romper; her waist-length hair in a flawless high ponytail that would've made Ariana Grande take notice.

And then there was Him. The third and final member of DJ Bacchanal.

He wore fitted blue jeans and a short-sleeved white T-shirt—a deceptively simple outfit that probably cost more than everything in his old wardrobe put together. And yet, for all his polish, I'd recognize him anywhere.

Aiden.

It had been so long since I'd seen him in person.

Even from a distance, I could see he'd changed. Where he'd once been narrow and wiry, his shoulders and arms had broadened with muscle. His hair, which he used to keep buzzed short, had been left to grow into tight black curls. I'd always told him he'd look great if he let it grow, and I was right. Someone more convincing than me must've gotten to him.

"Okay!" William said in a high-pitched voice. "I—I guess I'll go welcome them? Are you coming?"

I let out a laugh, like a bark. It was sharp and hard. It startled both of us. He'd completely forgotten my plan to check the villa, though to be honest, I didn't care anymore. "No, I don't think so.

12

You go ahead." I flicked my wrist in the direction of the window. "I'm sure you can take care of it. It's your job, after all."

"It's my . . . what the hell? Since when?"

"Isn't it?"

"Yes, but you've never thought so." William gaped at me. "Are you sick? You're scaring me."

I looked back at the window. "Stop stalling."

"I'm not stalling. I'm concerned."

Outside, Aiden hesitated next to the van, squinting up at the hotel's name emblazoned across the arch of the entrance. Why was he here? After we'd last spoken, I'd more or less resigned myself to the fact that I'd never see him again. I thought he'd done the same.

As if he'd heard my thoughts, his attention swung to my window. I jumped backward, letting the blinds snap back into place.

"You know I was only joking earlier," William said. "You don't look *that* terrible. If that's why you don't want to—"

"That's not why," I said, but I reflexively reached for my ponytail of messy curls.

Now that William had put the thought in my head, I realized Aiden absolutely could not see me like this. Not when we hadn't seen each other in two years. Not when he looked every inch the celebrity he'd grown up to be.

The office started to feel incredibly small. The walls too close.

I needed to get out of there.

"Go on." I hoped William couldn't hear the strain in my voice. "Unless you—you can't handle it on your own."

His spine stiffened. "Of course I can. I'm a professional." He scowled and marched toward the office door. "I certainly do not need a seventeen-year-old to do my job for me."

"Sure. You keep telling yourself that."

I wasn't surprised when he shut the door a little harder than necessary.

Finally.

Between gathering my things, I messaged Olivia. Still want to see my face?

Always, she answered.

THREE

When DJ Bacchanal first took off, I followed their journey closely.

Their success started with a simple upload to SoundCloud. Aiden and Fish, two no-name teenagers with tons of talent and a dream. By the time I'd discovered their song, "Hyperbolic" had gone viral, the boys already signed to a record label.

Within a few weeks, they'd rereleased the song, shot a video, and welcomed a new member, Leonardo Vale. "Hyperbolic" went to number one on several Billboard charts around the world, including in the US, and it parked there for six weeks. DJ Bacchanal became the hottest new act of the year, and the Grammy Award sealed it.

Their overnight success was wild. Aiden—the boy from down the street, the boy who cried during *Love & Basketball*, the boy who'd once bought me too many bags of red mango when I was sick because he knew I liked them—had a Grammy.

For six months, I watched every one of their interviews, read every article, listened to every song. I'd picked apart every lyric, cheered for every award. I was consumed by a potent mix of pride and pain, until I realized that these feelings I thought were bittersweet were actually toxic. Why did I need to know what he was wearing? Where he hung out? Who he was dating?

He'd moved on with his life; it was past time I did the same.

So I tried to cut him and DJ Bacchanal out of my life, which wasn't easy with them playing on the radio every ten minutes. Still, I tried, avoiding every mention of Aiden and the band, eventually blocking all outlets for celebrity news.

Of course, that meant I'd missed a few of the latest developments. Some of which had suddenly become terrifyingly relevant.

"How did you not know?" Olivia braced her hands on the counter. Behind her, Grace—Olivia's aunt and the owner of Grace's Seaside Grill—shuffled past the window to the kitchen. "Hailee Musgrove and Leonardo Vale have been together for a while now. It was pretty big news when it came out."

I pointed my fork at her. "You could've warned me."

"I thought you knew! Besides, whenever I bring up DJ Bacchanal, you get this look on your face—yeah, that one. It's not a good look, Reyna. I'd rather not deal with it."

I wasn't sure what she thought my face was doing, but I made an effort to stop. Sometimes I hated that she could read me so well.

When Olivia and I met, our first year of secondary school, we hated each other. As a gifted child, I was told repeatedly my talent for painting made me special, so meeting someone else my age who was just as gifted—or possibly more so—didn't go down well. She'd apparently felt the same.

We were rivals right up to the day Olivia got a low grade because her painting didn't address the assigned theme. I thought the mark was unfair, the piece was great anyway, and I told her so after class. We'd been friends ever since, even though elements of the rivalry still remained.

"Well, now I have to deal with it," I muttered, picking at my box of fried fish and seasoned fries. The lunch Olivia had used to bribe me here had gotten cold.

Aiden was here. In Tobago. In my hotel.

I still couldn't wrap my head around it.

"What am I going to do?" I wondered aloud, not expecting an answer.

Naturally, Olivia couldn't resist. "It's obvious, isn't it?" She put her hands on her hips. "You need to—"

"Olivia!" Grace dropped a food box on the window ledge. "I hope my business isn't getting in the way of your chat."

"No worries." Olivia smiled brightly, retrieving the box. "But Lord knows, it is not easy in this rush." She tipped her head toward the three people in the seating area. "Somehow we'll manage."

Grace's eyes narrowed. "Look, nah," she warned, her tone stern but her lips twitched with the start of a smile. "I done with yuh back chat. When it is you leaving for London again?"

"Lucky for you, just a few more weeks." Olivia's eyes met mine, and her smile dimmed at little. She looked down to read the receipt attached to the box.

I hated that she felt like she couldn't talk about London around me. But I was also thankful when she didn't.

"Forty-two!" she shouted toward the seating area.

A young woman dressed head-to-toe in Nike athletic wear collected the container.

When she left, I asked Olivia, "You were saying, I should—what?"

She blinked at me, confused for a second. Then it seemed to click. "Oh, yeah. I was saying, you should talk to him. Obviously. This is your chance to apologize. Get closure, so you can finally move on."

"I have moved on."

"Really?" She leaned against the counter. "Is that why you turn down every man jack who shows an interest in you? Because you've moved on?"

I didn't like where this conversation was going. "That's not true."

"You remember what happened with James Persad?"

"He was just joking around."

"Clinton Huntly?"

"I think he was drunk."

"Xavier Whatever-his-last-name?"

"You know how he is. He's naturally flirty."

"Naturally flirty?" she repeated, her nose wrinkled as if the

phrase carried a stench. "Please explain to me what is naturally flirty? An' how *for months*, he only did it around you."

"You're being ridiculous," I said. She was making it sound like I had guys falling for me left and right, which was not true at all. That didn't mean over the past few years there hadn't been a few interested. I usually pretended not to notice until they stopped. It was easier. Simpler. Safer.

Because I'd already been there, done that. I'd loved and lost, experienced heartbreak so intense I still felt the echoes of it today. The idea of putting myself out there, doing it all over again, wasn't just daunting. It was terrifying.

"Why are you so concerned about my love life anyway?" I asked Olivia.

"I'm not. I'm using your lack of one to prove a point."

"The point being . . . ?"

"You are not over Aiden!"

"Yes, I am," I said firmly.

Olivia threw her hands up. "Okay then. Prove it. Right here, right now."

"How?" I asked, with a sinking feeling.

"Number forty-three. The guy who ordered the shark and bake." She pointedly glanced toward the seating area. "He's not bad, right? Ask for his number. Or even better—ask him to stick around and have lunch with him."

I looked over to the guy. He was good looking, sure. But this whole thing felt forced and off-putting. "I can't have lunch with him. I'll need to head back to the hotel soon."

"Then just get his number," she insisted. "Or give him yours. Try a t'ing, nah."

"Olivia . . ."

"Forty-three!" she shouted.

"Olivia," I whispered through clenched teeth. "Don't."

She bowed her head to whisper back. "Admit you're not over Aiden and that you need to talk to him."

"I *am* over Aiden, and I do *not* need to talk to him."

"Then put your game face on. You've got to get Forty-three's number."

"I'll leave."

"Too late. You'll look rude." She straightened up, smiling at the customer. "Hi! So sorry, I made a mistake. Your order's not ready yet. But—hey, my friend here was just saying you look familiar. Have you been here before?"

Number Forty-three took a few seconds to answer. I couldn't blame him. I felt steamrolled as well.

"I have been here before," he said. There was a note of hesitation in his voice, but a glance at his face suggested it was born out of confusion rather than reluctance. He was smiling, amused. "But that's not how I know Reyna."

I coughed, surprise making me choke on nothing. When I cleared my throat, I asked, "You know my name?" I did not recognize him.

"I'm Nicholas. But I don't think you'd remember me." His eyes crinkled in a way that suggested he was a little embarrassed. "I was a year ahead of you in primary school. We never really interacted, but you were a legend after the Ibis Incident. After that, the whole school knew you."

"Ibis Incident?" Olivia asked.

I'd never heard it called that, but I knew what he meant. It was in primary school, a few years before Olivia and I met.

"The school was having an open house," he told her. "Some of us were asked to paint something for a small exhibition in the art room. The new teacher, a pretentious old man who thought he was critiquing master painters rather than ten-year-olds, decided Reyna's submission—a painting of a scarlet ibis—wouldn't be exhibited. He accused her of cheating. The painting was so good, she couldn't possibly have done it without help from an adult."

"What the hell?" Olivia frowned at me. "You never told me about this."

I shrugged. At the time, I remembered being embarrassed; the teacher lecturing me in front of the whole class about lying. When I'd gotten home that day, I went straight to my room. When Mummy asked what was wrong, I didn't even need to pretend I had a stomachache.

"So, what happened?" Olivia asked.

"The open house happened," Nicholas said. "Reyna's parents noticed her painting wasn't there, and the art teacher filled them in. They all start arguing. So Reyna, right there, in the art room, in front of everyone, finds a sketch pad and starts to paint another scarlet ibis. It was even better than the first one."

"No, it wasn't," I said.

It wasn't. There was no way it could have been. The first version had taken me weeks to get just right. It couldn't compare to something painted under the scrutiny of dozens of parents, teachers, and my classmates. I'd planned to let the entire thing go, but I'd seen the hint of doubt in Mummy's eyes and I knew I needed to do something.

I'd done my best to re-create the ibis. It wasn't great, but it was good enough to leave little doubt I'd done the original. When the art teacher apologized, Mummy had looked so relieved. Daddy had gotten the original painting framed and mounted it on the wall behind our couch.

"Okay, maybe it wasn't." Nicholas laughed, but there was a strained note in it. "I don't know, I never saw the original. But it was great for a ten-year-old. You must be insanely good now."

"I don't do that anymore." I used a napkin to wipe my mouth.

"Do what?"

"Paint." I stuck the fork into the food box and closed it. I'd had enough.

"Really? That's a shame. I was just going to ask if you wanted to join my after-school initiative." He shuffled his feet, pulling out his wallet. "A group of us volunteer twice a week to work with primary schoolers on their homework, or do fun activities like arts and crafts. It's mostly to keep the kids busy while their parents are still at work." He held out a card to me.

I took it and offered it to Olivia without looking at it. "Olivia's who you need. Now she's a painter. In fact, she's going to the University of Arts in London this September."

"Congrats." He sounded impressed. And he should have been—it was impressive.

"Thanks." Olivia glanced at me quickly, then backed away to retrieve a food box from the window. She looked uncomfortable, but that didn't stop her from smiling. It was like she couldn't help it. She set the box in front of Nicholas.

"But that means you'll be in London." Nicholas pulled the box toward him. "We only run during the school year."

Oh, yeah. Right.

I offered the card back to him.

He shook his head. "No, you keep it. In case you change your mind."

So Olivia would be learning from some of the best artists in the world while I taught kids to finger paint? Not likely. But rather than say that, I just wanted him to drop it. "I'll think about it."

"Great." Satisfied with that, he picked up his box, smiled, and left.

Once he was out of earshot, Olivia asked me, "Are you really not painting?"

I hopped off the stool and gathered my things. "Technically, I got his number." I held up the card before dropping it into my purse where I planned to forget it. "It counts."

"Reyna . . ." Her shoulders sagged.

"I'm going to head back to the hotel."

"And you're going to talk to Aiden?"

I didn't bother answering.

"Aren't you at least curious about why he's back here? It must be for a reason. What do you have to lose by asking?"

I almost laughed. What did I have to lose? Where to start?

My dignity? My head? My heart?

No, not my heart.

I'd been there, done that. Never again.

FOUR

Why was Aiden here?

The question haunted me. It was the last thing on my mind before bed, my first thought when I woke up. Olivia was right. I hated to admit it, but she was. I needed to know why he was here, if only to stop that tiny spark of something that made me wonder if he was back because of me. The very idea was silly, the likelihood near impossible, but the thought was still there.

That being said, I didn't have to talk to him right away. Now that I'd seen sense, a conversation seemed inevitable, but I needed some time to prepare first. I planned to write a script, too much unsaid between us for me to improvise on the spot. But coming up with the right words was more in line with his talents than mine.

While I figured it out, I avoided him and his group, spending most of the following day in Daddy's office. If I needed to go outside for any reason, I was fast, careful not to linger out in the open. Most important, I went nowhere near the villa.

It was only on my way home that evening that I realized Aiden might also be avoiding me. Not that I'd hoped or expected him to seek me out, but if he'd wanted to find me he could. I didn't know how to feel about the fact that he didn't.

As I walked up my driveway, a flurry of text messages came from Jake:

HELP!!!

Please

If you're free I mean

If you can't that's fine

No rush

I sighed and turned around. The air was pleasantly cool, so I decided to walk over to Pam and Jake's house. It was only five minutes away.

That evening, the brightly colored houses of Shell Haven village glowed in the pinkish light of the setting sun. Our house, the first on our street, was a three-bedroom bungalow painted burnt orange with white accents, the frangipani trees on our lawn bracketing the front gate.

On my way to Pam and Jake's, I called out to neighbors enjoying the evening breeze on their front porches. A handful of boys played football in the middle of the street, pausing for a couple seconds to let a car pass before they resumed their game. Yard fowls clucked from somewhere in the bushes, water trickling through the moss-coated drains that lined the roads.

At the end of my street stood the old Chandra house. Upon seeing it, I picked up my pace, trying my best to ignore the memories it brought back. No one had lived there since Aiden's grandfather moved to a nursing home in Trinidad. It was only slightly bigger than a shack, poised atop thick stilts that kept the front door level with the road. The body of the structure tipped forward slightly, cracked and worn but somehow still strong enough to hover above the sloping plot of land below.

Did Aiden plan to visit the old house? Would he be popping over to the sister island to see his grandfather? I could never tell if he and the old man were close. They used to bicker constantly, but they must have had some bond since Aiden spent so many of his school holidays here.

At the end of the street, I took a left and soon arrived at Pam and Jake's gate. Their house, a Spanish-style two-story with clay roof tiles and arched doorways, was perfect for the family of three (soon to be four). They'd been lucky to find someone selling a house, much less one so close to us. Here, houses were usually passed from one generation to the next. Daddy was the one who'd heard about the sale before anyone else, and Pam and Jake snatched it up.

Pam and I hadn't been close growing up, partly because she lived in Canada, but also because of the ten-year age gap between us. She was still a baby when my father's first wife, Aunty Helen, had gotten a job running an investment firm in Alberta.

As I opened the gate, Pam and Jake's rottweilers, Midnight and Terror, bounded toward me. I pushed the gate just enough to slip through without letting the little nightmares out. Terror— the more affectionate of the two—nuzzled her face against my thigh, her stub of a tail twitching wildly. I gave her a quick scratch behind the ears and relocked the gate. "Keep up the good work," I told the pair before jogging up the staircase to the front porch.

Jake answered the door wearing yellow dishwashing gloves, a tea towel slung over his shoulder. His pinched features relaxed when he saw it was me. I admit it did a lot for my mood to know my presence was appreciated.

"Oh, thank God." He ushered me in. "I'm so, so sorry to call you over, but I didn't know what else to do. Our usual babysitter has exams and—"

"Who are you talking to?" Pam called from the living room.

"Look who came over, babe," Jake said as we rounded the bamboo screen that separated the entrance from the living room. "Isn't this a nice surprise? Reyna came to visit."

Pam's dark-brown eyes narrowed. She sat on the wicker love seat, a loose peasant top disguising the slight bump of her stomach, her slipper-clad feet propped on the coffee table. Kesha, my niece, rested her head against Pam's shoulder. The last light of the day spilled through the window, illuminating them softly. I felt a thrill of inspiration, my first instinct to memorize and reproduce the scene on canvas later. But then I remembered there was no point. I'd never paint it.

"Reyna, you won't believe this," Jake said. "We were just talking about you. Crazy coincidence, right?"

"Jake," Pam said drily. "Look me in the eye—look me *right in the eye* and tell me you didn't ask Reyna to come over."

Jake wrung the towel in his hands. His gaze dropped to the floor.

Pam sucked her teeth. "Reyna, I'm so sorry. You didn't have to come over. We've got it covered."

"Now, hold on—" Jake started to protest.

"You go, and I'll stay home with Kesha," Pam said. "We don't need a babysitter. Case closed."

Hearing her name, Kesha raised her head. She blinked, her whiskey-brown eyes bleary. At a glance, the resemblance between mother and daughter might be missed. Jake was Jordanian and French Canadian, so he and Kesha shared warm beige skin and wavy dark-brown hair. Like me, Pam was Afro-Caribbean with jet-black hair and skin a rich shade of brown. But upon looking closer, it was difficult to miss the fact the Pam and Kesha had the same face with high cheekbones, upturned eyes, and full lips.

"Case *reopened*," Jake said, because he'd been a dad for all of eighteen months but already had the jokes down. "It's been a year since I've seen my sisters. As exhausting as they can be, I do want to see them." He fiddled with the towel. "I'd just really prefer if you came with me."

Pam's lips pinched. She looked like she was trying not to laugh at his distress. "It's just one quiet dinner at Le Tropique with your sisters. I'm sure it'll be fine."

Jake snapped off the gloves and dropped them on the counter. "You know there's no such thing as a quiet anything when it comes to my sisters. You know they're going to spend the whole dinner guilt-tripping me for moving here. Especially Eliza."

"Really?" Pam asked. "I would've expected it from Hailee. Even though you're older than her, I have noticed Hailee likes to treat you more like a son than her brother."

Jake huffed. "They both do. But Hailee's the kind, capable mom. Eliza's the type of mom that would try to run your life for you."

"And you want me to come along so they can guilt-trip me too?" Pam snorted. "No thank you. I get enough of that from my actual mom. She still ends each call with *are you sure about leaving the university? Really?*"

I bit my lip. It was a good question. Until two years ago, Pam had been on track to complete a PhD in theoretical physics, and Jake was a manager at one of his father's car dealerships. Then, out of nowhere, they decided to toss it all aside, elope, move to Tobago, and start a family. Now Jake worked as a scuba instructor, and Pam taught physics at a secondary school. I wondered about their life decisions too.

"Come on," Jake pleaded. "You know they like you more than me. They're not nearly so bad when you're around." He shot me a silent, wide-eyed plea for help.

"Go on." I approached Pam, arms extended. "Save your husband from his teenage sisters. I'll stay with Kesha."

"You do realize you're seventeen, right?" Pam frowned. "It's Friday night. You should be going out with friends, having fun."

"But spending time with Kesh is fun."

Pam shook her head. "You need a little more excitement in

your life, Rey. Maybe you should be the one going out with the girls and their friends tonight."

The thought struck me as so ridiculous, I laughed aloud. That was literally the last thing I wanted to do. Then I realized, she'd mentioned Hailee and Eliza's friends, and my laughter died. I'd thought the dinner was with the sisters alone.

I fought to keep my tone level. "Are they coming to pick you up here or are you meeting them at the restaurant?"

"Oh, we're meeting them there," Jake said firmly. "I am not ready to show them the house yet. They'll be nice and complimentary at first, then before you know it, they'll try to give it a makeover."

The knot in my chest eased.

"Sounds like it's all set then." I held out my arms. "Hand over the baby and get out."

Pam passed Kesha to me. "Fine, if you insist. It's not like I wanted to turn down a dinner where the food doesn't go flying across the table."

Jake mouthed the words *thank you*.

I laughed and brushed a loose eyelash off Kesha's cheek. "We're going to have so much fun. Isn't that right, Kesh."

Pam sighed, but she still rose to go get dressed. By seven o'clock, she and Jake were ready and about to leave.

Pam shuffled out of the bedroom. She wore a high-waisted, white cotton dress. Chunky blue beads dripped from her ears and circled her neck and wrists. She looked fantastic. Jake followed a few steps behind, dressed in a green short-sleeved shirt, faded black slacks, and sneakers—which was about as formal as I'd ever seen him. For the record, this was the guy who'd worn jeans to his daughter's christening.

"Call us if anything comes up," Jake said as he and Pam headed toward the front door. "I'm serious. Any problems at all."

Pam hooked her arm through her husband's and pulled him out the door. "Come on, babe. They'll be waiting on us."

"Even if you're not sure it's a problem," Jake continued to tell me as Pam pushed him into the car. "Just call. We'll come home right away!"

Kesha and I waved them off and blew kisses from the open doorway.

FIVE

After a rough dinner, where Kesha seemed determined to get food everywhere but in her mouth, and a bath that nearly flooded the second-floor bathroom, putting Kesha to sleep almost felt too easy. I'd only gotten halfway through the bedtime story—the trickster, Anansi, was about to con his way out of trouble once again—when Kesha nodded off on me. I closed the picture book and set her in her crib. I brushed the brown curls from her face, tucked the pink pony-themed covers around her body, and slipped out of her room.

In the living room, I collapsed onto the couch, scooped up the remote, and put on the TV. The cheers of a football match blasted through the speakers. I shot forward and shut it off.

Perched on the edge of the couch, I waited for the sound of Kesha's cries.

Seconds passed. Nothing.

I dropped the remote on the end of the couch. If only I'd

brought my laptop. Or my earbuds to listen to music without waking Kesha. Pam had shelves of books, but they were all physics texts and I wouldn't touch those with a ten-foot pole.

I dropped my head against the couch. The ceiling stared back at me, as white and empty as a fresh canvas. I hated silences like these. They were the most dangerous. Inevitably, my mind filled the empty minutes with images, and I'd get the itch to make something. A yearning to create, to escape.

"Reyna!" Jake bellowed. The front door banged against the wall. Seconds later, Jake barreled around the screen. He spotted me. "Hurry! Help me clean this place up. Pick up those pillows—quick!"

I sat up. "What's wrong? Kesha's sleep—"

"Jake, the place is fine." Pam shuffled into the living room. "They're right behind us anyway. Too late to do anything now." She grabbed two black harnesses from a wicker basket in the corner of the room and returned to the front door. "Be right back. I've got to put the dogs in."

I picked the throw pillow off the floor. "Who's behind you?"

The dogs started barking.

"Eliza and Hailee. And their friend." Jake sailed past me to the kitchen. "They wanted to come over to see Kesha. Without any warning!"

"B-but Kesha's already sleeping." I glanced in the direction of the front door with a growing sense of foreboding. "Which friend?" I asked, but my voice had dropped to a tight whisper.

"Like that's going to stop them?" He plucked the washed plates from the drying rack and popped them into an overhead cupboard. He snatched Kesha's towel off the edge of the counter, hesitated, then stuffed it into one of the utensil drawers. "I can't let them see the place in a mess. They always make fun of—"

"Which friend?" I swallowed against the tightness in my throat and tried again. "Jake, which friend?"

My pulse spiked. But by the time my self-preservation instincts kicked in, it was too late. Eliza and Hailee breezed into the room, Aiden close behind them.

"You must be Reyna." Hailee hugged me. The husky timbre of her voice seemed almost discordant with her lithe, willowy frame. Her black hair was pulled into a messy knot, exposing the elegant length of her neck. She wore just a hint of pink lip gloss and very little makeup. "Jake and Pam have told us so much about you. I'm so glad we could finally meet."

"Yes, finally." Eliza came over to hug me too, enfolding me in a cloud of fruity perfume. She wore another romper, this one black with white stripes. "Should've met you already at the wedding. But we didn't. Because, obviously, there was none."

Jake pinched the bridge of his nose. "Will you ever let that go?"

Eliza pulled out of our hug to face him. "My bridesmaid's dress was going to kill, Jake. Kill! I'll never forgive you."

Hailee shoved her hands into her jean pockets. "Should've known when Jake opted for something as conventional as a church wedding it wouldn't go through."

"Okay, you've made your point," Jake said. "Very sorry you couldn't wear your fancy dresses. Can we move on?"

"We never did get a refund for those plane tickets," I said. My delivery was off, my voice a little croaky, but they laughed anyway. I'd never seen Jake so flustered. He turned fire-engine red.

"Reyna," Jake whined. "Whose side are you on?"

"Ours, if she's smart." Eliza threw an arm over my shoulder and squeezed. "Come, meet our friend, Reyna. Wait—no! You two already know each other, don't you? Aiden just showed us where he used to live, not too far from here—"

"Yeah," I cut her off. This was the moment I'd been dreading. I forced myself to look at him. "Hi. Welcome back."

"Hey." He nodded stiffly, fiddling with the edge of his T-shirt collar. His hands still bore the same scars I remembered. An outline of a tattoo peeked under the edge of his left sleeve, an unfamiliar curl of black ink against his warm brown skin. His hand dropped and the sleeve lowered before I could get a good look at it.

Around us, polite conversation continued, the girls teasing Jake about the wedding that never happened. I stood there, clutching the throw pillow to my chest. Aiden didn't look at me. He said nothing. I said nothing. I didn't mean to stare, but now that I'd looked at him, I couldn't look anywhere else.

"Where's Kesha?" Hailee asked, pulling my attention. "We didn't get a chance to meet her yesterday. I'm dying to see her."

"Sorry, she's already asleep," I said.

"Oh, shoot. We did try to leave dinner early." Hailee turned to Pam. "Can I go take a peek? I promise we'll be quiet. Or we can always—"

"Thank you for inviting me," Aiden said suddenly, looking at his phone. All other conversation stopped. His voice was raspy and low, his vowels sharpened in an American accent. "But I, uh, have to take care of this."

An awkward silence followed his exit.

"Well, he is very serious about his work." Eliza laughed. "You know how it is with *artistes*. Never mind him. Jakey—you got any coffee in this house?"

"That's Jake. No *y*. And it's too late for coffee. You won't be able to sleep."

"Thanks for the concern. I'll sleep just fine." She wrinkled her nose. "When did you become such a dad?"

"Eighteen months ago," Jake said, and laughed at his own joke. His sisters groaned.

"That was awful," Eliza said. "Is he always like this now?"

I realized she was talking to me. "Uh . . . yeah?"

"Are you okay, Rey?" Pam leaned forward, looking at me. "You seem a little out of it."

"She does look a little peaky," Hailee agreed.

"Good," I choked out, then realized that made no sense. "I need to go check on Kesha."

Hailee set the glass on the counter. "We'll come with you."

"No! No, you—just stay here. I'll be a second. I'll be right—" I fled.

I closed the door and leaned against it. Safe within the bedroom, I drew what felt like the first real breath I'd taken since Aiden walked into the house. He'd stood right there. In my sister's living room. He'd spoken words and breathed and existed and left.

I glanced down at my blouse, stained with Kesha's dinner. Had I actually been worried about my appearance yesterday? That was nothing.

Not that it mattered. He hadn't even looked at me tonight.

It was like I hadn't been there at all.

Later that night, I walked up the driveway to my house, surprised to see Daddy's car wasn't there yet. After unlocking the door, I toed off my shoes and shot him a quick message. In my bedroom, I started undressing, noticed the dried food on my top again, and I collapsed onto my bed, drowning in mortification.

When I closed my eyes, I held a perfect capture of Aiden's face in Pam's living room. I couldn't read his expression. Had he been angry, sad, surprised, disappointed? All of the above? None of it?

Since the day he left, I'd imagined us reuniting in a thousand different scenarios. Some were quiet and sweet, others loud and dramatic. I'd thought up versions where we'd talk and part as enemies. Or friends. Or in my weakest moments, something more.

I couldn't shake the feeling I'd messed up tonight. I'd had my chance to fix things, to do *something*, and I'd lost it.

My phone buzzed with a reply from Daddy. He'd gone to pick up a friend at the airport. I was about to ask who the friend was when my phone started ringing.

It was a number I didn't recognize, definitely foreign. I don't know why I picked up, unless there was a small part of me that already knew. A part of me that was waiting for it. Regardless of any subconscious foresight, I answered, only to be stunned by the voice on the other end of the line.

"Reyna?"

I bolted upright. "Aiden?"

SIX

SIX YEARS EARLIER

I met Aiden in early July. It was my last day of primary school, the official start of my two-month vacation. After a year of intense studying for the Secondary Entrance Assessment, I was finally free to do nothing, and I planned to do just that for as long as possible.

Mummy, unaware of these plans, did not take me straight home after school. "Just a quick hello," she'd said. "Two minutes."

I knew this meant an hour in the hotel. Minimum.

She'd wanted me with her to welcome a particular aunty who came to stay at the Plumeria once a year. This aunty was an elderly Trinidadian who now lived in New York. She liked to pinch my cheeks a little too hard, and she smelled like she bathed in peppermint, but she told the funniest stories and loved giving presents. This time she'd brought me two boxes of toffees—a special brand, only made in an artisan shop in Brooklyn.

As Mummy pulled into our driveway an hour later, I mapped out the perfect hiding spot for the sweets. I decided on the farthest corner of the vegetable drawer, somewhere Daddy wouldn't think to look. When it came to sweets, he could not be trusted.

"It would be nice if you made Aunty Jen a card to say thank you," Mummy said, in the way that made it seem like she was only making a suggestion, but she wasn't. "She'd like that."

"But I told her thank you when she gave it to me."

Mummy cut the engine. "It would be a nice thing to do, Reyna. You like art. Why don't you draw something on it?"

I sighed and popped open the car door.

Calypso music flooded the vehicle. Upbeat and bouncy, the song blazing with roaring brass and snappy percussion. Mummy climbed out of the car and shut the door. "Haven't heard this one in a while." She tilted her head to the side, listening, then began singing along in English and Spanish.

"What?" I asked, confused.

"It's Calypso Rose."

"Oh."

She groaned. "No Spanish, no music history. What was I paying them to teach you at that school?"

I didn't answer. Mummy was big on protecting and celebrating Trinidad and Tobago culture and the community. That was why she often used the Plumeria and her resources to support and invest in local businesses—the art, furniture, and much of the foods at the hotel were sourced from the islands when possible.

"Listen good, Reyna," she said. "This is music. This is the sound of your roots."

I pointed to the end of Ixora Drive. "I think the sound of my roots is coming from Old Man Chandra's house."

"That's right," Mrs. Clay, our neighbor, answered from the other side of the fence that separated her yard from ours. A couple of plastic grocery bags hung from her hands. It looked like she'd just arrived home too.

"You telling me the old man is playing this?" Mummy laughed. "I didn't know he had such good taste."

"It's his grandson," Mrs. Clay said.

Mr. Chandra had a grandson?

Shell Haven was a smallish village. Everyone knew each other, if not by name then at least by face. But somehow, Old Man Chandra remained a mystery. In his seventies, he lived alone, kept to himself. A fisherman all his life, he left for the beach before dawn and returned from market well after dark. Sometimes he went unseen for months, the only proof of life were the lights that came on in his house at night. Up until that moment, I had no idea he had family.

"Young boy, about eleven or twelve now." Miss Clay drew closer to the fence, eager to share. "He's staying with Chandra for a few weeks. I think he came to help with the fishing."

"Did his mother come and visit too?" Mummy asked, surprising me. Clearly, she had more information on the situation than I did. "I haven't seen her since . . . before Reyna was born."

"It doesn't seem so," Mrs. Clay said. "But then, I'm not surprised after the way he kicked her out for getting pregnant. Not that any of us could say we didn't see that coming. That girl was always . . . *you know*. But I'm still surprised she let the child visit that man after everything."

Mummy's eyes narrowed. "Maybe she didn't have a choice but to send him here. Especially if she's still on her own." Her words took on a sharp tone.

Mrs. Clay didn't seem to notice. "I wouldn't be surprised if she was. You know, the apple doesn't fall far."

Mummy didn't answer, her gaze focused across the road. A boy about my age had stepped out of the bushes. He clutched a gray cinder block to his chest, then disappeared into the trees next to Mr. Chandra's yard.

"What is he doing?" Mummy asked.

"Who knows?" Mrs. Clay shrugged. "Pat said he was over by her earlier. Offered to cut her lawn for *fifty dollars*. What does he want that kind of money for?"

Mummy hmmed noncommittally.

The music changed to a Machel Montano song. I did recognize this one, and without thinking, I started swaying to the rhythm.

Mrs. Clay dropped her voice. "But how are you doing, Claire? Everything all good now? I see your hair is growing back in. It's lovely."

"Ah, thank you." Mummy gave her a tight-lipped smile and slicked down her sideburn. "But this still isn't mine."

My chest squeezed, and I stopped moving.

"Oh." Mrs. Clay drew backward. "Try cutting your hair on a new moon. It's supposed to make it grow faster." She lifted the grocery bags. "I need to pack these away. We'll talk later."

Mummy hmmed again, eyes still across the road. From the tilt of her head, I could tell she was planning something. I started toward our house, but she called out just as I hit the first step.

"Reyna, go next door and say hello to Mr. Chandra's grandson."

I stopped. "Do I have to?"

"It would be a nice thing to do." She crossed the lawn to meet me. "That poor boy . . . I know what it's like, having strangers judge you and your family. Growing up, it was just me and my mother." She took the bag from my hands. "When she was busy, I had to go stay with any family who would take me. It would've been so much easier if the people I met were nicer to me."

Before I could object, she removed one box of toffees and handed it to me.

"Give that to him as a welcome present," she said.

I gaped. My supply of toffees halved in a blink of an eye. "But these are mine."

"Don't be greedy, Reyna." She grasped my shoulders, spun me around, and nudged me toward Mr. Chandra's house. "Make sure and come back before dark."

I huffed, marching away from the her. *Before dark*, she'd said. Like I was going to spend any more than five seconds over there. None of this was fair. But it was *a nice thing to do*, which seemed to trump everything else in Mummy's book.

I walked down the street to the house. The music seemed to be coming from the backyard, so I plunged through the brush, skated down the sloping land, and stumbled into a hidden clearing behind the house. The grandson was there, sawing through a plank of wood. He had it balanced on top of a makeshift worktable, which he'd fashioned out of an old door and two overturned garbage bins. Three cement blocks were propped next to the back steps of the house.

The boy had jet-black hair shaved so short beads of sweat glistened on his scalp. His brow furrowed with concentration; his feet were bare and muddy. He was tall even back then, his limbs long and knobby, yet despite the awkward angles that defined his body, he moved with a surprising level of skill.

I noticed he acted older than he looked. Later I'd learn he'd had to, taking care of himself while his mom worked long hours as a nurse. It was only recently his mom and his grandfather reconnected, the old man agreeing to take Aiden for the holidays so Aiden wouldn't be home alone all day.

The boy looked up, saw me, and startled.

"Hi!" I said loudly. I didn't know if he heard me over the music. "My name's Reyna. I'm supposed to come over here to meet you and bring you a gift. You're Mr. Chandra's grandson, right?"

He didn't answer, retreating to the parked truck under the house. All the while he kept shooting me looks, like he couldn't believe I was there. That made both of us.

"That was a stupid question," I continued, raising my voice. "Of course you're his grandson. Why else would you be here in his yard? If you weren't his grandson this would be creepy."

The radio cut off a second before the end of my sentence. We stared at each other in the sudden silence.

He shut the truck door and walked over to me, his brows raised with surprise. I gripped the box, half-tempted to run off with it, stash it, then sneak it into my room when Mummy wasn't looking. But who was I kidding? She'd know.

She knew everything.

"Did you hear anything I just said?" I asked.

"Just the last part where you called me creepy."

"That's not—" I fumbled for words, embarrassed. "You didn't hear the whole thing. I was saying you were *not* creepy."

"Still seems like a weird way to say hello to a stranger."

"No. I swear, I didn't mean anything." Something had gone very wrong with this conversation. "I just—" I broke off when he started laughing.

He was messing with me.

I'd never met anyone with the ability to piss me off faster. Not before then, and not since.

"Here." I held the box out to him. "My mother told me to give this to you. You're welcome."

"Thanks." He took it. "These look good. That was nice of your mom."

"Yeah, she's a very nice person," I said, my voice flat. I turned to leave. "Welcome to Shell Haven. See you around." Or not.

"Wait—you want to stay a little bit?" he asked. "We can have some a' them? I don' mind sharing."

I froze and peered over my shoulder.

He held up the box.

"Okay . . ." Slowly, I returned to him. Maybe he wasn't so bad. Not if he was willing to share.

"I'm Aiden." He backed up and sat on one of the steps. "You?"

"Reyna," I said. "I live in the orange house. The first one after the turn."

"The one with the big front yard?"

"Yes," I said, not sure what qualified as a *big* yard or why he'd care.

Aiden picked at the plastic covering of the toffee box. He was taking forever. My fingers twitched, tempted to grab the box and unwrap it myself. I glanced around to distract myself.

The space under Old Man Chandra's house was cluttered. Around the car were stacks of boxes and shelves of tools, plastic containers, and fishing equipment. A rusted washing machine and dryer sat in the corner. A clothesline hung between two pillars. After a while, I started to feel weird standing while he sat, so I took the space beside him. I propped my feet on one of the cinder blocks. "What are you doing with all this stuff?"

"I making another step, right here so." He pointed at our feet. "The bottom one too high for Pa when he walking down. It giving him trouble."

Oh. Now that he'd said it, the lowest step did look a bit high. Not for us, but for a seventysomething-year-old, I could see why it might be a problem. It was actually a very sweet thing for him to do for his grandfather. He really wasn't so bad after all.

Aiden smirked. "He giving me a hundred dollars to make it."

Nope. He was just as bad as I suspected.

"You're making your grandfather pay you?"

He raised a brow. "I doing a job for him, so he paying me. That's how it works."

"I help out at my mummy's hotel all the time, but I don't make her *pay me*." I did it because the Plumeria was ours. That's what family did.

Aiden paused in the act of peeling the plastic from the toffee box. He looked me over. "What school uniform is this?"

I brushed my fingers along the folds of my skirt. "Nelson's Private Primary. Why?"

"That's what I thought."

"What does that mean?"

"Means you a Nelson girl."

"So?"

"You wouldn't get it. Your family have money."

I leaped to my feet. I'd heard what people said about kids who went to my school. Never had it said to my face though. "You think because I went to a certain school, you know me? I'm— what? A snob? Stuck up? I think I'm better than everyone?"

"*Do* you think you're better than everyone?"

I'd had enough. "I came over here to give you a gift."

"*Your mom* made you come over here to give me a gift."

"A gift that was supposed to be mine, but I gave it to you because I was being nice. You should try it."

I stomped up the incline to the road, never once looking back.

Without doubt, Aiden Chandra was the worst. The next time I saw him, I'd ignore him. That would show him.

The next morning, I woke up to the sound of a motor too close to my window. I stuffed my head under a pillow, trying to muffle the noise. When that didn't work, I sprang from my bed and threw open the curtains to find the source of my problem.

It was Aiden. For some reason, he was mowing our lawn.

The movement of the curtains must've drawn his attention because he looked right at my window. He paused, took a hand off the mower, and waved. I stood there, frozen, for far too long, then remembered my Pikachu pajamas and bedhead. Embarrassed, I dropped to the floor.

"Mummy!" I crept to the door, staying low so I wouldn't be seen.

I found her in the living room, tucking a tin of tuna and some Crix crackers into her purse for her breakfast later.

"Why is that boy cutting our lawn?"

"Good morning, Reyna," she said cheerfully. "Aiden came over this morning to thank me for the toffees and told me about his grass-cutting service. He seems like a resourceful young man, so I hired him." She zipped up her purse. "He asked if you'd be free to go to the beach today. I told him to ask you, but you can if you want." She smiled and kissed my forehead. "It looks like you've made a new friend."

Friend?

I wiped my eyes. "You're going to work now?"

"Yes, you don't have to come in today." She used her thumb to wipe her lipstick off my forehead. "Aiden seems like a nice boy. You two have fun."

Nice? Him?

"I'll be back around seven." Mummy walked to the door, car keys jangling as she plucked them off the counter. "Your father's in the bedroom working on his column, so try not to bother him until lunch."

I nodded. Daddy had been known to write through meal times if uninterrupted. He was a freelance journalist, regularly published with the biggest newspapers and local magazines. His passion project, though, was to write an extensive guide to the island. Sometimes he'd take Mummy and me on research trips to hot spots and landmarks, all the while telling us the stories behind them.

"Aiden's money is on the counter," Mummy said, on her way out. "You can give it to him when he's done."

"Yeah, fine." I held the door open, watching as she climbed down the steps and into the car. About half an hour later, after Aiden finished with the lawn, I met him on the front porch.

"What did you tell Mummy this morning?" I asked, handing over the money. "She thinks you're a *nice boy.*"

His brows lifted. "I am a nice boy."

I folded my arms. "You called me snobby."

"You called yourself snobby." He set Daddy's safety gloves aside and retrieved a backpack he'd left in the corner. He pulled out a familiar box and handed it to me. "This is for you."

I took the toffees without thinking, then felt bad. "You don't want them?"

"I don't really like sweets," he said. "I thought about trying an' resell it, but it's not worth it."

God, this boy was weird. How would he resell it?

But now that I'd gotten my toffees back, I felt a little more generous with my time. I sat on one of the porch chairs. "What do you need the money for?"

Aiden dropped onto the chair next to me. He pulled out his phone, and after a few swipes, handed it over. A picture of a guitar lit up his cracked screen. "A Gibson Acoustic Songwriter. My mother friend selling his for a thousand US. He giving me until the end of August to get the money."

A thousand United States dollars was about seven thousand Trinidad and Tobago dollars. That seemed like an impossible amount. "How much have you got so far?"

"One thousand, three hundred an' twenty-two dollars."

Yeah, no. He'd never make it in two months. Instead of saying that, I asked, "You already know how to play?"

"Mummy taught me some. And I learn some myself." He flexed his fingers. "But her guitar old-old. And I need my own instrument to write songs."

"You write songs?" That was kind of impressive. A small part of me didn't quite believe him. "Can I hear one?"

"I just said I have nothing to play it on." He rolled his eyes. "That's the whole problem."

"Can you play the keyboard? I have one. You can borrow it while you're here."

Aiden lit up. "For real?"

"Yeah." I didn't see why not. If Aiden was using it, maybe Mummy would stop hassling me to practice every night. It was bad enough she made me play the grand piano for guests at the hotel. My clumsy performances were embarrassing at best.

I brought the keyboard outside, and we set it up on the porch. Aiden's playing was impressive, especially when I realized he didn't need the music book. He listened as I played *Bach's Prelude in C Major*, his face serious, head tipped to the side, lashes lowered, dark-brown eyes trained on my fingers. I nearly fell out of the chair when he played it back to me a minute later.

"You're messing with me again, aren't you?" I asked him. "You take lessons. You've been practicing for years."

He tried not to smile, but I caught it.

I punched him in the shoulder.

He winced and rubbed the spot. "Okay, my friend's ma started teaching me in January. Never played this song before though."

"January?" I frowned. "No way. You had to be playing longer."

"Why? You think I'm good?"

"Shut up," I said, which only made his smile bigger.

It had taken me years of classes and hours of practice to play the song he'd learned in minutes *without looking at the music book*. I couldn't decide if I was in awe or I hated him.

"Show me something else," he said, attention already back on the keys. He shifted closer to me, ready for more. His knee bounced up and down, shaking the chair we shared. I couldn't help but get caught up in his excitement.

"Okay, let's see." I flipped through the music book. I usually avoided the more difficult songs at the back, but playing with him made me want to try. Stranger still, I found myself enjoying it.

SEVEN

Most people wouldn't guess I'm not a morning person. With every fiber of my being, I hated waking up early. Working at the hotel, I had to do it every day. Thankfully, the perky spirit I carried through my morning greetings to the staff and guests could be induced by a large mug of black coffee.

It was all part of the job. Perkiness was expected. People only really want to see smiles while they're on vacation. I'd had years to practice and perfect this, but that didn't mean some days weren't harder. If it weren't for the big conference we were hosting that day, I might've actually stayed home.

Who was I kidding? No, I'd still go.

I arrived at the Plumeria early. Instead of hanging around the front desk, catching up with the clerks and learning about the latest hotel gossip, I kept my head down and eyes on the floor as I headed straight into Daddy's office. As usual, Daddy wasn't there, so I took the seat behind the desk and started to answer emails. I nearly nodded off, the task boring enough on a good day, but this morning I was running on very little sleep. After Aiden called, I'd spent too long staring at the ceiling, replaying every word.

My phone vibrated with a message from Olivia.

Have you talked to him yet?

My fingers hesitated over the phone. I'd been dodging her since lunch at Grace's, sure she'd go on and on about how I was avoiding Aiden because I was still in love with him, or some version of that nonsense. The truth was I'd just wanted to save Aiden and me from a painful conversation—which was exactly what happened anyway.

I did, I messaged back. A second later she tried to call.

I wasn't in the mood for a line-by-line breakdown and analysis of the talk with my ex, so I hit ignore. If only I'd done the same with Aiden's call. No, instead I'd answered. Even he seemed surprised at the time.

"I didn't expect you to pick up," he'd said.

"But I did," I'd said, and we lapsed into silence. I'd wondered if he regretted calling. "How did you get my number?"

"Your dad gave it to me."

"Oh." I pressed my back against the headboard. "How—" I started, then thought better of asking him *how he was*. It seemed so trite, so empty. I really should've worked on a script. It was difficult to know what to say. I tried for something honest; a little more direct. "It was weird seeing you today."

"Yeah, it was," he said, then made a noise that might've been amused or sad. "That's why I called. I thought we should talk."

"I agree." I pulled my knees up and wrapped my free arm around them. My grip on the phone tightened as the apologies I'd been holding on to for years rose up to the surface like a balloon inflating in my chest. This was it. This was the moment.

"I want you to know being here was not my idea," he said.

"What?" I said, deflating. I'd been so ready to apologize; it was almost painful to pull it back.

Aiden seemed to be on a roll. I didn't think he even heard me.

"My friends planned the whole thing. Eliza and Hailee booked the hotel. I didn't even know where we were staying until we drove up to the entrance. It was all a surprise for my birthday. I don't know if you remember, but it's at the end of the month."

I remembered. I just hadn't put it together.

"They went through so much trouble for me," he said. "The last thing I want is for them to find out how bad they messed up. They didn't know that literally any other hotel would've been better."

I flinched. He might as well have doused me in freezing water. It was one thing to suspect he wanted nothing to do with me; another thing to actually hear it. All my hopes for clearing the air between us evaporated.

"That's why I haven't told them who you are . . . who you were to me," he said. "It's just easier. They know we knew each other growing up, but nothing more. I don't want to put that on them. It's not like we'll have to see each other while I'm here. If we're careful, we won't have to see each other at all."

"Sounds like a plan." I sank down to lie on the bed, numb.

"I'm glad you agree," he said after a pause. There was a hint of something that might've been anger in his voice. I wondered if *he'd* prepared a script. Aiden was never very talkative, this being the most I'd ever heard him say at one time. I wondered if he was mad because I'd agreed with his plan or because I'd thrown him off-book.

"But there is your family," he said, returning to the steady tone he'd had for most of the call. "When I asked your dad for your number, I got the impression he didn't know we had been together."

"He thinks we were just friends," I said, though I wasn't completely sure. For years, I'd thought Mummy had told Daddy, but after a while, I'd started to realize maybe not. I certainly hadn't talked to him about my romantic relationships. Or relation*ship*, since there was only ever the one.

"And Pam didn't seem to know," he said, anger creeping back in.

"No. She and I only got close about a year ago. Never saw any point in bringing you up."

"That should make things easy then." Yes, that was definitely anger. Good.

"Yes, it should. Olivia knows, but I'll make sure she keeps your secret." I sat up. "So, since that's settled, I really need to go now. I'm glad we got to talk this out. Good night."

I hung up before he could say more. Petty, yes. But it made me feel better.

Now my phone vibrated like crazy, Olivia sending one text after the other.

What happened????

Rey

What did he say?

Was it bad?

I could see on the screen she was typing even more. I sighed, caught in between stopping her and not wanting to talk about it. I guessed something like *he told me we should stay away from each other* would only make it worse. Instead, I sent a half lie.

It's fine. Closure achieved.

Fine was debatable, but the closure was definite. Aiden couldn't have made it clearer if he'd slammed a door marked "Our Relationship" in my face.

Olivia tried calling again. I messaged back that I was busy, then put my phone on silent. It wasn't her fault Aiden's words hurt me, but she *had* told me to talk to him, and look what happened. Because of that, she ranked just under Aiden as the last person I wanted to talk to at the moment.

"Hey!" William popped his head inside. "Good, you're here. Something's going on at the villa. They want someone to come over there to check it out. I need you to go take care of it."

My phone slipped from my fingers and landed with a thump on the carpeted floor. "Me?"

He retracted his head and shut the door. Apparently, that was the end of it.

I scooped up my phone and followed him. "Isn't there someone else who can go?" I fell into step with him as we crossed the lobby. "One of the clerks? You?"

"Today's the creative writing retreat, remember?"

"Of course I remember."

"Well, then you know I'm busy," William said, as we entered his office. "I've got to coordinate the staff and get the conference room ready. Everyone else is preparing for the guests' arrivals. Meanwhile, you're here and you're free, so . . ."

I lingered in the doorway. This was what I got for coming in early.

"I could fill in for you," I said. "I helped organize the retreat last year. I know—"

"One day." William dropped into his chair and let out a heavy breath. "For just *one day* can you please not fight me on every little thing? Your father told me you're already acquainted with the group at the villa. So as far as I can tell, you're only saying no for the sake of being contrary."

I opened my mouth to argue when his office phone rang.

He snatched up the receiver. "Hello? Yes, put them through." He held up a finger to me. "Yes, hello again, Miss Musgrove. Don't worry about a thing. Reyna is on her way as we speak."

"But—"

He pointed at the receiver. "She'll be there any moment now."

Unbelievable. Just last night Aiden and I made an agreement to stay away from each other, and I was violating the terms already.

Resigned to my fate, I stomped out of William's office, letting his door slam shut. I marched across the lobby, around the pool, and onto the main lawn. Shadowy clouds hovered overhead. The sea was a solemn gray-blue color, the water restless and choppy. I tried not to think about where I was going.

I'd just have to make it very clear that I was there for work. That I didn't have a choice. I'd get in, take care of the problem, and get out.

The heels of my black pumps clacked against the bricks of the path that cut across the lawn. By the time I finally got to the staircase that led up to the villa, my blouse was damp with sweat. I unbuttoned my blazer, drew a deep breath, then began the climb. As I ascended, the villa slowly revealed itself—the emerald-green roof down to the second-story veranda, the front porch, and finally the in-ground private pool. It looked like the girls and DJ Bacchanal had already settled in. All the downstairs windows were thrown open, swimwear and towels slung over banisters. Discarded shoes and empty glasses littered the poolside, the outdoor furniture disarranged.

I knocked at the front door. It opened.

Fish, the Grammy-winning, world-famous music producer opened it, wearing a T-shirt and sweat pants. Strands of his trademark silver hair hung over his pierced brow, his man bun askew. A thrill raced through me and I froze, starstruck.

I'd been so preoccupied with Aiden's return that I hadn't given much thought to the reality of coming face-to-face with an actual celebrity. Before I could shake off the shock, he grabbed my hand.

"Thank God you're here," he said, and yanked me inside.

EIGHT

Fish led me toward the living room. "In here."

"What happened?" I asked nervously.

It looked like a flea market had erupted: open suitcases, shoes, handbags, and toiletries scattered everywhere. Heaps of clothes were piled on the couch, some encased in transparent garment bags. I tiptoed around the items.

Footsteps thundered down the stairs behind us—Eliza. "Reyna! Thank God!" she said, panting. "Fish, this is Reyna. Remember we were telling you about her?"

"Yes, yes. Jake's sister-in-law." Fish rotated his finger in a *let's-move-this-along* gesture. "Do we really have time for this?"

"Right." Eliza seized my arm and tugged me toward the stairs. "Come quick. I've been keeping an eye on it."

"An eye on what?" I glanced around.

Fish lowered his voice, "Keep it down, yeah?"

"Where is everyone?" So far, I hadn't seen Aiden, which was

good. But their cryptic discussion was getting annoying. "What's going on?"

"In here." Eliza pulled me forward.

It had been ages since I'd been in the villa. It looked almost exactly as I remembered. All the bedrooms had been named after Mummy's favorite songs. The Calypso Queen room, which we entered, was startlingly bright, the tan curtains pulled aside, the dark wooden shutters open. Above the unmade bed hung a painting of three bèlè dancers with their overskirts thrown back, a drummer seated in the distance.

Above the painting, a lizard nestled into the corner where the wall met the ceiling. About six inches long, it had translucent, gray-spotted skin, almost blending into the yellow paint. If it weren't so big, I might not have noticed it at all.

"Oh God," Eliza whined. "Now it's even closer to the wardrobe."

I glanced from Eliza to Fish. "You know they're not dangerous, right?"

"So you say," Fish said. "But when I tried to catch it, it *lunged* at me." He shivered.

I suppressed my own shiver. Lizards weren't my favorite either. But did this really deserve a call to hotel management?

"It went straight for my face! My face is money." Fish circled the moneymaker in question. "I can't risk it. You need to get that thing out or move us to another villa."

Since the hotel did not have another villa, this would be a problem.

"Where are the others?" I asked.

"Leo and Hailee went down to get breakfast." Eliza lifted her phone and started filming. How helpful.

I tugged on my blazer. I did not dress to be on camera this morning. "And, um, Aiden? He left too?"

"He's sleeping," Eliza said.

"And let's keep it that way." Fish rolled his shoulders. "If he or Leo find out about this, they'll never let me live it down." He turned to Eliza and spoke directly to the camera. "Which is why this must never be posted."

"Oh, come on." Eliza pouted. "It's just my Instagram story. This is great stuff. Man versus beast."

"Eliza, I swear—"

"Fine, fine," she said. But when Fish turned his attention back to the lizard, she spun the camera to face herself and winked.

Fish set his hands on his hips. "So, what do we do?"

"We could . . ." I flinched when the lizard inched forward. God, it was huge. I did not want to touch it, but I didn't want to call for help either. The same way Fish would be embarrassed in front of his friends, I'd be embarrassed in front of the staff.

First things first, I needed some equipment.

Back on the ground floor, under the staircase, I pulled out a broom from a concealed supply closet. In the kitchen, I found a pot. All the while, Eliza followed me around with the phone. I did my best to ignore her.

Back at the Calypso Queen room, Fish hovered in the doorway.

"It moved," he said gravely.

The lizard had indeed crawled closer to the wardrobe. We had to move fast. If it got under the hefty piece of furniture, we might lose it.

"Okay, so this is what we're going to do." I held out the pot to Fish. "First, I'm going to chase the lizard toward the window with the broom. If it doesn't go for the window, then I'm going to try to knock it onto the floor. Fish, as soon as you get the chance, trap it under the pot. We'll figure it out from there."

Fish pushed the pot back toward me. "Why do I have to be the one who traps it? I don't want to get that close again. It already attacked me once today. That was enough."

I sighed. "Okay, take the broom." I handed it to him, trying not to roll my eyes. "Hit the wall and lead it to the window. We're trying to scare it outside. If you hit it directly, you might knock it onto the wardrobe or the bed, which we definitely don't want."

"Definitely," Eliza stressed. "I swear, Fish—you knock that thing on my bed, and we are switching tonight."

"Or we could share."

"Ha! In your dreams."

"Hey, it's either me or Aiden . . ." He snorted. "Actually, no. You would like that, wouldn't you?"

Eliza pinched his cheek. "You know me too well, Fishcakes. Now, do your job and get that thing out of my room."

Fish pulled away. He turned to the wall, took a deep breath, and tapped the broom next to the lizard. It scurried downward.

"It's heading for the bed!" I shouted to Fish.

"No, no, no!" Eliza said. "The window, Fish—the window!"

"I know, I know." He tapped the wall again. The lizard shot forward, in the direction of the open window. "Give me a second. I'm trying to—"

"Fish!" Eliza leaped onto the bed.

"I've got it—oops!"

The lizard dropped beside the night table. It scrambled along the wooden floor and disappeared under the bed. I dropped to my knees.

The lizard turned to look right at me.

"I see it," I told the others. I sat up to find both Eliza and Fish standing on top of the bed, their attention—and the phone's camera—focused on me.

"Okay," I said. "New plan. Fish, get down here and chase it out with the broom. Try to get it out this way." I pointed toward the door. "I'll trap it when it comes out."

Fish groaned as he climbed off the bed. He opened his mouth but stopped. His eyes popped. "Reyna . . ."

"What?"

"Get it!" Eliza shouted.

I looked down—the lizard was inches from my knee. When Fish climbed off the bed, the movement must've scared it out. Without thinking, I lunged. The rim of the pot smacked against the wooden floor. The lizard charged for the door. I missed. On my hands and knees, I scrambled after it, slamming the pot down again and again.

"Reyna!" Eliza shouted.

"You got this, you got this," Fish chanted.

I slammed the pot down one more time, capturing the beast in its ceramic nonstick cage. Then I lost my balance and pitched forward, hitting the ground with a thud. Pain shot through my elbows, but high on adrenaline, and the sweet taste of victory, nothing else mattered. "Got it."

"Yes!" Eliza jumped on the bed.

Fish cheered, swinging the broom over his head.

"What are you doing?" A raspy voice cut through our celebration.

My heart dropped.

Aiden braced a hand against the doorframe. His black curls were sleep-ruffled, his cheek marked with lines from the creases of his pillow. He wore only sweatpants, his torso bare apart from the tattoos scrawled across his brown skin. I tried to read the words inked into the inside of his upper left arm, but he folded his hands. "Reyna?"

My eyes skated up from his biceps. "Yes. Hi."

"Why were you screaming?" he asked Eliza. "I thought you were being murdered in here."

Eliza clasped a hand to her heart. "And you came to save me? What a sweet—"

"It was a lizard," I cut in drily. "A huge one. We were trying to get it out."

"Yeah, man." Fish slung the broom over his shoulder. His voice was noticeably deeper. "Sorry we woke you. But as you can see, we've trapped it. It's all good, I've got everything under control."

He had everything under control? Seriously?

"They called the front desk to ask for help," I said. "That's why I'm here. To remove the lizard." If it wasn't already obvious, I wanted to make it very clear.

He looked down at me, his attention as sharp as needles. "And they sent you?"

"There wasn't anyone else available." I tried to keep my tone professional. "I did trap it."

"You . . . trapped it? What . . ." For a moment we just stared at each other. Finally, he asked, "This is Tobago. There are lizards. This is how you handle it?"

No. Usually, I called Daddy and he handled it.

Aiden folded his arms. "What are you going to do with it now?"

I swallowed, my throat dry. "I was going to use a lid to cover it and take it outside."

"Where's the lid?" he asked.

My skin warmed. "I mean, if you have a better idea—"

Aiden bent forward and reached for the pot. I jerked back, every cell of my body vibrated at his proximity. I stilled, afraid to move or breathe, terrified of what my expression might betray to Aiden or his friends. Or the camera.

Aiden lifted the pot and scooped up the lizard in one smooth move. He cupped the wiggling creature in his hands, turned, and disappeared into the hall.

Slowly, I rose to my feet, eyes on the empty doorway. Why did I come here? I knew seeing Aiden would be bad, but this was even worse than I expected.

"My hero." Eliza sighed loudly as she jumped off the bed.

"Whatever," Fish muttered. "At least we're done here."

I couldn't help but agree. At least we were done. Now I could go back to the original plan.

Stay away from Aiden and his friends.

NINE

When I was younger, I believed the laundry of the Plumeria was a magical place. To get to it, one had to venture through the labyrinth of the maintenance workshop, sneak past the vigilant security sentinels, and descend the dark tunnel that linked one world to another, this new land filled with light and sound and movement.

Sunlight spilled through the open ventilation blocks of the walls, several standing fans coordinated to circulate the hot air and fumes. Giant machines vibrated and rumbled like hungry beasts, waiting to be fed. The housekeepers were split into two troops: one sorted and washed, the other dried and folded. Their movements were sharp yet graceful; a well-practiced performance, no superfluous actions or seconds wasted.

When I was a child, Mummy had forbidden me from going down there. So, of course, I snuck in every chance I got.

Looking back, I understood her logic. It was dangerous for

a child, alone and unsupervised among the hot machinery and detergents. Not to mention it must've been annoying for the housekeepers to keep an eye on the boss's daughter while trying to do their jobs.

This must've been why Miss Pearl, the head of housekeeping, intervened during my little adventures. Like clockwork, she'd appear and gently lead me from the main floor to her office, a small room on the upper floor. She'd make me tea, and for an hour or so, we'd sit and sip while she told me stories that combined fairy tales, folklore, and—though I wouldn't realize it until later—episodes of the old local soap opera, *Westwood Park*.

After the disaster at the villa, I needed comfort. I couldn't think of anyplace better.

"Well, I haven't seen you in a while." Pearl handed me a cup of tea. "For a second, I thought you forgot me."

"Sorry." I carefully balanced the cup and saucer. "It's busy lately. Or, I guess *busier*." I inhaled the sweet smoke that curled from the amber-colored liquid. "I really needed this."

Pearl reached for a pack of jub-jubs from the bowl on her desk. She made the sweets and frequently gave them out as presents during birthdays and holidays. She opened the plastic wrapping and popped one of the sugar-coated candies in her mouth.

"Is it your father?" she asked.

I shrugged. Yes and no. "Daddy's still being Daddy."

"He's doing the best he can."

"I know." I just wished his best was better for the hotel.

It was frustrating how easily he shook off his responsibilities to the Plumeria, letting them fall to someone else. Lately, he seemed more distracted than ever. He'd probably started writing again. Even though he'd given up on freelancing to manage the hotel, he still worked on his guide to Tobago from time to time.

I took a sip, the taste sharp and bittersweet. "Orange?" I guessed. "And cinnamon?"

"Very good." She nodded. "I'm reworking the old recipe— something simple but bold. They say orange peel is supposed to be good for warding off a cold." She smiled slyly, swirling the steaming cup in her hand. "And eases stomachaches. Some even say it relieves tabanca."

I choked. The hot liquid scalded my tongue and throat. I set the cup and saucer on the desk between us. "What?"

Pearl coolly regarded me over the rims of her glasses.

I slumped in my chair. "How did you know?"

"Why would I not?" She tapped the side of her head. "You think the moment one of them girls mentioned the Chandra boy's name it wouldn't click?"

I fiddled with the handle of the teacup. "That was a long time ago."

"Two years is a long time?" She sucked her teeth. "It would seem long to you. You young people are the only ones who don't realize your youth is fleeting. Blink and it passes. You collect regrets like stones, and you don't even realize all the bad choices you've made weigh the same as the good ones you've missed—"

"I got it," I said, interrupting her. If I didn't, she might've gone on for a while. In addition to her masterful teamaking, she was a consummate romantic, as evidenced by the fact that she was currently on her fourth husband.

"Do you?" She watched me with narrowed eyes. "Do you remember me telling you about my first husband?"

"The mechanic?"

"No, the farmer," she said. "I was about your age when I married him. Look, nah—I already see you setting up your face, but that's how it was back then. And you have to understand, both my parents were emigrants from Guyana. When they died, I was brought up by British nuns at one of the orphanages. He was the first real family I had."

Pearl pulled her teacup closer, her gaze somewhere over my shoulder. "It's been fifty years since he died. *Fifty*. God is good—he brought love into my life again. But . . . even though I can't recall his face without looking at a picture, things does stick. I still remember how he made me feel. Safe. Loved. And when I tell you he was a sweet man—the kind of man who'd go thirty minutes out of his way every evening just so we could walk home from work together. He used to hold my hand the whole way."

Pearl gave me a small smile. "We had two years together, Reyna. Two years is not a long time."

My phone chimed, the screen lighting up with a new message from Daddy.

My office now

"Sorry," I said, pointing to the phone in my lap. "I have to go."
She waved off my apology.

I set the cup down, stood, then hesitated for a second. Even though she didn't seem upset, it felt rude to leave right after she'd shared something so personal. I didn't want her to think I didn't appreciate it. "Thanks for the tea and talk."

Pearl's eyes crinkled. "You'll think about what I said? About Aiden?"

"Yes," I said firmly. "But it's not tabanca. It's just . . . complicated."

As I left the office, she chuckled. "It usually is."

William was at the front desk. As I crossed the lobby, he paused his conversation with one of the clerks to point to Daddy's office door. "They're waiting for you in there."

"I know," I said, even though I didn't know who *they* were. I pushed the office door open. It knocked against someone's back, and I stopped. "Oh, sorry!"

Hailee turned around. "Oh—no, it's my fault." She stepped away, rubbing her arm where the door hit. "I shouldn't have been standing there."

I looked from her to Eliza and Fish standing near the window, then to Daddy sitting behind his desk. There was something about my father's expression that caught my attention. It was the same look he wore when reading over an article of his that was published, or when I used to show him a finished painting—a look of bone-deep satisfaction.

"What's going on?" I stepped farther inside the office. The door clicked shut behind me. "Is everything all right? It's not another lizard, is it?" I smiled to show the last question was a joke, but Hailee didn't laugh.

Instead, her brow pinched. "Another lizard?"

"Actually . . ." Fish stepped toward me. "We do have a problem. Your father says you can help."

"Of course," I said, smiling politely. "I'll do what I can. What's the problem?"

"Well, first," Hailee said, taking the seat across from Daddy. "We should explain that this holiday is a birthday surprise for Aiden."

I almost admitted I knew that, but caught myself.

"He'd had no idea where we were going until we got to the airport." Eliza laughed. "You should've seen his face when he realized. Actually—you can. The video will be posted in a couple of weeks."

"The thing is," Hailee said. "Eliza and I were planning to come see Jake and his family this year anyway. I started thinking it would be great if Leo could meet them too. And since Aiden is from here—"

"We got the idea—" Eliza cut in only to be corrected by Fish.

"*I* came up with the idea. Since we had some time off around his birthday, I thought we could make this a group trip."

"And *we* made a plan." Eliza shot him a dirty look. "Stay here for three weeks, hire a tour guide to show us around, then end with a big birthday party."

"Well, sounds like a really great surprise." I was trying so hard to hold my smile my cheeks hurt. "You're really good friends to do all that for him."

"Yeah," Eliza said. "It was amazing how it came together. The guys got time off, then Jake and Pam got us a booking at a hotel—where it turns out Aiden's childhood friend works." She beamed at me. "It was almost too perfect!"

That was certainly one way of looking at it.

"And what did you need my help with?" I asked. "Is it the birthday party planning? I can definitely take care of it." No doubt it would be weird, planning a party for my ex-boyfriend who wanted nothing to do with me, but I'd do my job.

"The tour guide they hired can't make it," Daddy finally spoke. He leaned back in his chair, hands clasped over his stomach. "They asked if I could recommend someone. I thought of you."

"Oh." I racked my brain. The guides I knew offered one-time trips to specific places. From the sound of it, they wanted someone for the duration of their stay. "Would you be okay hiring a few different people?"

"No . . ." Hailee shot Daddy a look of confusion. "We'd prefer one person. Someone trustworthy. The more people we involve, the more likely someone will betray our location or take photos to sell or post on the internet. We'd like to keep a low profile while we're here."

"Yeah," Eliza said, smiling. "Someone who knows the island and can keep up with us."

"And someone fun," Fish added. "It doesn't hurt if they're cute too."

Eliza swatted the back of his head.

"Ouch—I was complimenting her."

My heart dropped. "Wait—you mean me? You're talking about me?" I looked at Daddy. "I'm not a tour guide."

"But you could be," Daddy said. "You know the island. You know where to go, how to get there, where to eat, where to lime—"

"Lime?" Fish frowned.

"It means to hang out," Daddy said helpfully. "Plus, it would give you a chance to reconnect with Aiden."

A bubble of panic in my chest expanded, pressing against my ribs. "What about Aiden?" He wouldn't like this idea at all. "Why can't he be your tour guide?"

Fish snorted. "I asked him something like that last year. We were talking about making a trip over here, and he said something along the lines of *don't ask me. I wouldn't know the first thing about the type of sh—stuff tourists would be into.*" He winced. "Sorry," he said to Daddy.

I bit back a laugh. That sounded like something Aiden would say.

"Plus, the tour is part two of the surprise," Eliza said. "He doesn't know about it or the party yet."

Well, it was definitely going to surprise him. Just not the way they were hoping for. "Like I said, it's cool that you planned all this for him. And it sounds like fun. Normally, I'd love to, but I can't show you around. I don't have time."

"Yes, you do," Daddy said.

I gaped at my father. Obviously, I didn't have time to play tour guide. I already had a job *working for him*.

"Don't worry," Daddy said. "After the conference over tomorrow, we get a bit of a lull. You can take some time off." He offered Hailee a smile. "Reyna will start tomorrow morning."

"Awesome," Fish said. "I'm glad that's sorted. Anybody else hungry?"

"Yes," Eliza said. "The desk clerk told me about this place where we can get the best curried crab and dumplings. I've been thinking about it all day."

While the others left the office, Hailee hung back for a few seconds. "Thank you for doing this, Reyna. Having you with us is going to be way more fun than some random stranger." She squeezed my arm. "Aiden's going to flip."

I forced a smile. "I bet."

The instant the door shut behind her, I spun to face my father. "I can't do it."

"Why not?"

"Because . . ." I struggled to put into words what seemed so obvious. "I can't take time off now. I just started this job. How will it look to the rest of the staff?"

Daddy reclined, and the chair wedged against the wall behind him. "You just started the job officially, but everybody know you been working around here for years now. None of them would blame you for taking a little time off."

"I don't need time off."

"That so? Tell me nah—when was the last time you took

time for yourself? I never see you painting or going out with your friends anymore."

I snapped my fingers. "I had lunch with Olivia a few days ago."

"And apart from that?"

I folded my arms and reverted to my original point. "I do not need time off."

"As general manager I giving it to you. Go on—take a break. Is no big t'ing. Them kids just need someone to make sure they don't get lost or confused. Besides, there are a few places in my travel guide I haven't visited in a while. You can check on them for me. Let me know how they looking."

"So you are still working on the travel guide?"

He smiled, but it was sad. "I trying. Maybe one day I'll finish. In the meantime, take some notes for me and I'll update it again."

I wrung my fingers together. It looked like I might actually have to do this. "Aren't you worried about me—your teenage daughter—hanging around with a group of male musicians?"

"You?" His brow furrowed. "Not really."

My shoulders sagged. Fair enough.

"Reyna, what really going on?" Daddy rocked forward in his seat. The space between his brows pinched. "I thought you'd jump at the chance to spend time with Aiden. The two ah you were such good friends."

"We were."

Daddy picked up a pen and rolled it between his fingers. "I know . . . this time of year not . . . easy for you. It hard for me too.

I do not think is a good idea for you to be at the hotel right now."

"I don't—" My words caught in my throat.

"Please, Pumpkin." His eyes softened. "Take some time for yourself. If not for you, then do it for me."

And how was I supposed to argue with that?

The correct—and maddening—answer was obvious.

I couldn't.

TEN

The night before my first day with the group, I returned Olivia's call. I didn't particularly want to talk about my current ex-boyfriend problem and would've happily avoided it forever, but that was proving to be impossible. So I gave Olivia a brief recap of Aiden's phone call and my recent appointment to tour guide, hoping for a little compassion—a little bit of sympathy—from my best friend.

"You done?" I asked, when she'd finally stopped laughing. "Got it all out of your system?"

"I just don't see the problem," she'd said, with a gleeful air of condescension. "If you're so over Aiden, spending a few days around him shouldn't be an issue."

"Would you like to spend three weeks with your ex-boyfriend?" I asked.

"If it came with an all-expenses-paid vacation with Leonardo

Vale—yes! That boy is gorgeous. From what you've seen, how serious are he and Hailee?"

"Why did I call you? I can't remember."

"Because you're panicking," she said. "Now you have to spend time with Aiden, and as much as you trying to deny it, you're still in love with him."

"I am not!" How many times did I have to say it before someone believed me?

"All right, nah." She laughed again. "I'll stop, yes. You say you're not, then you're not. Maybe you did move on. But, Reyna, you are going to be spending a lot of time with him. And you know what the old people does say: *Old firestick easy to catch*."

I grabbed a pillow and squished it against my face. Voice muffled, I let her know, "I'm hanging up."

"Wait!"

"What?"

"Once you're done with your celebrity friends, you want to come and slum it with my regular ass? I could take the afternoon off."

"Don't." I sighed, sitting up. "You'll get in trouble."

"No, I won't. What's Aunty Grace going to do? Fire me? Mammy would involve herself, and Aunty Grace is totally afraid of her younger sister. Worst thing Aunty could do is dock my pay."

Exasperated, I tugged the pillow off my face. "Pay that you need. Come nah, Olivia. You need to save up. London isn't cheap, you know."

There was a beat of silence, during which I realized Olivia

might mistake my concern for condescension. It was unintentional, really. But I knew it was too late.

"Wow—that's brand-new information," she said. "Thank you, Reyna. What would I do without you? How else would I ever have known *London isn't cheap*? Is not like that's the whole reason I have the job in the first place."

"I didn't mean—"

"You coming by Grace's tomorrow or not?"

"No," I said, feeling like the worst friend ever. When did it become so easy to say the wrong things to each other? "The group has lunch plans somewhere else. Then they want to go to the beach after. But maybe another day?"

"Right," she said.

Before I could apologize again, she hung up.

"Reyna!" Hailee called as I approached the villa the following morning.

At first, I didn't understand what I was looking at. Hailee was arched in the air, Leonardo stretched below her. He held her right hand and her right foot, his left foot pressed into the middle of her back, her left foot and hand lifted to the sky. They reminded me of a sculpture, elegant and unreal. It must've taken an insane amount of strength and flexibility to hold themselves together like that.

"Uh . . ." I approached the couple. "Good morning?"

They opened their eyes and both looked toward me as if on cue. Their perfect coordination was mildly disturbing. They wore tight athleticwear, skin shining with sweat.

"Good morning," Hailee said. "You haven't met Leo yet, have you? Leo, this is Reyna, Aiden's friend. Pam's sister."

"Hi," I said shyly.

Leonardo Vale's generous mouth broke into a smile. He lay on his back, bare-chested, muscles on display. Unlike Aiden and Fish, the dark-brown skin bore no tattoos—at least not as far as I could see.

Here was the guy whose face had become a meme based on how unearthly handsome he was. I found myself more than a little tongue-tied.

"Hey, nice to finally meet you, Reyna," Leonardo said. "I'd shake your hand, but . . ."

"Oh, no. No problem." I waved my hand, flustered. No one that handsome should sound that sincere. It was too much. "Just please don't drop her."

He laughed, his body and Hailee's shaking.

"Leo," she warned. *"Focus."*

"Sorry." He exhaled slowly, the muscles of his arms flexing. "So, Reyna, what brings you here so early in the morning?"

"What do you mean?" I frowned. "You have your horseback ride this morning."

Hailee's eyes popped open. "That's this morning? Eliza said it was tonight."

"No. It's this morning." I checked the time on my phone. "In an hour from now. Why would the ride be at night?"

"Why wouldn't it?" Hailee asked. "The empty beach, moonlight glittering on the sea. I thought it sounded lovely."

"So, no one's ready?"

"Eliza's in the kitchen," Leonardo said. "Sounded like she was on a call with her agent. More than likely the others are still sleeping."

"Great." I bit back a groan of frustration. "Do you all still want to go today? If we move quick, we could still make it."

Hailee pursed her lips as she exhaled loudly. "Fine . . . Give us ten minutes to finish up. We'll be right in."

"Okay . . ." I'd have preferred now. But at least they'd agreed.

Inside, I found Eliza slumped against the kitchen counter, working on her laptop and nursing a cup of coffee. She was dressed in shorts and an oversized lime-green T-shirt, her hair pulled back into a limp ponytail.

"Eliza?" I approached her. "Hi! Sorry to bother you, but—"

She held up a finger, then tapped the wireless headset nestled around her ear. "No, Jimmy. We both know it's a little more than a cameo. I can play Cecilia. I'd nail an audition if they'd give me a chance. Which one do you like better?"

She poked my shoulder. I realized the last question was directed at me.

"Which one?" She pointed at the laptop screen where two photos were displayed. In both, Eliza sat on the steps outside the villa. In one, she leaned forward, her hair draped over a shoulder. In the other, her head was tipped back.

"I like the first one," I said, but my artist's eyes couldn't help but nitpick. "But there's a shadow over your feet. And the lighting's better in the other one." I shook my head. Wait—what was I doing? "That's not why I'm here. Do you remember the horseback riding?"

But it was no use. She was already distracted, swiping the trackpad. With a few deft taps, the first photo transformed, taking on a sunset glow. She removed the offending shadows, sharpened the hazel of her eyes, then blurred away the shine on her cheeks, chin, and shoulders.

"Eliza," I said a little louder. "The horseback riding—"

"That's not going to work for me," she said.

"What?"

She pointed to her headset again. "Jimmy, look, I understand they want someone with more experience, but how can I get experience when no one will give me a shot? Have they seen my subscriber count? I come with a built-in audience. Don't ask me— it's your job to convince them!"

She yanked the headset off and slammed her hands onto the counter.

I jumped.

"Sorry, Reyna," she said, after a few deep breaths. "Just dealing with some business. Did you want something?"

"The horseback riding," I said gently. "It's this morning. But we can cancel. That's fine."

Eliza pushed her hair back from her forehead. "Sorry, I thought it was tonight."

"Don't worry about it. It's in less than an hour. If we hustled, we could still probably make it. But since it looks like Fish and Aiden aren't even up yet, maybe I should cancel."

Not to mention this had the upside of putting off dealing with Aiden for another day.

But Eliza was shaking her head. "No, we'll still go."

"If you're sure . . ."

"Yeah." Eliza's lips curled into a smile. She stood up straighter, her whole face brightened. "We'll just have to wake them up." She took a swig from her mug, then set it down in the sink. She took my hand and pulled me toward the stairs. "Come on, this should be fun. We can film it."

"I—I really don't think this is the best use of my time. I should go call the stables. Let them know we might be a little late."

"In a minute. Right now, I need your help. You can film."

"Is that really necessary?"

"My fans expect a new post every day, Reyna. It's not easy coming up with new ideas all the time. I've got to snatch inspiration whenever it pops up."

"Not that. I mean, wouldn't the guys mind us barging in like this?" Or more specifically *me* barging in on them.

Eliza let go of my hand. "Nah—they won't care." She disappeared into the Calypso Queen room, then returned a few seconds later, hair down and a fresh shirt on. She shoved her phone at me. "Okay, I'm ready."

With a sigh, I started recording.

"Morning, lovelies. We're going horseback riding today! I know you're as excited as I am. The only problem is—we've got two late sleepers holding us up. You want to say hi to the fam, Reyna?"

"I'd rather not."

Eliza laughed. "She's funny, right? That's Reyna. We're excited to have her tagging along with us for the next few days."

More like being *dragged along*, I'd say.

"Right now," Eliza said. "I'm going to show her some tricks I've learned to wake these guys up. Let's start with Fish since he's the easiest."

I drew a steadying breath and followed her to the Yellow Bird room.

Eliza threw open the door without knocking and walked right in. I had the camera trained on her as she moved toward the sleeping body wrapped in red sheets on the bed. A thick comforter and all but one pillow had been knocked to the floor.

Eliza stopped at the edge of the bed. "Max Martin is overrated!"

Fish bolted upright. "Why don't you say that to my face, you—" He blinked, squinting at us. "What the hell, Eliza?"

"We have horseback riding at ten," I said, when Eliza wouldn't stop laughing. "Please get dressed. We need to get going."

"Otherwise we leave without you!" Eliza said.

Fish dropped back onto the bed. "Fine," he said to the ceiling. "But only for the horsies."

Eliza snorted. She took my hand and tugged me back into the hall. I didn't even have time to brace myself before she burst right into the Hot, Hot, Hot room. I made a mental note to lock the door if I found myself staying with Eliza in the future.

"Time to rise and shine, cowboy!" Eliza padded across the carpet and yanked aside the white curtains. Sunlight flooded the room. "We've got another surprise for you."

The human-shaped mound beneath the comforter shifted. Eliza drew closer to the bed. I wanted to bolt.

Above the headboard, a mural of an immortelle tree stretched along the wall. Depicted at the height of blooming, the orange-red flowers burned like flames. If someone looked closely though, they'd notice something off. If they pushed the bed forward, they'd see the mural wasn't finished.

"Not another one," Aiden rasped. "I swear, if I pull off this cover and you're filming, I'm throwing your phone over the balcony."

Eliza knelt on the end of the bed and leaned over him. "So mean." She pouted. "Why deny the people your pretty face? Do you want your fans to die of thirst?"

"I'm serious, Eliza. Right over the balcony. And you along with it."

"I think your pillow talk needs a little work, hon." Eliza snorted. "And just so you know, you're wrong—I'm not filming."

"Sure you're not." Aiden pulled the covers from his face. His head appeared, framed by a mess of curls. He smiled crookedly as he squinted against the sunlight. Then he glanced toward the doorway, saw me, and sat up, startled.

I stopped recording and lowered the phone. By this point, Eliza had gotten more than enough.

"We're leaving in twenty minutes," I said, pushing past the bile burning the back of my throat. "Be outside or we will leave without you." I didn't wait for their reply, already turning away.

Olivia was right. It took seeing Aiden flirt with Eliza for me to realize it.

I was not over him.

Aiden C. of DJ Bacchanal and Eliza Musgrove dating? Repeatedly spotted together, the hot new music producer and the C-list vlog-tress have tongues wagging. But is it a summer fling or a PR thing? Then again, who says it can't be a bit of both. . . .

There it was in black and white. Well, actually black and hot pink on the gossip site. Not the most reliable source, but searching for Aiden and Eliza together mostly brought up fan shipping or articles about Hailee and Leonardo. There were a few pieces, like this one, that hinted at the possibility of them dating. I dreaded finding something concrete, but at least then I'd know what I was working with.

While I leaned against the side of our rented van, frustratedly clicking through gossip-site links, the others trickled out of the villa. Eliza had shown up first, dressed in an emerald-green beach dress, the straps of a black-metallic bathing suit tied around her neck. She and our driver chatted politely until Hailee, Leo, and Fish joined us.

Aiden strolled through the doors last. He wore a wrinkled white T-shirt, knee-length maroon swim trunks, and an obnoxiously huge pair of sunglasses that concealed half his face. His hair was a mess, curls in every direction. For all the time it took for him to get ready, it looked like he'd just rolled out of bed and pulled on the first clothes within reach. It wasn't fair how good that looked on him.

"Here he is." Eliza sprang to his side. "Nice glasses. Can I borrow them?"

"No." He dodged her hand. After greeting the driver, he stood there for a moment, hands shoved in his pockets. "So . . . horseback riding. You guys really did not need to do all this."

Eliza slung an arm around his waist. "Sure we did."

"I call shotgun!" Fish pulled open the passenger-side door and climbed inside. Leonardo and Hailee followed him.

"Reyna . . ." Aiden approached me.

My eyes snapped up to his face. I'd been staring at the spot where Eliza's hand rested against his stomach. I prayed neither of them had noticed. "Yes."

"You really coming with us." He didn't say it like a question, but I answered anyway.

"I really am," I said.

Eliza let go of Aiden, and the knot in my chest eased a little.

"It took a little convincing," she said. "But Reyna has agreed to endure our group of dumbasses for the next few weeks."

Eliza turned her smiling face toward Aiden. They were almost the same height—well-matched in this aspect. I didn't want to think about any others.

"Isn't it great, though?' she said. "Now you two have all the time to catch up and chat about the old days."

"So great," Aiden said. His tone somehow straddled the line between enthusiasm and sarcasm, so neatly that Eliza seemed to totally miss the latter.

I did not.

"Don't you have a job?" he asked me.

"I do," I said, pointing to the van. "This is it."

"How—"

"Your friends asked my father."

"I see."

"Yeah."

We didn't say anything for a beat. And then another.

Despite my better judgment, I felt a prickle of amusement worming its way through the awkwardness and silence. It was funny, in a way. His friends were trying so hard to give him a perfect vacation; all Daddy wanted was for me to have fun. Even though Aiden and I had agreed to stay away from each other, we'd failed thanks to the very people who wanted to make us happy.

Did Aiden find it a little funny too? I couldn't tell. Not through those massive sunglasses he was wearing. Once upon a time, we used to have a similar sense of humor, so maybe he did. Or maybe not. How different was this Aiden from the boy I used to love?

And then there was Eliza. The influencer. The girl Aiden was probably dating.

Eliza, whose wide hazel eyes bounced between Aiden and me, her expertly shaped brows inching upward, almost disappearing behind the cut of her bangs. Clueless as she may have been at the moment, she was bound to get suspicious if we drew out this silence any longer.

"After you?" I pointed to the van.

Without another word, we climbed into the idling vehicle. Aiden took the spot next to Eliza in the middle row, which left me in the back with Hailee and Leonardo. Unfortunately, this meant I'd be staring at his and Eliza's heads for the whole ride.

"Finally!" Fish said as the van door slid shut. "Let's put on some music! What do you want to bet we'll find one of our songs playing on the radio?" He twisted. "Hey, Reyna—I hear we're big with the Trinis."

"Not that big," I muttered, then realized where I was, and how insulting that might've sounded. "No offense."

Fish inhaled sharply. "Yes, offense. You take that back."

"I didn't—" I started to apologize, then beside me, Leonardo smothered a laugh against his fist. I glanced over to see Hailee smiling too. Relieved I hadn't crossed some line, I pretended to consider Fish's order. "No."

Fish stared at me, mouth open.

Leonardo burst into laughter. "Where did you find this one?"

Eliza twisted around. "We got lucky, right? We might need to bring her home with us if she can shut Fish up like that."

"Hey!" Fish called back, while Leonardo and Eliza snickered like preteens in the back of a school bus.

"Behave, children," Hailee said, even though she was obviously trying not to laugh too. "You're going to scare her off. And it's just her first day."

Just my first day. Of three weeks.

As the van pulled out of the parking lot, I found it difficult not to regret every decision that led to that moment.

ELEVEN

The stables were tucked into a back street, a good distance from the main road. Thankfully, the driver knew where to go. If we'd been on our own, we might've missed the driftwood gates at the entrance.

I'd never been, but the horseback ride looked exciting in the pictures—the powerful chestnut-colored animals galloping through a pristine blue sea, the riders beaming like they were having the time of their lives. Mummy had loved recommending the place, and Plumeria guests gave it nothing but rave reviews.

We parked and got out. My sneakers sank into the soft ground. The air smelled of freshly cut grass and manure. Heather Gunther, who I knew through Tourism Association events I'd attended with Daddy, came out to greet us. She was an older woman with waist-length graying hair divided into two neat braids. She enfolded me in a hug before leading us into the office.

"Welcome, all of you." Heather showed us to a set of chairs and handed us forms to sign. "Before we get started, I need to ask—how many of you have ridden before?"

Everyone but me lifted their hand. Great.

While we filled in the forms, a preteen girl bounced into the office with a box of key chains. She crossed the room to Heather, took one look at the boys, and shrieked.

"Ma, do you know who this is?" She ducked behind Heather. The key chains tumbled to the floor. "It's DJ Bacchanal!"

"Who?"

"Ma, come on. You know, they sing that song you like." And then she started to sing "Hyperbolic," rocking her hips to the rhythm.

"Okay, okay." Heather spun her daughter toward the door. She shot us an apologetic smile. "Thank you, Lauren. Please go help get the horses ready. We'll be out in a second."

"Uh-huh . . ." Lauren backed out of the office, eyes on the boys. She lifted her hand in a small wave. All three boys waved back.

Lauren squealed and fled.

Aiden laughed, and his dimples deepened. He'd finally taken off the shades. I hadn't seen him laugh like that since he'd arrived.

It took me a few seconds to realize Heather was speaking to me.

"Sorry, what?"

"I'm happy you finally made it here," she said.

"Oh. Thanks." I handed her my finished form. "We're sorry for being late. I hope it's not too much trouble."

"No problem," she said. "This is Tobago. It's only when people early I worry. But that's not what I meant. For years, I promised your mother I'd take your family out on a trail. Bless her soul, she never did make it here." Heather clasped my shoulders. "She was such a lovely woman. Very no-nonsense, but very kind."

"Thanks," I said, my throat tight.

"Well," she said. "At least I finally got you here."

I nodded. When she moved to collect the rest of the forms, I let my gaze fall to the floor. She was trying to be nice, and I appreciated the sentiment, but I would rather not think about all the things Mummy never got to do. It wasn't fair she wasn't here, and nothing could make up for it.

Ten minutes later, our group had been outfitted with helmets and boots and assigned to horses. Mine was Lydia, an ex-racehorse from Trinidad who'd decided one day there was no point in leaving the starting gate. So she retired to Tobago, giving the occasional visitor a ride along the beach. Heather mentioned that Lydia didn't go out on the trail as much as the other horses, and I could tell. The second I mounted her, she turned away from the others and returned to her stable to eat more feed.

"You need to relax," Heather told me. "If you're nervous, she's not going to listen. You've got to convince her you know what you're doing."

"But I don't know what I'm doing," I pointed out. After observing the others, I didn't see that what I was doing was so different. I tugged the reins, clicked my tongue, encouraged her to *walk on*.

Eventually, Heather got tired of watching me struggle, retrieved me and Lydia, and led us back to the others.

She instructed everyone to stick close to the group, especially through the woodsy part of the trail that led to the beach. "There are a few alternate paths," she said. "We don't want you wandering off."

With the introduction finished, we set off. The horses filtered through the open driftwood gates one by one. Hooves clacked against the road, the group moving at an easy pace. Hailee and Eliza were out in front, Heather and I at the rear. Heather's daughter and two other assistants walked alongside us.

Overhead, delicate wisps of clouds did nothing to ease the glare of the midmorning sun. It was a weird feeling, sitting high up, rocking with each jerky hoof fall, all the while conscious of the huge living, breathing animal beneath me. I gripped the reins tightly, certain I was about to fall off at any moment.

"Relax, Reyna." Heather rode alongside me. Since I was the least experienced, she seemed to be sticking close to me. I was both appreciative and embarrassed. Every time one of the other riders looked back at us, I wanted to disappear.

"Don't worry about them," she said, probably noticing my discomfort with being left behind. After a few beats of silence, she said, "You're Tobagonian, right? Born here, in the country of soca? I'm guessing you know how to wine. To dance with your hips?"

"Yes." But I couldn't remember the last time I'd danced. Or gone to a fete or anywhere where wining would take place.

"Use that then. Visualize yourself dancing. Feel the rhythm

and go with the flow. Go ahead and sing your favorite song if you need to."

I decided against singing aloud. This was to both spare myself from further embarrassment as well as Heather from having to listen to it. But I did start quietly humming Shurwayne Winchester's "Don't Stop." It felt a little weird at first, but soon the beat of the song started to blend into the click of the hooves and I leaned into the groove, bobbing along. At some point, I stopped focusing on how to stay on the horse and started enjoying the ride.

"You're doing great!" Heather said.

I looked over to find her smiling at me. "Thanks."

At a small fork in the path, Lydia went left. Heather's horse followed. It took a few seconds for me to be sure, but the riders in front of us were definitely on a different path. I tensed up again. "Um, Heather? I think we made a wrong turn."

"No worries. Lydia wanted to take a shortcut. We'll meet up with the others at the beach."

"Oh." I watched the rest of the riders disappear behind the trees. I felt a twinge of FOMO, but there was no reason for me to feel excluded. I already knew I wasn't really part of their group, just the guide. They probably wouldn't notice I was missing anyway.

"You're tensing up again," Heather said. She was right.

I tried humming music again, but "Hyperbolic" kept invading my brain, like the irritating earworm it was. Instead, I tried distracting myself with the scenery—the azure sky, the verdant trees. Along the grassy trail, warm sunlight dappled through the shadowy leaves, making me think of Claude Monet's painting, *Garden Path*.

A short while later, I heard the sounds of waves and the chatter of sea bathers. Heather led me through a patch of sea grape trees, the horses weaving their way around trunks, arched roots, and low hanging branches. Finally, she stopped, dismounted, and helped me down.

She led Lydia over to a palm tree, and the horse started eating leaves. "I'm going to leave you two here in the shade while I check on the others. The beach is just on the other side. Let Lydia graze for a bit. I'll be right back."

I nodded, then watched as she mounted her horse and rode off again.

"Well, I guess this outing wasn't *so* bad." I patted Lydia's neck. She ignored me in favor of what must've been a very tasty patch of grass.

"Wait—stop here for a moment." Eliza's voice came from the other side of the trees. "We're getting really far ahead. Do you think Reyna's okay? I haven't seen her in a while."

I was about to call out to her when Aiden answered, "I'm sure she's fine."

Something about his dismissive tone made me pause.

"I feel bad though," Eliza said. "It's her first day with us, and we've already ditched her. She's only here because we asked for her help."

"Yeah, about that," Aiden said. "I've been meaning to ask— whose idea was it? I get you wanted a local guide. But her?"

"Why not her?" Eliza sounded confused.

Yes, why not? I also wanted to know. After making sure Lydia was still occupied with her grazing, I crept forward to hear the answer he came up with.

"You don't know how she is," he said. "The Plumeria is her life. I have no idea how you guys talked her into taking time off from it. Your intentions were good, but my guess is Reyna's hating every second away from her precious hotel."

"Stop it, Aiden." Eliza laughed. "You make her sound so boring."

"Well . . ."

"You know what? I think I see it. The way she dresses *is* kind of dull. And you should've heard how worried she was about getting us here on time. She gave me serious type A vibes. I hope she isn't going to be so rigid with the schedule for the whole trip. We are on vacation, for crying out loud!"

Me? Boring? Rigid?

I waited for Aiden to dispute this. Eliza didn't know me, but he did.

"Exactly," he said instead.

My mouth fell open, and I glared in the direction of their voices. I understood why he might try to talk his friends out of including me, in fact there was part of me that hoped he succeeded, but that was no reason to slander me like that.

Unless he thought it was true.

I glanced down at my outfit: a pair of stretched-out jeans and a plain white T-shirt. To be fair, we were horseback riding. I'd thought it would be sensible to dress with a focus on comfort, not style. But, then again, I did tend to choose comfort over style most days.

In my defense, I was trying to run a hotel. Who had time to worry about things like that?

"Honestly," Aiden said, sighing. "I don't think she's going to be able to keep up with us. I know she definitely can't keep up with you."

My heart sank. I recognized that tone. He was flirting.

"No one can keep up with me," Eliza said with a laugh. "Not even you. Though I do like to watch you try."

"Oh really?" Aiden said, his voice ripe with challenge and something else I did not want to name.

The pair started to move again, the hoof falls of their horses picking up pace and quickly fading. I was relieved to miss the rest of that conversation. Frankly, I'd heard too much already.

We returned to the hotel after sunset. The fading light in the sky cast an orange-gold glow over the villa as we pulled into the driveway. After we finalized the plans for the rest of the week, Hailee walked with me to the front door.

"Definitely calling it an early night," Hailee said. "I'm exhausted."

"Yeah, me too." I laughed lightly.

"It was fun though, right?"

"So fun," I agreed, waving to her as I headed down the steps. The second she was out of sight, I gave up the pretense of walking normally.

The muscles of my thighs were on fire. I was dying.

After the horseback riding, we went for lunch. Then to the beach. It took everything I had not to cut the outing short. But that would've proven Aiden and Eliza right—I couldn't keep up. Even if every step I took burned like hell, I'd be damned if I let them see it.

Every time I thought about what I'd overheard, it stung a little more. It was bad enough seeing Aiden and Eliza together all afternoon without their discussion about my boringness ringing in my ears. So far, I'd been spared any unambiguous physical displays of their affection, but I knew that couldn't last.

To my relief, I spotted Daddy's car in the main parking lot. Thank goodness. I did not want to drive home like this. He'd have to take me.

No longer caring who saw me, I shuffled toward Daddy's office, my knees bent at an outward angle. I would not call my movements crablike, but I couldn't honestly deny the descriptor either.

I opened the door and froze on the threshold. "Aunty Helen?"

"Reyna, oh my!" She stood up, turning toward me. "Look at you. How are you, darling? You're more beautiful each time I see you."

I shut the door behind me. Why was she here?

Pam and I had a running theory—her mother and my father hadn't actually been attracted to each other back in the day, only hypnotized by each other's brightly colored plumage. Apparently, their unique style was not something that faded with time. She wore a sleeveless blue-and-yellow-polka-dot dress; a large yellow bow tied around her head; her makeup a vivid blend of maroon, brown, and gold. When she pulled me into a hug, the edges of her chunky shell necklace jabbed into my chest.

"It's so good to see you," she said.

"You too." I looked at Daddy over her shoulder. "I didn't know you were here." Her relationship with Daddy, as far as I knew, was cordial but not too friendly. Had that changed? And if so, since when?

Daddy shot to his feet. "Yes, and thank you, Helen." He crossed over to the door and opened it. "I appreciate all your help. We'll talk soon."

"Soon," she agreed, and let me go. "Call me if you need anything else." She hooked her gold, diamante-studded purse over her shoulder and walked to the door. "Take care, Reyna. I'll see you at the party."

Daddy mumbled a farewell and shut the door behind her.

"What party?" I asked. "The rum punch party?"

Daddy returned to his desk, pulled out a drawer, and rifled through it. "What? Oh—yes. The party, yes."

"Why did we need her help? Is something wrong?"

The Plumeria's rum punch parties were a longstanding tradition where hotel guests, staff, and specially invited friends got treated to a night of live music, free food, and endless drinks—the main draw, of course, being the notorious rum punch. We used the same musicians and vendors every year, and I'd already booked them. There shouldn't have been any problem.

"Is nothing." Daddy shut the drawer. It seemed like he hadn't found what he was looking for. "But forget about hotel business, how was your day with the horses?"

"Fine . . ." Something still felt a little off, but the intense need to sit overwhelmed my suspicion. "I took some notes that may be useful for the guide." After dropping into a chair, I pulled out my notebook and flipped to the first page. "For one thing, they recommend coming thirty minutes early, if possible. And they do have specialty tours for more experienced riders, but you've got to ask for them—"

"Reyna," Daddy said, holding up a hand. "All that is good, but did you enjoy it?"

I lowered the notebook. "What?"

He raised a brow. "Did you enjoy it?"

Did I enjoy it?

Well, I was thoroughly exhausted. And the muscles of my thighs were screaming out in anguish. Oh, and I'd overheard my ex-boyfriend call me boring. But in terms of the horseback riding itself . . .

"Honestly?" I thought of Lydia and smiled. "I liked the ride. It was . . . calming. My horse was a sweetheart, and Heather was an awesome instructor. She was very patient with me. Overall, I'd definitely do it again."

"And what about lunch?" Daddy asked.

"We went to the Black Bean Café, like you recommended. I had the oil down and loved it. Couldn't convince the Americans to try it, though. They said it looked too slimy." I laughed, remembering Hailee's face when she saw my plate. "They really seemed to enjoy the geera pork, though."

"Now that is what I want to hear!" Daddy sat forward. "I want you to have fun. Enjoy these outings. Not report back with facts I could find on the internet." He stopped as if something just occurred to him. "You do know it's okay to have fun with this, right?"

I rolled my eyes. "Yes."

"Really, Reyna. You would tell me if you were ever unhappy with something?"

"*Yes.*" His concern felt suffocating, like a heavy blanket. "I'm happy. It just feels wrong to not be at the hotel, helping. Planning the rum punch party—"

"Will go on as usual. And you will wholeheartedly enjoy your time off. Promise me you will try."

Given the current situation, I didn't see how wholehearted enjoyment was possible. But Daddy looked so hopeful.

"I'll try," I said.

TWELVE

FOUR YEARS EARLIER

Growing up, I loved all kinds of music. It was hard not to, living in Tobago. My playlists were a mishmash of local calypso and soca, Jamaican reggae and dancehall, a bit of Bollywood, and a ton of America's hip-hop, R&B, and pop. I even liked a little classical music, though no one would have been able to tell from the way I played it.

"That note did not sound right," Daddy said, from the kitchen. He'd paused, knife lifted, in the middle of chopping tomatoes for our breakfast of sardines and coconut bake.

"It is," I lied, and kept playing.

I shouldn't have set up the keyboard facing the window. My attention strayed outside too easily. That day was clear and warm, the front lawn a lush green. The frangipani tree would bloom any day now; the bougainvillea, ixoras, and zinnias had already erupted in starbursts of purple, red, and pink flowers. Looking at all that color, I felt intoxicated. I wanted to touch it. Paint it.

Then suddenly Aiden blocked my view.

I jolted upright, my fingers smashing against the keys.

"Ay!" Daddy turned from the fridge to face me. "Now, I know that not right."

"No, it's—"

I looked back at the window. Aiden had vanished.

This was the first time I'd seen him in months. Every school holiday, for the last two years, he'd stay with his grandfather. During these days, we limed together constantly. Almost inseparable. His visits were so part of a routine—*our routine*—I was confused when it hit mid-July and he hadn't shown up.

Yes, I could've messaged him. Asked when he planned to turn up, if he planned to at all. But then that might make it sound like I cared. Like I missed him.

Just the idea that he might find out about my crush left me weak with mortification. That he might realize, if he didn't already— and sometimes, the way he looked at me, I did wonder—that a glimpse of him was enough to rouse butterflies in my stomach. That, as I sat there, at the keyboard, staring at the window, I was smiling like a fool, holding back the impulse to run outside.

I didn't know when, but at some point, liking Aiden turned into *liking* Aiden, and I had no idea what to do with it. All I knew was I'd die if he found out. Or, even worse, if he found out *and* rejected me. I'd die twice.

Exhaling slowly, I attempted to wrestle the stomach butterflies into submission. I lifted my hands to the keys and continued to play.

And there he was again. I shot him a look that I hoped conveyed annoyance, but if Aiden got it, he ignored it. He made a circular gesture with his hands that indicated I should keep playing. I did—or tried to—but it got harder when he started dancing, his moves so cheesy and out of time, I didn't know whether to laugh or die of secondhand embarrassment.

Finally, I couldn't take it anymore. "Okay, I'm done. Can I go outside now?"

"Your mother said you need to practice for at least thirty minutes," Daddy said, removing the toasted bake from the oven.

"I must've passed that." I'd been practicing for ages before Aiden showed up.

"It's been twelve minutes."

"What?" I groaned, then looking at Aiden, I shook my head.

Aiden pouted.

"Okay, nah." Daddy sighed loudly. "Jus' go. But remember your mother wants you at the hotel for two o'clock. She has someone she want you to meet."

"Yes!" I leaped to my feet.

"Take your breakfast first." Daddy came over to hand me a brown bag. "Is one bake for you and one for Aiden. I was going to ask if he wanted any, but he always hungry anyway."

I froze. He knew Aiden was outside?

Daddy laughed, heading back toward the kitchen. "Be back before dark," he said. "And tell your boyfriend if he mashed up any of your mother's zinnias with his little dance routine, there's nothing I can do to save him."

"Will do," I said, then sprinted out of there, embarrassed. Daddy hadn't used the word *boyfriend* in front of Aiden yet, but it was only a matter of time. He thought it was *so funny*.

I met Aiden on the front porch.

"I hope you're happy," I said, trying to sound annoyed. I didn't know how effective it was. I was just so happy to see him. "You ruined my piano practice."

He stood, dusting off his swim pants. "The way you were murdering *Clair de Lune*, someone had to."

"Funny." I handed him the food, and we descended the steps.

Now he was back, the holiday could start for real.

When we got to the beach, it was packed. Dozens of people were scattered along the sand, running, playing, digging. Swimmers waded, splashed, and sliced through the sea. We sat together at the water's edge, the low tide lapping lazily at our feet.

"Stop moving." I squeezed his elbow, yanking it closer. I know it was asking a lot; Aiden was rarely ever still, constantly twitching or tapping, the only exception when he was writing. "I'm almost done."

He groaned. "You said that twenty minutes ago."

I looked up at him, checking to see if he was really upset. Or, as I suspected, complaining for the sake of complaining.

He was looking at the sea, his profile toward me. I couldn't help but notice the length of his dark eyelashes, or the sprinkle of sunlight caught in his short wet hair. For a second, I couldn't breathe, the butterflies in my stomach on the loose again.

Aiden caught me staring. "You're done?"

"Almost." I dropped my eyes quickly. It took a second for me to resume my drawing, my heart racing. "You were saying something before? About money?" I laughed. Did I sound nervous? "What do you want to buy now?"

Two years ago, he hadn't made the deadline to buy the expensive guitar. Instead, he'd gotten a hand-me-down from his music teacher. Apparently, she'd offered it as a gift, but Aiden insisted on paying its worth. I wasn't surprised when he told me; Aiden would never accept something he felt he hadn't earned. But in doing so, he'd drained his savings.

"New laptop and recording equipment," he said.

"I'm not even going to ask how much." If the guitar had been impossible . . .

"No, see—I have a plan this time."

"And I'm listening, but you need to hold still. You're going to ruin it."

"Come nah." Aiden frowned at the image I'd inked into his arm. "It have to be flowers again?" He tried to twist his body to get a better look, but I held his arm right where I needed it.

"Yes. Now stop moving."

"You can't make it something more manly?"

"Manly?"

"Yes. Please."

"Okay . . ." I moved on to the blank canvas lower down his

arm. "I see what you're saying," I assured him. Then I proceeded to write the word *manly* in flourishing cursive, weaving roses and sunflowers through the letters.

"Yes," he said drily. "That's exactly what I meant."

He turned his head away, but not before I caught the edge of a smile.

"You know about the Crown Bago Festival talent competition?" he asked. "This year I'm going to enter. First prize is five thousand dollars."

I nodded slowly. "Ah."

"At least pretend you think I have a chance."

"You have a chance." Of course he did. But the competition was a big deal. A lot of people entered. I didn't want him to set his hopes up for nothing.

"Remember I told you about Miss Bee, my music teacher?" he said. "She's helping me. I'm just having problems with the lyrics."

"Why?" I swiped at the sweat that gathered at my temples. The heat was starting to be too much, but I didn't want us to move yet. I loved the moments like these, where it was just us, sitting, talking, being. "What's it about?"

Aiden squinted up at the sea. The glare of the sun reflected off the water. "The music would suit something like a happy love song, but I'm not feeling particularly romantic at the moment."

Ouch. This right here—sitting on the beach, drawing on his arm—felt pretty romantic to me.

"I broke up with Alanna," he explained.

"Oh." I didn't need to fake my surprise. Sympathy was a bit trickier. "I'm sorry."

Aiden's lip twitched. He watched me from the corner of his eye. "Why are you sorry?"

The heat of embarrassment snaked up my neck and chest. I returned my attention to the drawing. "Excuse me. I was being sympathetic. Remind me not to be nice to you next time you break up with someone. I will not be making that mistake again."

"You're rambling," he said. "But do you mean it?" There was a strange tension in his voice. "Are you sorry?"

"Of course."

I tried to laugh off his question with a lightness I did not feel. I glanced at his face. He was watching me, searching for something. My stomach clenched. Could he see right through me?

"I know you really liked her, so yes. Do you think I want you to be sad?" I quickly finished filling in the last petal. "Okay, done."

"You really mean that, don't you?"

"Yes, it's really done." I looked up. He was still watching me intently, his gaze less probing now, but softer. With no reason to hold his arm anymore, I let go. His warmth and the impression of his skin lingered on my palm; I closed my fist in an attempt to keep it a little longer.

"That's not what I meant," he said.

"Hold on." I reached for my phone. "Let me take a picture of it before you—" The time on the screen read ten minutes after two. I scrambled to my feet. "I've got to go."

"What? Wait."

"I can't." I grabbed my bag off the ground. "Mummy told me to meet her at the hotel at two. I've got to go. Now."

"I'll go with you."

"No." I zipped my bag shut and threw it over my shoulder. Mummy wouldn't appreciate him tagging along. Plus, after all this talk about his ex-girlfriend, I needed some space. "She wants me to meet her friends. It'll be boring, and I don't know when we'll be done. You stay here. Maybe some inspiration will hit."

He looked toward the sea then back to me. "But I was trying to tell you something."

"Tell me later!" I started for the steps to the main road.

"Don't you want to know why I broke up with her?" he called out.

Hell, yes. But I needed to sort out my feelings first. "Later!"

When we met up the next day, he never told me. Later came and passed. I thought of asking, but something held me back. It was okay though. A few months later, I'd have a pretty good idea what he'd been trying to say anyway.

THIRTEEN

A few days after horseback riding, I went to meet Hailee and Eliza at the villa. They'd asked me to show them around the hotel property so we could decide on the perfect spot to hold Aiden's birthday party. I thought their poolside would've been perfectly fine, but they wanted *options*. On my way, I stopped at the restaurant to grab them two coffees and one for myself.

Approaching the villa, I was happy to see the folding front doors pulled open, the front porch a mess—all signs that the girls were up and about. If they were ready to get going, it would limit my chances of bumping into Aiden.

So far, I hadn't really worked out how to be a normal person around him. I was constantly on edge, conscious of my every word, every action. I didn't bring up our past. Never stood too close or looked at him too long. When he and Eliza flirted, I did my best impression of complete indifference. Sometimes, I could feel myself fading into the background. No doubt this made me just as boring as Eliza said, but what else could I do?

On the front porch, I noticed a thin notepad flipped open, several crumpled sheets of paper stuffed into a bin beside the chair. A laptop sat open, a set of expensive cordless headphones tossed to the side. The computer screen idled on a program I'd never seen before, but with tags like *track*, *kick*, and *clap*, it didn't take a genius to work out it was some sort of music production software. Fascinated, I leaned in for a closer look.

"What are you doing?"

I jumped.

Two of the cups flipped out of my tray onto the floor. Coffee spattered in every direction. My first thought was *oh, thank God it didn't land on the laptop.*

My second thought was *ouch!*

I glanced down. Brown stains soaked into my left sleeve and down the front of my shirt. I pulled the fabric away from my skin. "Oh, it's hot!"

"Are you okay?" Aiden cursed, took the tray from me, and set it on the table. "You got burned? Come, you need to run it under cold water." He reached for my arm and pulled me inside.

In the kitchen, he turned on the tap. The water erupted at full blast, bounced off a bowl in the sink, and sprayed upward, soaking us both.

"Shoot! Sorry." Aiden turned the pressure down.

I flicked the water from my face. "It's fine."

"I'll get you a towel," he said, then took off.

While he was gone, I peeked under my neckline. The skin of

116

my stomach stung a little, but I didn't see any burns. I rolled up my sleeve to find a faint pink splotch. I stuck my hand under the cold water.

Aiden returned. "Here." He handed me a towel.

"Thanks," I said, wiping my face, neck, and arms. "I'm fine."

"Are you sure?" he asked. "You should still take off your shirt."

My head shot up.

We stared at each other for a long moment.

Something flashed in his umber-colored eyes, and he stepped back. He cleared his throat. "Honey," he said, moving toward the adjacent counter. "You need honey. It would help with the pain and scarring. But we don't have any here."

"I don't need it," I assured him. "I really am fine."

He nodded, still searching through a few drawers. He returned with a handful of takeout napkins and started to clean up some of the water that had splashed around the sink.

I ran the towel over my arm, watching him from the corner of my eye. We'd been touching on instinct, moving in each other's spaces like we belonged there. I instantly missed his nearness, the warm weight of his hand. I didn't even notice how close we'd been, but now that he was gone, I wanted it back.

He'd been so careful, so kind to me. I knew he wasn't the type of person to not act when someone was hurt, but a part of me wanted to cling to the notion that it might be more than that.

"Reyna? Here you are." Hailee entered the kitchen. Her eyes widened as she took me in. "What happened to you?"

"I had a small accident. All my fault." I glanced at Aiden. He was still turned to the sink, taking a long time to clean up a little bit of water. I gestured to my shirt, now soaked with coffee and water. "I'm okay. Though I cannot say the same for my clothes."

Hailee gave me a sympathetic smile. "Don't worry about that. We just need to get your top soaking in hot water to make sure it doesn't stain. In the meantime, you can borrow something to wear."

"It's fine. I can go home to change."

"Not if you want to make sure you get that stain out. And I didn't see your car outside, so you must've parked by the main entrance?" When I nodded, she lowered her voice and leaned closer. "I'm guessing you haven't realized yet. Your shirt is more than a little see-through at the moment."

I crossed my arms over my chest. "I'll take that shirt. Yes. Thank you. But I highly doubt I'm going to fit into the same clothes as a supermodel."

She led me to the stairs. "Don't worry, we'll find something."

As we left, I turned to look at Aiden. He still had his back to us, facing the sink.

Hailee led me to the Tempo room, my favorite in the villa. It was open. Peaceful. Painted in soft blues and decorated with a few pieces of rattan furnishing. Soon as I entered, I crossed over to the balcony overlooking the sea. That morning the water was so clear and calm, I could make out the dark shapes of the rocks at the bottom.

I turned back to Hailee. "You got the best room."

"That's what I said!" Hailee laughed. She quickly flicked

through her wardrobe, examining each piece, then sliding it aside. She pulled out a red top with lace around the collar. "Here—try this."

I eyed the scrap of fabric with skepticism. "I don't think this will fit me."

She handed it to me. "Try it. The color will look great on you. I swiped it from a shoot in Manila."

"Okay. Thanks." I held the shirt to my torso. The neckline seemed a little wide, but it would do. "Are you allowed to take clothes from photo shoots?"

"Not usually." She turned her back to give me some privacy. "But the designer was a friend. Really, the whole shoot turned into a party. We ended up visiting a bunch of places. Palawan. Cebu. Boracay."

"It sounds amazing." I started undoing the buttons of my shirt. "The Philippines is definitely on my list. Well, to be fair, everywhere that's not Tobago is on my list."

"You've never left this island?" Hailee asked, shocked. "Not even to Trinidad? But it's right there."

I tried to laugh it off, embarrassed. "I know, right? It's only a twenty-minute flight. But it just never worked out. I was supposed to go with my class on a field trip once. We were meant to visit Pitch Lake and Caroni Swamp, but it got canceled."

"And you're okay with that? Staying here?"

I shrugged. "It's just how it is." And it didn't look like it was going to change anytime soon.

"Wow," Hailee said. "I can't imagine. Getting to travel is

probably the best part of modeling, even if it is usually for work. Out of everything, it's going to be the thing I miss the most about it."

I pulled my stained shirt off. "Why would you miss it?"

"You don't know? I haven't made an official announcement, but I thought Jake might've told you. I'm putting modeling on indefinite pause. Next spring, I'm off to college."

"Really?"

"Yeah." Her words rushed out with excitement. "I put it off for a year, but college and law school has always been the plan. Modeling is something I fell into. You should hear my mom boast about her daughter, the future lawyer. She's so relieved I'm going back to school."

"Your mom?"

Desiree Ahura? The former model and actress? The woman best known for briefly dating that guy from *Dawson's Creek* and playing a string of femme fatale characters in the nineties?

"Yeah." Hailee snorted. "I know what you're thinking. Truth is she tried really hard to discourage Eliza and me from following in her footsteps. She's much happier running her cosmetic company than she ever was in Hollywood. Mom hates the idea of Eliza going into acting, but . . ." She shrugged.

"Eliza seems to be doing well though," I said. "Her videos get a lot of views. She's got tons of followers."

"Yeah, but followers aren't the same as fans." Hailee sighed. "I'm not saying she isn't talented. Lord knows she can be charming when she wants to be. And I guess she is stubborn. The type of person to push *and push* until she gets what she wants. Trust me, it's incredibly annoying, but helpful in show business. When it comes to gigs—or guys—I tend to pity anyone who tries to get in her way."

Good to know. Not that I had any plans to get in her way. I doubted I could even if I'd wanted.

A quick glance in the mirror assured me that the top did fit, the shoulders a little loose, the style way too flirty to mesh with my black pencil skirt, but the color *was* nice on me.

"Okay, I'm dressed," I said.

Hailee turned around. "It looks good!"

"It doesn't look like me."

"So?" She stood beside me, looking over my reflection. "Still try it. Experimenting with looks, playing with different personas—it's my favorite part of modeling. You might discover a new you."

"I thought the best part of modeling was traveling."

"Yeah. That too." There was a note of wistfulness in her voice.

"Are you going to miss it? Modeling?"

"Yeah," she said, meeting my eyes in the mirror. "But I'm ready to move on. And excited." She plucked the wet shirt out of my hands. "Why don't you go down and join the others? Let me put this to soak, then we can head out."

When I returned downstairs, Fish and Leonardo were sitting on the couch. The face of a singer I vaguely recognized filled the widescreen TV. Through the window, I spotted Aiden sitting at the table on the porch. He had his hands buried in his hair, his head bowed as he concentrated on the laptop screen. As if he could feel my attention, he turned to the window. I quickly shifted my eyes, readjusting the neckline of Hailee's shirt, which had slipped over my shoulders.

Fish and Leonardo were watching music videos. Clips of a woman running through a barren landscape full of melting clocks were intercut with a skull-like image miming along to the lyrics. I leaned against the back of the couch to watch.

"They're referencing something," Leonardo said. "But I can't remember what."

"Salvador Dalí," Fish and I said at the same time.

Fish shot me a quick smile before smacking Leonardo on the knee. "How do you not remember? I dragged you and Aiden to see his stuff while we were in Figueres. We spent four hours in the art museum."

"You asked Aiden to go to an art museum?" I joined them on the couch. "And he went?" I couldn't believe it. Back in the day, he'd shown zero interest when I'd tried talking him into going to art exhibitions.

Leonardo snorted. "We sure did. Fish used his preferred method of persuasion. He annoyed us into saying yes."

"Hey," Fish said. "Don't knock the methods. Especially when they get results." He wrinkled his nose, then added, "I will admit, Aiden did prove to be a harder target than usual when it came to the museum. In the end, the only way I could convince him to go was to promise I'd introduce him to Nicola Love. I'd done a charity spot with her, and she'd given me her number."

"Nicola Love?" My chest clenched. "The singer?"

"Yeah—hey! Aiden!" Fish called out. "You remember Nicola Love?"

Aiden lifted his head. "What?"

"I said, do you remember Nicola Love?"

Aiden rose from his seat and stood in the doorway. "Why are you asking?" He folded his arms, his black T-shirt stretched across his chest. The outline of one of his tattoos peeked out from under his sleeve.

"I was just telling Reyna about the time you begged me to introduce you to Nicola Love. Then you went out with her once and never called her again." Fish leaned closer to me and mock whispered, "I try to help, but no one ever seems good enough for him."

"And why are you talking about that?" Aiden asked.

"We weren't," I said quickly. I didn't want him to think I was fishing for information on his love life. "We were talking about the time you guys went to the Dalí museum. Fish just made a verbal detour."

"Sure did," Fish said, shifting to face me. "I totally forgot to show off my Dalí-inspired tattoo. You want to see it?"

I eyed the bit of his tattooed half sleeve not covered by his T-shirt. I couldn't make out anything similar to Dalí's style. Then Fish reached behind his head and yanked his shirt off.

Like, whoa—give a girl a warning!

There was suddenly a lot of uncovered muscle and inked skin.

He had way more tattoos than Aiden, but for some reason, they were all on the left side of his body. Over his chest, I spotted the double image—from one perspective, a couple with their heads bowed close, but when you pulled back, took it all in, their figures formed a skull. It was haunting, and really well done. The longer I looked, the more seamless the transition between one image and the other.

"Seriously, Fish?" Aiden asked.

I yanked my hand back from Fish's arm. I didn't realize I'd touched him. "I am so sorry."

"No problem." Fish smirked. "What? You think I got the tattoos for me to admire?"

Leonardo snorted. "One day, that is not going to work."

Fish shrugged. "Hasn't not worked yet."

I blinked at them, confused. "What?"

"Nothing," Aiden said sharply. At some point, he'd moved to stand behind the couch. "Fish didn't realize that you're really, *really* into art." To Fish, he added, "That's all. She's a painter." For some reason, he sounded like he was trying to make a point.

"Oh?" Fish stretched his arm along the back of the couch. "You have to show me your stuff sometime. I'd love to see it."

"Seriously?" Aiden asked again.

I glanced back at him. What was his problem? "No, sorry. I don't do that anymore."

"Do what?" Fish asked.

"Paint. I don't paint anymore."

"What?" Aiden sounded pissed. "Why? Since when?"

"I don't know what to tell you, Aiden," I said. His anger had started to fuel my own. "It's been a while. I grew out of it. Got new hobbies."

Why did he care?

"I'm going for a walk," Aiden announced suddenly. "There's no way I'm going to get any writing done with you guys messing around." He crossed the room and headed right out the door.

"Sorry!" Fish called out. He pulled his shirt back on, which was a shame. Aesthetically speaking.

Leonardo set the TV remote aside. As soon as Aiden disappeared down the steps outside, Fish shot to his feet and jogged over to the porch table, Leonardo right behind him. Fish flipped Aiden's laptop open.

I followed them. "What are you doing?"

"Nothing." Fish typed in a password.

I narrowed my eyes at them. It definitely didn't look like nothing.

Leonardo sighed. "Aiden's been working on songs for our second album," he said. "We're checking to see how it's going."

"And Aiden would be okay with you doing that?" I asked.

Fish opened the saved files. "We're his groupmates, Reyna. His songs are our songs."

I folded my arms, still suspicious.

To be fair, Aiden used to share his unfinished songs with me all the time. In fact, some of my best memories were of us working on our latest projects together. I'd be painting, lost in the act of pulling an image out of my head and putting it onto the page, all the while he'd be strumming the guitar, creating melodies in the background. In those days, so much of us bled into each other's work. Artist and muse, we shared both roles, in constant collaboration without ever officially collaborating. I missed it.

I missed getting so wrapped up in our little world of music and color everything else disappeared. I'd never felt that close to anyone before, and I didn't know if I ever would again.

It did make sense Aiden would share his unfinished music with his groupmates now. It made me jealous, but I understood. That being said, the way they were going about it still seemed shady.

"If that's true, why did you wait until he left?"

"We're trying not to pressure him," Leonardo said. "He's dealing with a lot of expectations from the label. From our fans. We're trying not to make it harder for him, but it's our careers on the line too. I'm just relieved to see he's finally writing again."

"He's been blocked?" I asked.

"Majorly." Fish slipped the headphones over his ears.

"We were hoping, by bringing him back here, he'd feel a little more inspired," Leonardo said.

"I thought you brought him back for his birthday."

"We did," Leonardo said. "But we could've taken him anywhere for his birthday. We specifically brought him home—back to his roots—for this reason. In fact, it's the only reason the label let us have this time off."

Fish shrugged. "If he has a good time while we're here, that's great. But if he happens to write a few new songs because of it, that's even better."

The whole thing sounded a little manipulative to me. But, then again, did I want Aiden to be creatively blocked? If they really thought this would help him, then I was on board one hundred percent.

Even though I couldn't listen to his songs anymore, there were the days where the knowledge that he was still making music sustained me. It meant—for as much as I missed him, for as badly as I'd ended things—at least he was doing what he loved. At least he was happy.

"Has it been working?" I asked.

"Let's find out." Fish tapped the touch pad. "He's definitely been writing more, so it could be—" He stopped, then listened for a few seconds, hands pressed over the earpieces. The color leeched from his face. "Uh-oh."

Unable to wait anymore, Leonardo snatched the headphones off Fish's head and slipped them on. Fish stood so Leonardo could take the seat. Leonardo listened for a few seconds, then collapsed into the chair.

Fish started pacing. "I can't believe this."

Leonardo stubbornly stared at the laptop. Slowly, he slid the headphones off. "He's done this before."

"I thought he was done with it."

"What's wrong?" I asked. "Is it that bad?"

"It's not bad," Leonardo said, and Fish snorted in disagreement.

To my surprise, Leonardo held the headphones out to me. I shouldn't have, but curiosity got the best of me. I glanced at the stairs to make sure Aiden was nowhere in sight, then tugged the headphones on. My ears were immediately assailed by a brash, electric drum beat. The bass wasn't bad; it had a certain groove to it. But everything else was terrible. It was like all the instruments were in an argument with each other, everyone trying to shout their piece at once.

I had to side with Fish on this one.

"It has potential." I removed the headphones and rested them on the table. "With some time, he could make it better."

Fish stopped pacing. "He's been working on this exact song since we met."

"Oh."

Fish tipped his face toward the sky. "I thought he'd finally given up on it, but now it's back. This damn song never goes anywhere. He never finishes it."

Leonardo blew out a frustrated breath. "I have noticed he tinkers with it whenever he's feeling blocked. Or uninspired. Or—"

"Sad," Fish finished softly. "I really thought coming back here might spark something."

"It'll pass." Leonardo continued to stare at the screen. "It has to."

"Leo, we don't have time for him to be stuck!"

"At least he's working on something." I pointed to the laptop, moved by an urge to defend Aiden. "You may not like the song, but it is *something*. He's not completely blocked."

"Honestly, Reyna," Leonardo said. Bitterness laced his voice. With a flick of his wrist, he snapped the laptop shut. "If this is all he has, it might be better if he was."

FOURTEEN

My father has always insisted the only real way to experience a steel band is live. Not just for the stunningly crisp sound and the energy of being in a crowd, but to see the joy in the players' faces and the liveliness of their movements, to feel the passion they put into every note.

That night's outing was Sunday School, a street party that was rumored to have originated as a lie the men of the village told to get a break from their wives. They'd tell them they were attending "Sunday School," then gather for gambling and drinking. Tonight, the steel band was on fire, playing energetic renditions of the latest soca songs.

I wished I could keep my eyes on the players, enjoy the live music the way Daddy recommended. But like a bug to a zapper, my attention was continuously drawn to the spot where Aiden and Eliza were dancing. It stung every time.

We'd arrived at around nine, Pam and Jake joining us a few

minutes after. I'd asked Olivia to come too, but she'd said she had errands to run early in the morning. Her evasiveness with the details of said errands led me to believe it had something to do with her plans for London, so I backed off easily. Watching Aiden and Eliza now, though, I did wish I'd pressed her a little harder. I could've used some emotional support, or a little more distraction.

Pam, bless her, did occasionally nudge me with her elbow and say, "Ay, why don't you go dance with him," pointing to a random guy. But for the most part, she and Jake, like Leonardo and Hailee, stuck to each other, leaving me the odd woman out, sitting between the couples.

I couldn't pin down Aiden and Eliza's relationship. Initially, I'd thought the rumors were right, but they never kissed or held hands. Now though, they were dancing together, holding each other closer than "just friends" would. I didn't know what to think.

I shouldn't care either way. Aiden wasn't mine, after all. So, I forced myself to watch, let the image of them sear into my brain, burn until I became numb to it.

"Looks like fun, right?" Fish said over my shoulder.

I tipped my head back to look at him. "What?"

As soon as we'd arrived, Fish headed for the food carts. I hadn't seen him since then.

"I said it looks like fun, right?" He tugged on the black cap covering his very distinctive hair. "The dancing?"

"Okay," I said, then returned my attention to Aiden and Eliza. For a second, I thought Fish had left again, but then I heard the scraping of iron against concrete—Fish pulling a chair into the tight space between Leonardo and me.

"So," he said, once he was seated. "You paint?"

"No. I said I used to paint. I don't do that anymore."

"Why not?"

I sighed, hoping he would get the hint to change the subject or move on to someone else. "I don't have the time."

"You'd be surprised." Unfortunately, he sounded far from deterred. "Most people who say they don't have time don't realize how much of their day is wasted on trivial stuff."

"Like this conversation," I muttered.

Fish made a choking noise.

"Sorry," I said quickly. "I didn't mean it. I'm just not in the mood for talking right now."

"No, no. You said it, and you meant it." He blinked. "I don't think anyone besides Eliza has cut me down like that. Not in a long time."

I winced. "Sorry."

"No, no. It's all good, really. I'm just . . . having a major revelation about myself." Then in a rush of breath, he asked, "Do you want to dance with me?"

"Um, no?" I caught Leonardo's eye and sent him a silent plea to intervene, but he only laughed. "Fish," I said slowly. "I just told you I'm not in the best mood. I don't even want to talk to you, but you still ask me to dance. Does that make sense?"

"We won't be talking if we're dancing."

"I'm sure you'd find a way."

He made the wounded noise again. Seriously, why did he keep doing that?

"I need you to dance with me," he said. "Please."

"Why?"

"Because you've just destroyed me, Reyna, and I don't think I'll ever recover unless you dance with me."

I looked at Leonardo, seeking some explanation. Or confirmation that Fish had lost his mind.

Leonardo shrugged. "I've found it easier to just go with it when he's like this. He will keep asking. And, yes, it can get more annoying."

"Fine." I stood, my resignation giving way to reluctant amusement when he offered his hand like we were characters in some nineteenth-century novel.

Pam called out, "Yes, Reyna!" as we joined the other dancers. Thankfully, Fish led me to a spot not too near Aiden and Eliza. As we danced, I only caught glimpses of them at first, then lost track of them altogether.

Fish was not a great dancer, but he was very enthusiastic. He really loved spinning, whether it was me, himself, or the elderly woman who danced next to us. We danced and laughed, at each other and ourselves. When our lungs were as exhausted as our feet, we returned to our seats.

"Do you want anything to drink?" Fish asked.

"Yes, please." I sagged into my chair. "Water."

He nodded. "And then we can talk?"

"Sure."

His face lit up, and I rolled my eyes in response.

When he left, Pam nudged me with her elbow again. "Look at you flirting."

"That wasn't flirting," I said. No, *flirting* was whatever Aiden and Eliza had been doing all night. I hadn't looked in their direction while Fish and I were dancing, but now I couldn't help myself. I couldn't find them.

I sat up. "Where are Aiden and Eliza?"

It was almost eleven, and the crowd had started to thin.

"They took off a while ago," Pam said, standing up. She patted Jake on his shoulder. "Actually, it's time for us to go too. Come on, babe."

They said their goodbyes, and I mumbled a reply, my attention now on Leonardo. "Did Aiden and Eliza head back to the hotel?"

"I don't know." Leonardo said. "They didn't say."

Hailee, who had her head rested on his shoulder, added, "I think Eliza said something about the beach."

"How long ago was that?" I asked.

Leonardo paused, about to sip. The can of soft drink rested against his lips. He lowered it slowly. "About twenty minutes ago. Why? Does it matter?"

"No," I admitted.

Fish handed me a bottled water and took his seat. "What's going on?"

"Aiden took off," Leonardo said. "With Eliza."

"Oh." Fish laughed drily. "So, the usual?" He smiled at me, but it was tight. "Taking off in the middle of a party is what Aiden does. Sometimes it's with a girl. Don't worry. They'll turn up."

But they didn't.

Not long afterward, the band stopped playing and the players packed up. A lot of people started leaving. Dance music started piping through the speakers, the vibe of the evening changing into something like an outdoor nightclub. We were ready to leave, but Aiden and Eliza still hadn't returned. Hailee messaged them.

"They're at the beach," she said, pocketing her phone. "They're going to hang out there for a while. They said to head back without them."

I wanted to object, but I couldn't come up with a reason. At least, none I could admit to.

On the drive back, Fish tried to talk to me. Distracted, I couldn't give more than one-word answers. I kept picturing Aiden and Eliza on the beach, Eliza dashing in and out of the glittering sea, Aiden standing on the shore, his lips quirked with amusement. The picture in my head was so clear, I could've painted them together, bathed in soft moonlight.

Eventually, Fish gave up on me. I couldn't blame him.

FIFTEEN

I made it a policy to avoid Pigeon Point when possible. Don't get me wrong, the beach is stunning. Google Tobago and it'll be one of the first photos that pops up. For good reason too; its crystal-blue waters are the stuff postcards and dreams are made of. But for a Tobagonian looking for a peaceful dip in the sea, there were other beaches; alternative spots less crowded and quieter. Unfortunately, this was where the boat tour departed.

I didn't like it. The more people around, the higher the risk of DJ Bacchanal and the Musgrove sisters getting recognized. On the way to the beach, I brought it up in the van. They were quick to brush off my concern.

"You'd be surprised," Hailee said. "People rarely recognize our natural faces. When we're not in makeup."

No surprise. This did nothing to ease my worries. First of all, Hailee had to be wearing at least a little foundation. I refused to believe anyone's skin naturally glowed like that, unless they were part phytoplankton. Second of all, I recognized them. So had quite a few people on the hotel's staff. So far, we'd been unbelievably lucky, flying under the radar of social media. I didn't want to test it.

"Hailee's right." Fish twisted around in the front seat. "If we act normal, and I keep my hair covered, we tend to blend in. Except for Leo." He leaned forward to shoot his groupmate a cut-eye. "The face that launched a thousand memes. If anyone's going to get us in trouble, it's him."

Leonardo frowned. "Hey!"

"If only we could make him less pretty." Hailee sighed, staring at her boyfriend. "Wait! I've got it." She dug around in her bag, pulled out her sunglasses, and slid them onto his face.

I stretched forward in my seat to get a better look.

Well, damn. "I think you made it worse," I said.

Hailee hmmed in agreement.

"Oh, for—" Aiden, who'd been quietly looking out the window until now, unclipped the panama hat that Eliza had on her beach bag and handed it to Leonardo. "Y'all are ridiculous. Here."

Leonardo put it on. For a few seconds, we silently contemplated the look.

"Well . . . ," Hailee said finally. "I think this is about as *not good* as he's going to get."

I agreed, hoping it was enough.

"Wow, that's really Leonardo Vale." Olivia's voice was pitched higher than I'd ever heard it.

My hope took a hit. "What the hell?"

Olivia had clocked him right away. It didn't seem to matter that most of his face was covered, or that he'd stood with the rest of his friends at the shoreline, a good thirty feet away from us.

"Can you really recognize him?" I asked. "Like if you didn't already know he was here?"

"What?" Olivia wasn't exactly hiding behind a palm tree—the trunk was too narrow for that to be possible—but she was definitely attempting to. "Yeah, okay. *Wow.* You've been hanging out with Leonardo Vale. How are you functioning?"

"Um . . . the usual way? Did you want to come and meet them?"

"Oh, hell no." Olivia peered around the trunk, then shrank backward again. She gestured to her grease-stained uniform. "I look like I've been roasting lamb all morning. I smell like it too."

"They won't care."

"I do. Besides, I've got to get back to Grace's soon anyway. Of all the places to ask to meet up—Pigeon Point? It might be a five-minute drive from the restaurant, but you know what it is to find a parking space here?"

I winced. Okay, so this may not have been the best time for a meetup, her on a lunch break and my boat tour about to start any minute. But I'd gotten an idea into my head and I needed to follow it through. Since Olivia got accepted to the university, we'd been growing distant. I knew most of it was my fault; I was jealous. The dream we were supposed to share, she would be taking it on her own. But that wasn't her fault.

For a while now, I'd been trying to think of a way to show her she had my support. That I was happy for her. The answer didn't come to me until last night.

It was so obvious. I don't know why I didn't think of it sooner.

"I'm sorry," I said. "But it'll be worth it when you see your gift."

Olivia folded her arms. "We'll see."

I handed her a slim black case. "This is for you."

Olivia rolled her eyes, but she smiled as she took it. Quickly, she unrolled the paintbrush set, her excitement melting into confusion. "What—" She looked them over. "Didn't your father buy you these?"

"Yes. Last Christmas." I remembered the day I'd shown them to Olivia. Her eyes had lit up in admiration. "They're really high quality. Never used. I thought you could take them with you to London."

She looked up at me. "These are your brushes."

"And now they're yours."

"But I don't need new ones. I have my own."

"Yes," I said, confused by her reaction. Since when she didn't like gifts? "These are—"

"Not mine."

"It's a gift." Why did she sound angry? I was trying to show her I supported her art. That I was okay with her leaving. "Use them. Otherwise they're just going to sit around and rot."

"Then *you* use them," she said.

"You know I'm not going to."

Olivia rolled the case up and held it out to me. "Here. Take them back."

"They are yours for—"

"Take them back," she repeated, teeth clenched. When I didn't do as she said, she let the brushes drop onto the sand.

"Hey!" I picked them up. "What is your problem? Why are you mad at me?"

"I'm not mad at you," she said. A blatant lie. "I have a lot to deal with right now. Working at Grace's. Getting things ready for school. I don't have time for this."

"Okay, nah. Sorry." I held up my hands. "I shouldn't have asked you to come out here now. I could've given you the brushes later. But it was the only free time I had today. And for real, I want you to have them."

"Do you?" Olivia's eyes roamed over my face, searching. Her anger seemed to fade, her voice softer when she asked, "Can you honestly tell me this is all about me? That it has nothing to do with the fact that you want to get rid of the brushes?"

"What?" I asked. "Why would I do that?"

"I don't know, Reyna. Maybe because they're tempting you? Rotting away, reminding you of the things you wanted to do but convinced yourself you can't anymore?"

"That's not . . . ," I started, then swallowed. It was hard for me to hold her gaze. "Does it matter? End of the day, I'm not going to use them. I don't want to waste them."

"You're the one wasting them," Olivia said, then exhaled loudly. "If you want to give up painting, fine. Throw the brushes out, let them rot—I don't care. I can't tell you what to do, but I don't want any part of it."

"Olivia—"

"Enjoy your boat trip, Reyna," she said, leaving.

I watched Olivia walk away, until she disappeared around the corner of the beach facility. Absentmindedly, I dusted sand off the case, so it looked shiny and new again. Now what? I hadn't expected to leave here with them.

A black garbage bin stood a few feet away. I could dump them. Did it make a difference if I got rid of them one way or the other?

But even as I thought it, my heart twisted. It really was such a waste.

Walking past the bin to join the others, I stuck the case into my bag. I'd give the brushes to someone else eventually. Someone who could actually use them.

"So, is it Manolo like the shoe?" Fish asked, two minutes into our boat trip.

Honestly, it took him longer to ask than I thought it would.

A short, well-muscled man in his sixties, Manolo was an ex-employee of the Plumeria. He'd worked as a gardener for twenty years, then decided he loved the sea more than land. Mummy lent him money to help buy his first boat. Since then he'd bought four more, and now Manolo's Tours was one of the most popular boat tour companies on the island.

"No." Manolo kept his eyes on the horizon. "Manolo, like the designer."

Eliza laughed behind her phone, filming the whole thing. Fish stuck his tongue out at her. Eliza returned the gesture before leaving to join the others on the roof. Fish, Pam, Jake, Kesha, and I stayed with Manolo on the lower deck.

Wind whipped against our faces as the boat sliced through the formidable block of inky-blue ocean. The water churned and frothed in our wake. Behind us, the stretch of beach contracted until it blurred in the distance. As we drove farther from land, the large panes of glass affixed to the bottom of the boat revealed glimpses of aquatic wildlife beneath. I held Kesha on my lap, pointing out the small silvery fishes that appeared every now and then. There wasn't much to see just yet, but it was more than enough to keep Kesha's interest.

I inhaled the salty air, the knot in my gut that formed during my argument with Olivia starting to loosen. When was the last time I'd been to the reef? Was I ten? Eleven? It was sad, but I'd forgotten what it felt like to have a life beyond the hotel. Even though certain dynamics of the present company weren't ideal, excitement started to bloom in my chest. Today might actually be fun.

I nudged Fish's foot with my own. He rested his head against the rail, his feet propped on the bench. His lashes fanned out against his cheek as he dozed lightly.

"I thought you, of all people, would be more excited about this trip," I said.

His eyes opened. He watched me for a few seconds, as if considering something. Then he said, "I'm plenty excited. It's just the motion of the sea makes me drowsy. It reminds me of all the boring-ass parties on my dad's yacht. God, those were dull as hell.

The best thing to do was hide in the cabins and sleep through them."

"For a guy who doesn't love the sea, you picked a weird nickname."

"What do you mean?" He pressed a hand to his chest like he was offended. "It's a genius name. Have you ever met anyone else named Fish?"

"No. But, you know, there might be a reason for that."

"Rude," he said, but he was smiling now.

"Why do you call yourself Fish?" My curiosity had been sparked after reading all the interviews where he'd dodged this very question. Why bother keeping something like this a secret? From the smirk he gave me, I got the feeling I wasn't about to find out.

"I told you. Because it's genius. One of a kind." He scratched his shoulder, shifting but not sitting up. "Hey, I'm sorry if I went on about painting too much the other night. I could tell you didn't want to talk about it. It's just . . ." He laughed. "I'm curious. About you."

"About me? Trust me, there's no story here. I used to love it, but things changed. I don't like to talk about it."

"Oh. Like a bad breakup."

I laughed.

"Ah. That sounds like the laugh of someone with experience in this particular area."

Well, he was not wrong. "What about you?" I asked, in an

attempt to turn the attention away from my past—who was sitting on the upper deck, right above us. "I'm guessing it would take someone with experience to recognize it."

Fish shrugged. "I've had a few breakups. But none I'd call bad." He fingered the end of his T-shirt. "There was this one girl, though. We were never together. I wanted her, she wanted someone else."

"Yeah. It sucks when that happens."

He quirked a brow. "You've got experience with that too?"

"No, I meant, it sucks in theory," I said. Fish was proving to be more perceptive than I'd expected.

"Definitely a story here," he said.

Time to cut this off. "There's no story. Just me."

"Just you is good too."

"Okay." I shifted Kesha's weight on my lap. Was he flirting with me? Because it sounded like he was flirting with me. I didn't know what to do with that.

I let the conversation lapse into silence, then turned to listen to Jake and Pam. It took a few seconds for me to catch what they were talking about, their voices just above whispers.

"Didn't you see them dancing at Sunday School?" Pam was telling Jake. "How can you be so oblivious? I'm telling you, something's going on between Eliza and Aiden."

Jake stretched his arm along the back of the bench, one of his sandaled feet propped atop his knee. "Nah."

"Are you kidding me?" Pam said. "You can't possibly believe that."

I dropped my eyes to the floor. A thin layer of seawater sloshed on top of the glass on the bottom of the boat. A wave of nausea churned my stomach. I wasn't surprised they'd noticed Aiden and Eliza's flirting. Something was definitely going on. I didn't get why Jake doubted it, though.

I looked at Fish to see if he'd had a reaction to hearing any of this, but he'd closed his eyes again.

"Eliza flirts as easily as she breathes," Jake said to Pam. "It's her primary form of communication. If something were going on, everyone on the planet with internet access would know by now."

"Still, I'm sure there's something there," Pam said. "Or if not yet, there will be. Some people take a little longer to catch on to their feelings. Take you, for example."

"Me?" Jake jerked backward. "What do you mean? I loved you the second I saw you!"

"But I asked you out."

Jake took her face in his hands. "Only because you talk faster."

I saw the kiss coming and blocked Kesha's eyes just in time. "Think of the child! You two are disgusting." I made a loud retching noise, and the pair broke apart.

"Hey!" Eliza came down the steps, Aiden just behind her. "Someone seasick down here?"

"No." Pam glared at me. "Just someone suffering from a severe case of immaturity."

I rolled my eyes.

Eliza and Aiden took the bench opposite us. They sat close but not touching. I eyed that sliver of space between their thighs with great intensity, as if I could expand it with my will alone.

"Why aren't you still upstairs?" Jake asked them. "You've still got time. We're a good way out from the reef."

Eliza examined her phone. "I need a break from the sun. Can't see with the glare on my screen."

"And I just need a break from the sun." Aiden looked over at Fish and smiled softly. "Fish and boats. Reminds me of those babies that fall asleep in cars. He can't help it."

Eliza eyed Fish. "He's got to be faking."

The boat bounced on an extra-high wave, and Fish's head knocked against the railing. He startled, sitting up, blinking at the rest of us. For a few seconds, no one spoke. And then he asked, "What?"

We broke into laughter, while Fish sputtered with bewilderment.

My ears tuned to one specific laugh, like a radio caught on a particular frequency. I glanced up, tracing it to its source, and found Aiden watching me. Our smiles slipped simultaneously, but our stares did hold, not long enough to call attention to them, but just long enough to cause some forgotten, fragile feeling to flutter in my chest.

I looked away first.

SIXTEEN

We spent the rest of the afternoon at sea. First, snorkeling at the Buccoo Reef, exploring the vivid, alien world of coral castles and its Technicolor inhabitants. The rainbow-colored parrotfish were Kesha's favorite, their turquoise blue-green bodies highlighted with brilliant pink, yellow, and orange streaks. Every time one appeared, she'd point and babble, and check to make sure everyone else was watching too.

Later, we swam in the Nylon Pool, a spot in the middle of the ocean where waist-high icy blue waters covered chalk-white sand.

"They call it the Fountain of Youth, you know," Manolo called out to those already in the water. "They say you mus' rub the sand on your skin. It's supposed to take ten years off."

Eliza immediately covered herself, diligently scooping the sand from beneath the water and rubbing it against her cheeks.

Hailee sniffed a small amount and tested it on her arm. "Smells weird."

"That's how you know it works!" Aiden told them, then shared a grin with Manolo.

I snorted, standing on the lower deck. Pam held her excited, squirming daughter while I helped secure Kesha's floaties.

"Leo, I see you!" Fish called out. And, sure enough, Leonardo was in the process of rubbing the white sand on his arms.

"I'm sampling the local culture," he said very calmly. "Don't be rude, man."

Fish continued to give him crap anyway, though from where I stood, I could see Fish covertly scooping up his own handfuls of sand beneath the water.

While Kesha and Pam joined the others in the sea, I stayed on board. For the moment, admiring the water—stunning in clarity and color, like the finest aquamarine gemstone—was enough to keep me occupied. It stirred the strongest temptation I'd faced in a long time to pick up a brush. As I sat there, with my elbows resting against the railing, sea breeze tickling my skin, the irony didn't escape me that the very seas that inspired my need to paint were the same ones that cut off my means to seriously pursue art.

It was a beautiful bubble I lived in. The island was imbued with a warmth, separate from the reach of the sun. It would be difficult for me to describe exactly, but heard in a neighbor's *good morning*; in the smell of pelau on the stove; in the way that Aiden and Manolo, who never met before, easily carried on a conversation about their pasts and people they have in common. In the way a boat ride and a clear blue sky can distract a broken heart, even if it's for a short time.

The island is not a perfect paradise. It is likely anyone who says so does not live here. It has its flaws, the isolation, one of many. But it is my home. The only place I've ever known. Likely the only place I'll ever know. It had my heart, even when my dreams were somewhere else.

By the time we returned to Pigeon Point, the beach had grown crowded. People gathered on the sand, the passengers of another tour boarding. Our boat chugged into the shallows and we disembarked one by one.

With Manolo's help, I stepped into the water, as lightly as I could to minimize the splash. "Thanks again," I told him, letting go of his hand. "Don't forget to bring us your new call cards. You can drop them at the desk when you come to the party tonight."

"Will do, Boss Lady," he said.

I waded out of the sea, my bag and towel held high to avoid the water. "Later!" I called back to him. Once I got far enough from the water's edge, I set my bag on the dry sand, let my hair loose, and used the towel to dab the water out of it.

"Hey! Did someone forget something?" Aiden called from the boat.

No one answered him. When Aiden didn't say more, I assumed he'd sorted it out.

I shook out the towel and wrapped it around my shoulders, glancing up in time to see Aiden hopping over the side of the boat. As he trudged out of the water, I was reminded again of the ways the last two years had made him broader, taller. I shaded my eyes like I was protecting them from the glare of the sun off the sea surface, but really, I didn't want to look like I was gawking. Whereas Fish had made his body a canvas for art, Aiden's was a manuscript, tattooed with words, lyrics, and quotes; I wanted to take the time to read each one, to ask about the reasons behind them. Why *Art is never finished. Only abandoned* on his back, or *limitless* on the inside of his upper left arm.

As he drew closer, I recognized the black case in his hands. My paintbrushes must've fallen out of my bag. I hadn't noticed.

"Yours?" He stopped in front of me, dripping onto the sand. He held out the brushes, and I took them from him.

"Thank you." I picked my bag off the sand, then took my time stuffing the case inside, but he didn't walk away like I thought he would. I straightened up and pushed my hair back. "What?"

"I'm just wondering why paintbrushes. A strange choice for a boat trip. Extra weird for someone who claims she doesn't paint anymore."

Claims? Did he think I'd lied about it?

"Why is it so hard to believe? People do change, you know."

"Said the girl walking around with paintbrushes."

"They're not mine. Well, no, they are. But they were supposed to be a gift for Olivia. She didn't want them."

"So that was Olivia this morning," he said. "I thought it looked like her. She didn't want to say hi?" He scratched his cheek, laughing drily. "No, I suppose not. She probably hates me now."

The *because of us* went unsaid.

"She doesn't hate you." I held my bag to my chest. "Why would she? You didn't do anything wrong."

Aiden went very still. "You didn't—"

"Aiden!" someone shouted.

We turned toward the sound. Oh, Lord. They'd finally been recognized.

My entire body tensed as a guy in a Sweet Lime Tours T-shirt jogged toward us. He appeared to be about our age, with wide shoulders, and hair shaved in a clean-cut high fade.

"You back an' you en' even call me?" The Sweet Lime guy approached us, a smile on his face.

Aiden's face broke into a smile too.

Oh. This was a friend, not a fan.

The guys crashed into a hug, fists thumping each other's backs. It looked a little painful to me, but both guys were laughing.

"I tried to call." Aiden pulled back. "But your number changed?"

"It didn't change. *Your* number changed. I don't answer unknown callers. You could of left a message. You know what—it don't matter. Is good to see you. How you doing? How the music t'ing going?"

Aiden grimaced, rubbing the back of his neck. "Well . . ."

"I joking with you. I's tell everyone—I know that boy in DJ Bacchanal, same boy who used to thief pomeracs from Miss Danbi's yard."

Aiden laughed. "That's not true. I en never thief nothing. You the one climbing the tree. All I did is hold the bag open. Not my fault if the fruits land inside."

"Aiden, you going to introduce us or . . . ?" Fish asked as he and the others joined us.

"This is Darren," Aiden said. "We went to school together. His mother taught me music."

"Until he deserted us for America," Darren finished. "Never forgave him."

While the others greeted Darren, I hung back. I knew about him, but we'd never met. He was one of Aiden's oldest friends. From Aiden's stories, it sounded like their childhood antics all ended in blood, tears, or being chased by old ladies with cocoyea brooms. There was a good chance, if I'd heard about him, he'd heard about me too.

Darren's smile dimmed a little. "You know Ma won't forgive you if you don't come and see her. You know she still think you're her son."

"I don't know." Aiden glanced back at us, lingering on me. "Is not just me though. I have my friends here . . ."

"So?" Darren asked. "Bring all a' dem!" To us he added, "You're all welcome, of course. We have more than enough room." He smacked Aiden's shoulder. "Unless you feel you too good for us now?"

"As if that's possible," Aiden said. "Your ma is a queen, and she knows it."

Darren laughed. "She'll be happy to hear that."

"Boy!" one of the workers from the Sweet Lime boat called

over. "Look—I not playing with you. Get over here! We not pay-ing you to lime with yuh friends!"

"I coming!" Darren grimaced and started for the boat. "Call me nah!" he shouted back to Aiden. "I'll answer this time. We'll set somet'ing up."

"Yeah . . ." Aiden waved Darren off. A sad smile tugged at his lips, like he'd just made a promise he thought he couldn't keep.

After the boat tour, I went home to get dressed for the rum punch party. I'd planned to wear one of my work outfits, but tonight I wasn't working. Plus, knowing Hailee and Eliza were definitely going to dress up tonight made me want to try a little harder. Too bad everything in my closet felt *wrong*.

On impulse, I went to the laundry room and pulled down a small suitcase tucked on the topmost shelf. A few of my mother's things were stored inside. Things I couldn't bear to give away. They used to smell of her perfume—the sweet scent of oleander. Now they smelled of must and mothballs.

There was the washed-out green, spaghetti-strapped house-dress she used to wear in her rare time off. The dress had a small hole under her arm, which she always forgot to mend.

There was the turquoise blouse she saved for church.

The black dress with gold sparkles she wore on Old Year's Nights.

And the white dress suit she wore to parties.

I don't know what compelled me to pull the suit on. It smelled awful, looked wrinkled, itched, and hung far too big on my frame. One glance in the mirror was enough to inspire me to take it off. I stuffed it—and everything else—back into the suitcase, then returned it to the shelf. Back in my room, I changed into my black work dress and covered it with my blazer.

I don't know what I expected to find in my mother's clothes. Was it comfort? Courage? Acceptance?

All I'd done was waste time.

SEVENTEEN

THREE YEARS EARLIER

"Look at all that food!"

I faced the two guests—a mother and daughter from New York. Even though Mummy had introduced us earlier that week I couldn't remember their names. They eyed the huge pile on my plate. For this year's rum punch party, the kitchen had gone all out on the seafood spread. I'd taken two of everything.

"Is that all for you?" the mother asked. She bent forward and her voice inched higher, the way some adults do when they speak to a child. It didn't seem to matter that I was almost fifteen and we were the same height.

I started to excuse myself, but it didn't matter. She'd spoken too loudly, drawing Mummy's attention back to me, just when I'd finally lost it.

For the party, Mummy's outfit was stunning as usual, her white suit adorned with a necklace of silver and pale-pink gems. Her straightened hair hung loosely around her shoulders. She approached us, eyes on the contents of my paper plate. "You know how much teenagers can eat," she told the women. Her arm rested on my shoulder as they launched into a conversation. I couldn't leave.

"Claire?" Pearl said, appearing at Mummy's side.

The housekeeping manager had dressed up for the night, donning a glittery purple shirt and white slacks, a sizable peacock pendant pinned to her chest.

"I'm surprised to see you down here," she said to Mummy, her expression pinched with worry. "I thought they would've called you."

Mummy's arm on my shoulder stiffened. "Why?"

"I just passed by the front desk, and it look like somebody causing a commotion. Shouting about lawsuits." Pearl lifted a shoulder. "You know what, since they didn't call you, is probably not'ing."

"Excuse me," Mummy said, pulling her phone from her purse. She headed for the main building, her stride quick but not fast enough to draw attention.

Pearl whispered in my ear, "I also passed by the gazebo. There's a very lonely looking young man sitting there alone."

"Thank you," I whispered back.

She winked and swiped a crab cake from my plate.

I excused myself, plucked two sporks from a pile on the table, and slipped away from the party.

The trek to the gazebo was dark, the light from the pool area weak from this distance. My new shoes sank into the soft grass. I still hadn't gotten the hang of walking in my new sandals, but they were my first heels so of course I took any excuse to wear them.

Aiden waited right where I'd left him, no longer alone. Three girls, about our age, formed a semicircle on the steps. They wore the standard vacation outfit: spaghetti-strap tops over swimsuits, shorts, and rubber slippers. I wasn't surprised by the sight of girls flirting with Aiden; it had become irritatingly familiar. At some point over the last year, Aiden's limbs seemed to have decided taller-than-average wasn't enough, and he'd shot up six more inches. That, coupled with the muscle he'd earned from long hours on the fishing boat, made the girls staying in the hotel take notice.

"Hello!" I squeezed past them to sit on the bench.

Their conversation stumbled for a bit, shaken by my arrival, then it continued to roll on without me. I listened to them, amazed, as always, by how good Aiden was with strangers. At least, when he wanted to be.

He had a laid-back charm, somehow asking just the right questions to seem interested, dropping just the right responses to be interesting. There was no doubt he was listening, invested in the details. I don't know if anyone else picked up on this subtle tactic for steering the conversation away from himself. Only when someone did manage to turn the tables on him, he disengaged instantly, suddenly shy for some reason. Sometimes I wanted to shake him and shout, *Why can't you see all the ways you're amazing, sweet, talented? Why can't you see you the way I do?*

These girls were more than happy to keep the focus of the talk on their recent trip to the rain forest, and their plans to hit the beach tomorrow, dangling an open invitation for Aiden to join them. Aiden didn't take the bait, and finally they left.

Aiden raised an eyebrow. "What happened to being nice to guests? I think that's a rule. A big one."

"I was nice. If anything, they were the ones being rude, not talking to me."

Aiden walked over. "They might of talked to you, if you weren't bad-eyeing them the whole time." He peered down at me with something that should've been disapproval, but he had trouble not smiling. "Are you pouting?"

"No." But I was.

He laughed and pointed to my plate. "Are you sure this okay?"

"Stop worrying." I patted the bench next to me. "I told you it's fine."

He sat, his body slumping with exhaustion. I didn't need him to tell me he'd had a hard day out on the sea. I'd taken one look at his sunburned face, and the fresh bruises on his hands and wrists, and I knew I had to cheer him up.

Every year it seemed to be harder for the fishermen. The fish just weren't where they'd been in previous years. This meant longer days and trips farther out to sea. This meant Aiden took on more work when he visited Shell Haven, picking up the slack as his grandfather's arthritis worsened. We didn't know it then, but a year and a half later, Old Man Chandra would hang up his nets for good.

"I shouldn't of let you bring me here tonight," he said, even as he eyed the plate in my lap with unconcealed interest. "I don't want to make your mother mad. You should go back before she notice you gone."

"She too busy to notice." I hoped.

"You know she will, and she'll blame me for taking you away." Aiden toed at a crack in the floor. "Is it even safe to be here? I thought this thing was falling down."

"It's fixed." The renovation of the gazebo had been finished a few days before. Unfortunately, a few days was all it took for the floor to start cracking again. "The contractor said there might be an old cavern below, which is why the ground is weak."

"That supposed to be reassuring?" Aiden tapped the post behind his head. "Maybe you should break it down. Pa said pirates used to run this bay. Maybe there's buried treasure in the cavern."

"If there *is* a cavern," I corrected him. "We don't know for sure. Besides, Mummy would never tear this thing down. She loves it too much."

"Reyna, I'm talking about buried treasure here. *Buried treasure.*"

"You're right! What am I saying?" I held up a spork. "We can start digging right now."

"Yes!" Aiden plucked the spork from my hand. "Right after the crab cakes." He frowned at the plate. "Only one?"

"The price to leave the party."

He gave me the look he sometimes gave me—something between confusion and amusement. It was good to see him relax.

He never admitted how stressed he was about his grandfather, but he didn't need to. Aiden had changed a lot in the last few years: he was taller, broader, but his smiles weren't as quick and his laughter was edged with something harsher. If he told me crab cakes were the solution, I was ready to risk Mummy's fury to get more.

I watched him take a bite, then hold the spork between his lips.

"What?" he asked.

"Nothing." My stomach filled with butterflies. I scooted closer and used the second spork to reach for the plate.

"Hey!" He pulled the plate back. "Get your own crab cake."

"I got this one." I yanked on his arm, but he didn't budge. "Come on. We'll split it."

With our faces a breath apart, we stilled. My eyes crossed a little as I took him in. My heart beat so rapidly it resounded throughout my body. In my chest, my limbs, my fingertips. I don't know who moved first, but our lips met in our first kiss. Nothing more than a soft press of lips. It wasn't the dramatic stuff of movies, but it was cautious, precious, sweet. Easy in a way that made it feel inevitable, all the time we'd spent together building to this. We both pulled away smiling.

"Reyna!"

Aiden and I sprang apart.

Mummy. She sounded close.

"Reyna, is that you?" She marched up the steps. "What are you doing out here in the dark? Is that Aiden with you?"

I leaped to my feet. "I'm sorry. I was just—I was coming back."

She brought her shoe down, the heel clapping sharply against the floor. "You will come back to the party with me right now. Aiden, go home."

"Yes, Aunty." Aiden scrambled to his feet and fled. He hadn't taken the plate I'd prepared. It sat on the bench, the sporks on the floor.

I watched his retreating back. "Can't Aiden come to the party too?"

"No." Mummy started to cross the lawn.

"Why not?" I hurried to follow. "Isn't the party open to everyone? Why not him?"

"He can't come dressed like that. There *is* a dress code."

"That's not fair."

Mummy stopped and faced me. "You know what's not fair?" she asked. "Every year I work my fingers to the bone to make this party a success. To show the Plumeria staff and guests how much they mean to us. Do you have any idea the amount of time I put into this? How much care? All I ask is for you to be there. Is that too much?"

"No," I muttered.

"Good." She started walking again. "And pay attention. One day, you'll be in charge of all this. Then you'll really understand how much trouble I go through. Boys come and go, Reyna. You need to start focusing on what really matters, because one day I won't be around to set you right."

For the rest of the night, I played her silent shadow. She wanted me there—fine. I'd be there, and nothing more. She noticed of course, her returning silence sharp and icy. It might've been then the first of the cracks in our relationship appeared, like those on the floor of the gazebo. We'd try to cover it in the coming months, but the foundation was busted. We were never the same again.

EIGHTEEN

The second I saw William's face I knew something was up. Not that he'd ever been particularly happy to see me. In fact, if there wasn't some hint of irritation at all, I'd have been surprised.

The look of abject horror he wore this evening though—that was new.

Looking at William's face, I could tell he'd not expected to see me. I wasn't even that early, the party set to start soon. I slammed my car door, making a beeline right for him and the guy he was talking to. As I got closer, it became clear this guy was not staff, and his overalls were part of a uniform, so he wasn't a guest. Another contractor brought in to tear down my gazebo? It would explain the traitor's panic.

"Listen nah, I just want to drop them off," the guy was telling William.

William's eyes bounced from me to the man. "Yes, so go wait at the back gate." He made a series of shooing motions with his hands. "I told you someone will be there at any moment."

"And I told you I been waiting back there for fifteen minutes. We have a schedule to keep. I need to drop dem t'ings off now-now."

"Hi," I said, closing in on them. "William."

"Reyna," William said nervously. "You're here."

"Yes." To the stranger, I asked, "Is there something I can help you with?"

The guy looked me up and down. He seemed to be in his fifties, tall even with a stoop to his posture. "You?" He sucked his teeth, then turned his attention back to William. "I'll drop it off in front here if I have to."

The label on his breast pocket read *Simona Limited*.

"We're expecting a delivery?" I didn't remember any big orders. In fact, this particular beverage company wasn't local, so we would've tried to limit our dealings with them period. "You sure you have the right place?"

"Listen nah, man." He spoke to William, ignoring me. "Sort it out later. Just open the gate so we can drop off the rum punch."

"Rum punch?" Slowly, I turned to William. He'd buried his head in his hands. "As in for the party tonight? What happened to Shirley's?"

The delivery man cleared his throat. "Service gate."

"Right, one minute." William nodded, then took off.

I chased after him. It wasn't easy in my sandals. "Simona? Are you serious? How dare you bring that generic, watered-down mess into my hotel!"

"Have you ever tasted it?"

No. But that wasn't the point. "We've been ordering from Shirley's for years. Shirley and her family are good friends of ours."

"It's not personal, Reyna." At the front desk, he summoned one of the clerks. "Go see what's up in the back. Vernon isn't answering, and we need the service gate opened now."

The clerk ran off.

"This is a betrayal," I said. "Since the hotel opened, we've tried to support local businesses. Now you want to throw away years of tradition, buying our rum punch from some faceless international corporation?"

William sagged against the desk. "Why do you always have to make things so difficult? You're acting like we never buy imported goods, which you know is not true. It's impossible to survive without them."

"But if we have the option to go local—"

"Shirley's has been raising their prices every year. Is that personal for them? No, it's business. Simona is less than half the price. Shirley and her family do what they have to do to survive. We should too."

"So, we pay a little more. It's real, authentic rum punch. It's what our guests expect."

"It's fruit juice and alcohol."

"They'll notice the difference!"

"I bet they won't. In fact—" His eyes opened. He considered me for a few seconds. "Let's do just that." He shifted away from the desk. "Let's bet on it."

That threw me. "What kind of bet?"

He looked around, but no one was in hearing distance. "I bet the guests won't notice anything wrong with the drinks. In fact, I bet tonight's party will be one of the most successful the hotel has ever had."

I snorted. That seemed like quite the escalation, from drinks to the whole party. Then something awful occurred to me. "Did you make more changes?" I'd left him very clear instructions for the party. But if he'd changed the rum punch—the very core of the party—who knew what else he'd done.

He held up a hand to stop me from going off on him. "Hear me out. I bet the guests will come, get drunk, and have the time of their lives. They'll love the punch, and we'll save ourselves a ton of money in the process."

"I don't care about the money."

"Well, you should, seeing as we're running a *business*." He hissed the last word through his teeth. "Look, I'm saying if I'm wrong about this, I'll lay off the gazebo."

"Forever?" I needed him to be clear about this. "You'll stop trying to tear it down? No more sneaking in contractors. No more consultations behind my back."

"Yes. Hell, I'll even advocate for having it fixed. Even if it is a stupid waste of money."

"And if you win?" I asked.

"It comes down."

"No way." Not when the risk was so high.

"Why not?" he asked. "If you're so sure your way is the only way, what's the risk? The party is happening tonight anyway. You can't change it now. This is your chance to prove me wrong once and for all. You win and your precious gazebo gets fixed, and I'll stop fighting you on your decisions for the hotel."

I examined his face for any signs of deceit. I only found determination. "You'll stop going to Daddy with ideas for drastic upgrades? You'll leave the hotel as it is? No changes? Nothing?"

"Nothing," he agreed. "Unless the party tonight is a success. Do we have a deal?"

I stared at him for a long time, wavering. The price was high, but the prize was too sweet to resist. Besides, I knew I was right.

I held out my hand for us to shake on it. "We have a deal."

At the villa, I met Leonardo in the entrance.

"Hey, Reyna," he said, smiling. "You look nice."

"Thank you," I said, well aware he was only being nice. I was dressed the same way as any regular workday, just with a little more lipstick. He, on the other hand, stunned in a white dress shirt. "You look all right."

His eyes crinkled when he laughed. "Have you seen Hailee?"

"I just got here. Haven't seen anyone else yet."

"Oh." He glanced over his shoulder, then frowned. "Actually, there's something I need to talk to you about. Do you have a second?"

"Yes, but only a second."

"I'll use it wisely," he said, then stayed silent for a good while.

"This is way more than a second."

He leaned against the doorframe. "Yes. But I'm not sure how to put this."

"Uh-oh. Are you dumping me?"

He turned his head to me, smiling. "Oh, Reyna. It's not me, it's you. Or more specifically, it's you and Aiden."

Uh-oh. "What about me and Aiden?"

"I think you know."

I suspected I did too. Oh, God. I needed to explain. "Leo—"

"Hey, no." He put up his hands. "I'm not going to tell anyone. It's not my business. And . . . who knows? We might get some songs out of it."

"Hey!"

"I'm joking. Sort of." He held out his arm. "Help a guy out?"

I helped him with the buttons. "How did you find out?" Had I been obvious? It couldn't be Aiden who'd given us away. When we were with the group, I might as well have been invisible. He'd only had eyes for Eliza.

"Aiden may have dropped some hints a while back," Leonardo said. "Like he had an ex-girlfriend back in Tobago. That she liked to paint. Her parents owned a hotel. Her name was Reyna."

"Those are some big hints."

"To be fair, he'd just gotten his wisdom teeth removed. He'd been drugged out of his mind." Leonardo offered me his other cuff. "He talked a lot. Said things about himself, I don't think he even realizes. I've never told anyone what he said, not even him."

"Well, now I'm just curious," I muttered, buttoning the other cuffs. "There. Done."

"Thank you." He straightened his collar, smile softening. "You know, Reyna, I had my doubts about this birthday trip, but it may turn out to be exactly what Aiden needed. The thing is, when Aiden was drugged up, despite all the rambling and drooling, I got the impression you meant a lot to him."

"When was this?"

"Almost a year ago."

Oh. A year. So before the Grammy. Before Eliza.

"I think he's made it pretty clear he doesn't still feel that way," I said. "But I do think he is enjoying the vacation." Despite my presence. "Even if it isn't really the type of vacation I would've thought he'd like."

Leonardo's brows rose. "And what kind of vacation would you have planned for him?"

"I don't know, something more laid back. No schedule. Fewer outings. More time visiting his old friends, like Darren." I shrugged. "But at the end of the day, you guys are here with him, and that's really what he wants. To spend time with the people he loves."

The sound of voices and footsteps came from the direction of the stairs.

"Do you think the others know?" I whispered.

He snorted.

Before I could ask him to elaborate on that, Fish, Hailee, and Aiden found us. Hailee wore a knee-length lavender cocktail dress, whereas the guys had donned dark jeans and short-sleeved shirts—Aiden's midnight blue and Fish's hibiscus red.

"There you are," Leonardo said. "Took y'all long enough. We've been waiting."

"Sorry," Aiden said. "*Someone* was hogging our bathroom. Kept me back."

"I said I was sorry," Fish muttered. "Hey, Reyna. You look great."

"Sure," I said, then laughed. I don't know why they were bothering with compliments. I really did look the same.

"No, really, you do," Hailee said. "I love the lipstick. The red is so good on you."

"It is," Aiden said.

What the—? Aiden too?

Was the lipstick magic?

Beside me, Leonardo made a noise—something between a laugh and a groan. "I think it's time for us to go," he said.

"Where's Eliza?" Hailee asked.

"I'm here!" Eliza stepped around the corner from the living room, dazzling in an emerald green strapless dress. "I'm right here. You ready?" She linked her arm through Aiden's. "Let's get this party started!"

NINETEEN

The party was well underway by the time we arrived. On the lawn, long rectangular tables were covered by white linen cloths, adorned with tiny seashells, vases of dried sticks and leaves, and handmade clay lamps that held the darkness at bay.

The food had been set out on sparkling silver platters, woven palm-leaf place mats, or freshly cut banana leaves. They offered spicy Jamaican patties, sticky guava pies, mini potato rotis, and slices of crisp watermelon and pineapple. Honey-glazed barbecued shrimp had been skewered on thin wooden sticks. Salt-fish cakes and balls of fried pholourie were piled around bowls of tangy tamarind sauce. In one corner, a small bar had been set up with frosted bottles of rosy-pink rum punch on display. Exactly how Mummy used to do it.

Except for the brand of the punch, it seemed that the rest of the party had been spared William's meddling. Or so I'd thought.

I stumbled to a halt. "What the hell is that music?"

"It sounds like . . ." Fish tilted his head to the side. "*Step aside and welcome the king. Let me hear everybody in here sing. This ain't just hype-hype-hyperbolic.* It's us!" He beamed. "You know what? I think I kind of like this instrumental version of the song better."

Aiden nodded, a thoughtful expression on his face. "It's actually not bad."

"It's terrible," I said.

"Wow, Rey." Fish frowned. "Tell us what you really think."

William. He'd messed with the music. I'd expected changes to the food, to the decor, but not *this.* The only thing worse was if he'd removed the party from the hotel altogether. We'd had the same steelpan player, playing the same calypso setlist, for the past decade. He had no right to change it.

"You know I enjoy our banter, Reyna," Fish was saying. "I serve it up and you shut me down. Fun. But there are some lines—"

"Excuse me," I said, spotting William at the edge of the party. He wore a slim-fitted gray suit, a glass of rum punch in his hand. I walked right up to him.

"Drinking at work?" I asked.

It was a mistake to let him handle this party. The bet was a huge mistake.

"Oh, this?" He held up the glass. "This drink that your father handed to me, just before he patted my back and told me *good job on the party*? I figured it was okay." He gestured to the people around us. "And, as you can see, the party is more or less running itself anyway."

I wanted *so badly* to believe he was lying about the drink, but it sounded like something Daddy would do.

"Who is that?" I pointed at the pannist. Obviously, this was not our regular player. This guy was too young, too flashy, in a pair of skintight black pants and an unbuttoned silvery shirt. Thick silver chains hung around his neck. His skills were nowhere near the level of our usual pannist.

"Oh—we hired someone new this year. It was actually Aunty Helen's idea, and your father approved."

"Aunty Helen?" I remembered the day I'd walked in on them in Daddy's office. Was this what she helped with? "Did Aunty Helen have anything to do with switching to Simona punch too?"

"She recommended it, yes." William sighed. "What, Reyna? Are you going to make a problem out of this too? You wanted a pannist—that's a pannist."

"He's supposed to be playing classic calypso. The guests are expecting an authentic experience."

"And by authentic, you mean old? Look around you, Reyna. Everyone is enjoying themselves. The only one with a problem is you."

I shook my head. No, that wasn't . . .

I looked over to the gaggle of dancers. Yes, they were dancing. Yes, they were smiling. But only because they didn't know any better. The music was all wrong, too loud, too electric. It was nothing like it was supposed to be.

William smiled smugly. More than anything, I wanted to wipe that sparkle of victory from his eyes. But I couldn't think of a thing to say.

"Reyna, love." The last person I wanted to see at that moment—Aunty Helen—wrapped an arm around my waist, pulling me into a cloud of mint and coconut oil. She wore a burgundy dress and a matching headwrap. Gold hoops hung from her ears. She pulled William into her other side.

"Will," she said. "You did a wonderful job with the party tonight. C'est magnifique!"

"Thank you, Aunty," William said.

Will? Aunty?

What the hell was going on here?

"Looks like De La Iron is a hit." William nodded toward the pannist. "Thank you again for recommending him. His music is exactly the type of fresh, modern upgrade I was looking for. Reyna was just talking about his playing."

"Isn't he divine?" She tried to get me to sway with her. "A talented young man. Your father and I heard him playing at a bar on the beach. He had everyone on their feet."

I didn't move, my feet rooted to the ground. Why was she still here? Didn't she have a business to get back to in Canada? Why was she all up in mine?

"Come, Reyna. How does that saying go?" she asked dreamily, then proceeded to answer her own question. *"Music expresses that which cannot be said, and on which it is impossible to be silent—*I've always found it to be true. N'est-ce pas?"

"Sure," I said, squirming out of her hold.

Without missing a beat, Aunty Helen used her free hand to

snatch Eliza's arm as she and Aiden passed. "Eliza! And it is Aiden, yes? I'm a big fan of your group."

"Really?" Aiden failed to hide his surprise. "I mean—thank you."

Aunty nodded enthusiastically. "'Hyperbolic' is number one on my workout playlist. I love the beat. It gets me *Hype-hype-hyped*!" She shimmied her shoulders. "Why aren't you both dancing?"

Eliza bit her lip, obviously trying not to laugh. "We will in a bit."

"Don't wait too long. The dance floor waits for no one." Aunty Helen slipped her arm through William's. "Shall we? I'm ready to show you youngsters how it's done." She winked at us. "Feel free to take notes."

Eliza and William laughed. Even Aiden cracked a smile. Was I the only one who thought she was trying too hard? Really?

William handed me his drink, and I took it reflexively. "Try to enjoy the party," he said, before they sauntered off to join the dancers. If my glare could burn, he would've been incinerated on the spot.

Eliza laughed. "So, what do you think?" she asked Aiden. "You want to dance now? Or get something to drink first?"

I glanced at them, just long enough to see Eliza latch onto his arm. I quickly switched my attention to the dancers. My father had joined them, dressed in a shirt printed with surfing turtles. William stepped back so Daddy could pull Aunty Helen into his arms. Together they swayed in time with the rhythm, smiling and dancing to the type of music Mummy would never have had at her party.

I stared at the glass in my hand. There had to be something wrong somewhere. If not with the music, at least with the punch. I sniffed the drink, then sipped. The flavor was sweet and tart. It wasn't actually that bad. Damn it.

"Or we could take a walk?" Eliza said to Aiden. "Head down to the beach. It's a nice, clear night. We should make the most of it."

I knocked back the rest of the punch in one gulp. It hit the back of my throat and burned like hell. I covered my mouth to stop myself from spewing it right back out.

"Whoa!" Eliza laughed. "Reyna!"

Aiden stepped out of her hold. He took my glass just before it slipped. "You okay?"

I forced myself to swallow. "Great."

"Well, look at you." Eliza set her hands on her hips. "First lipstick, now this. You're really letting your hair down tonight!"

I shook my head. "I think I'm going to . . . sit for a while."

"You sure you're okay?" Aiden asked again.

I brushed past him. Since when did he care? I couldn't be around their flirting a second longer.

For some generic punch, the Simona messed me up. I weaved through the cluster of dancers and took one of the empty plastic chairs near the buffet tables. As I sat there, watching the guests and staff, my thoughts slowed. My mood sank into something dark and heavy.

Daddy and Aunty Helen. Eliza and Aiden. Hailee and Leo.

Fish and the random female guest he was dancing with. Everyone had somebody. And what did I have? A hotel that didn't need me anymore? I'd put so much of myself into this place, and it ran just fine without me.

Suddenly, I couldn't stand it. I rose to my feet on shaky knees. No one would notice if I left. Why would they?

In the darkness, I crossed the lawn alone, seeking out my safe haven. The one place that brought me peace. The place I was about to lose forever.

I dipped beneath the caution tape and sat on the bench in the gazebo. It was cold and hard. Several cracks perforated the floor like nerves. Sitting there, I could almost pretend no time had passed. When I closed my eyes, I remembered better days: back when there was only calypso music, and Mummy and Daddy were the ones dancing together. I could even see Aiden sitting beside me. Everything as it should be.

I heard the rustling of tape and opened my eyes.

"I knew you'd be here." Aiden's hands were shoved into his pockets. He took in the gazebo, his brow pinched. "How is this thing still standing? I thought you'd have it knocked down by now."

I made the shape of a T with my hands. "Timeout, please," I said, eyes burning. "I know you hate me, but I can't deal with you right now. Can you just—" My voice broke, and I bit my lip to stop a sob from slipping out.

"Are you crying?"

I covered my face. "No."

I breathed deep, waiting for the sounds of his retreat, but they didn't come. No, that would be too easy. Instead, his footsteps drew closer.

"I don't hate you, Reyna," he said. "But I think I'm entitled to be a little angry."

"A little angry?" I couldn't control the words as they tumbled out. "Having you here has been a nightmare. You know what? No. I don't want to talk about this right now."

Back at the party, the pannist started to play his version of "California Gurls."

"Oh my God!" I blinked furiously, unable to stop tears from slipping down my cheek.

"Come on, don't . . ." His voice hitched with a hint of panic. "What's wrong? Do you want me to get someone for you? Your father?"

"No, don't! He's the one who said yes to this music in the first place."

"A Katy Perry song is the problem?"

"Yes! It's the song, it's the pannist, it's the punch. Everyone's having a great time, and I'm going to lose this gazebo."

"Because . . . of a Katy Perry song." There was an edge of humor to his tone.

"Yes, because of a Katy Perry song!" I glared at him. Nothing about this was funny.

Aiden wasn't laughing though. He seemed to be contemplating the roof. The darkness softened the lines of his face, reminding me of the boy he'd once been. For a second, I could almost pretend I was fourteen again.

"Do you remember that time you snuck out of the party to meet me here?" He seemed to be thinking along the same lines. "Then your mother found us. She was livid."

"Yeah, I remember the way she ran you off."

Mummy had invited Aiden to the party the year after, but he wouldn't go. Not after the way she'd sent him home. There was nothing I could say to convince him she'd wanted him there.

"I was so mad at her for that." I snorted. Who was I kidding? "I'm still mad at her for that. And I know it's unfair because she's gone. But I'm mad at her for that, too, so . . ." I looked to the ceiling, furiously wiping tears from my eyes. "Pretend I didn't say that."

When he didn't answer, I looked at him. He was watching me with a gentleness in his expression that made my chest ache. "I didn't need to come to the parties, Reyna."

I wiped under my cheek, my chin, under my nose. I must've looked like a mess. "You should've been able to."

"There was only one reason I would've gone."

"Crab cakes?"

"Two reasons," he corrected himself. "I would've gone to be with you. Wherever you were, that's where I wanted to be."

Then why did you leave? I wanted to shout at him, but I held on to the words. They burned in my throat. Everything he said was past tense. What good would it do to bring it up again?

"Besides," he said. "The parties always seemed a little stuffy to me. Except for the music." He smiled. "I remember the music was good. I could hear it from here. Lots of older stuff like Kitchener and David Rudder."

"Because they were her favorite calypsonians," I said. "I know Mummy could be a bit . . . but she loved these parties. She worked so hard to make them perfect, with all her favorite foods and songs. It was her way of sharing a little piece of her heart with everyone."

Aiden was silent for a moment. "Her birthday was around this time too, wasn't it?"

"She would've turned fifty-one next week." I pressed my heel against a crack in the floor. It was a struggle to keep the tears away.

"I'm sorry," he said softly.

His shadow slid along the floor, and when I looked up, he was gone. I sat there in the silence, staring at the spot where he'd stood. It would've been easy to pretend he hadn't been there at all.

A few minutes later, the steelpan stopped and the electronic accompaniment cut. Near silence filled the air, the only sounds the light chirping of insects and the crashing of waves on the bay. When the pannist started to play again it was very different.

The intro sounded familiar, but I couldn't place it. It was fun, upbeat . . . It picked up quickly, the notes tumbling after one another, the original tune flawlessly adapted and injected with a vibrant, chaotic edge that I hadn't heard from the pannist earlier. "Trini To De Bone" by David Rudder—of course. It seemed obvious to me now.

I rose to my feet in a daze, moving without thought. I trailed the song back to the main lawn, where the party had ground to a halt. I wove through the bodies like water around reeds. Even though I knew who was playing, the sight still stunned me.

Aiden's sleeves were rolled up to his elbows. His nimble hands played the pan with a level of skill and strength that was as breathtaking to hear as it was to watch. Beads of sweat had already bloomed across his brow, but he ignored it, too caught up in the performance to notice anything but the music. He wasn't just good—he was amazing. No one could look away. He had the entire party hypnotized.

The moment the song ended, everyone burst into applause.

Aiden looked up from the instrument, startled. He bowed his head and smiled, flustered by the attention. I never understood that about him. For someone who worked so hard mastering his art, learning how to entertain and impress, he seemed almost shy in the face of praise, even when he deserved it.

He handed the sticks back to the pannist. They exchanged a handshake and a few words. Everyone gravitated toward them, including me.

Eliza beat us all, though. She lifted her face to his, her smile bright and brimming with admiration. She was speaking, waving her hands.

Then, without warning, she kissed him.

TWENTY

Even before my phone chimed, I awoke with a sinking sense of dread. Sunlight sliced through the gaps of the curtain and shot past my lowered eyelids, boring right into my brain. I rolled over, burying my face in the pillow. My head throbbed viciously, memories of the night before returning with cringe-inducing clarity.

I snatched my phone off the bedside table. Olivia had sent a ton of messages overnight.

> Ok. I just want to say I get it now. Aiden playing the steelpan is HOT!?!
>
> Sorry. I messaged that before I saw the end.
>
> Are you ok???
>
> I'm so sorry. call me

I let the phone drop and dragged myself to the shower. The night before, I'd fallen right into bed. Remains of the party lingered on my body—my hands sticky, my tongue tainted by a bitter, sugary taste. The scent of dried sweat, sweetened fruit, and alcohol permeated my hair and clothes. I wanted to stay in the shower forever, let the hot water wash away the feeling of grime and humiliation stuck to my skin.

I didn't want to talk to Olivia. Or anyone.

For a flicker of a moment, while Aiden had been playing that song, I'd thought *maybe*. It was foolish. Apparently, all it took was one sliver of kindness from him to turn me into a fool. What was it going to take for me to realize everyone moved on except for me?

It wasn't until later, after I'd gotten out of the shower, dressed, and grabbed breakfast, it hit me.

How did Olivia know about Aiden playing the steelpan in the first place?

"I want it on the record, it was not my fault this time," Fish announced to the office.

"Not now." Hailee yanked him into the seat next to her. "That's really not important at the moment. Don't you think?"

She tipped her head toward Eliza, who stood near the door.

A guest had filmed Aiden and Eliza last night. They'd captured the performance and the kiss, and posted it online. It took no time at all for it to start trending. In less than twelve hours, the video raked in more than a million views, spreading faster and generating more buzz than any of Eliza's posts ever did. Eliza hadn't said more than a handful of words the entire morning, her phone glued to her hand.

She was upset. They all were.

Sympathy bled through my numbness. I'd taken a peek at

the comments earlier. It wasn't pretty. When Aiden and Eliza's rumored relationship was page three of the comments section on a gossip blog, no one paid attention; now their kiss was *E! News* headlines, people had something to say. Aiden's fans, in particular, were the most vocal of all.

> No one would even know who she was if it wasn't for her sister.
> Talentless—did you hear she's actually trying to get big movie roles now? Not a chance in hell.
> She's not even pretty. At all. Not without makeup on.

It was sexist. And cruel. No one said a word against Aiden. Just Eliza.

It was probably a good thing Aiden and I had never worked out then. If his fans treated Eliza Musgrove this way, what would they have done to a nobody like me? I didn't know if I could handle it.

There, I thought. The thinnest of silver linings.

Unsurprisingly, it did not make me feel better.

"It's no one's fault," Daddy said. "We just need to work out where we go from here."

I peeked through the office blinds. At the entrance to the hotel, our security escorted two preteen girls from the premises. They were both dressed head-to-toe in DJ Bacchanal merch. The second the security guards returned inside, the girls started to assess the side wall, probably trying to decide if they could scale it.

"Reyna?"

I let the blinds snap shut. "Yeah?"

Daddy's brow furrowed. Today's shirt was a colorful balloon print. "What did the private security firm say?"

"They'll send some people from Trinidad on Monday."

"So what do we do until then?" Leonardo asked. He stood behind Hailee's chair; their hands locked over her shoulder. Aiden was leaning against the wall beside them.

"Until then, we can't guarantee your privacy," I said. "I'm sorry, I don't think you can stay here."

"So where do we go?" Fish sat forward. "Another hotel?"

I thought of my contacts at other hotels. "I'll make some calls and find out."

"Won't the fans just find us again?" Hailee said.

"Not if we don't go to another hotel like they'd expect." Leonardo twisted around. "What if we stay with Aiden's friend? Darren? Didn't he invite us to his house yesterday?"

Aiden blinked. "I don't know." He scratched his cheek. "That's a lot to ask of them. Especially last minute."

"He did say we were all invited." Leonardo arched a brow. "It would only be for the weekend. You do want to visit them, don't you?"

"I don't know," Aiden said again. "It might be—"

"I think we should go," Eliza said.

Aiden's mouth snapped shut. He turned to look at her. We all did.

"If you think it'll be okay." Eliza's words were soft. Uncharacteristically hesitant. "It would be cool to meet your friends. See

185

where you grew up. Meet the woman who taught you music."

Aiden frowned. "Are you sure?"

Eliza lifted her shoulder in a small shrug.

Aiden dragged his fingers through his hair, silent for a few seconds. Finally, he let his hand drop. "Okay, yeah. I'll ask him."

Eliza gave him a tentative smile. It was fleeting, but there. The first we'd seen from her that morning. Aiden smiled in return.

I turned back to the window, furiously biting down a surge of bitterness. No doubt Aiden only agreed to this because Eliza asked him. If I hadn't seen them kiss, this small, sweet act would've confirmed their relationship more than anything else.

"Aiden, where does your friend live?" Daddy asked.

"Speyside."

Daddy nodded. "Good restaurants on that side of the island." He stood, his chair rolling backward. "There's a new one that jus' opened I really want Reyna to try. She'll go with you, of course. You can continue your outings while you're staying up there."

What? No. I'd wanted a break. At least one weekend without the group. A chance to pull myself together, away from Eliza and Aiden. "Daddy, I don't think—"

"She can come," Aiden said, shifting his feet. "I mean, if Darren says we can all come, it should be fine for her to come too."

I was too shocked to speak. And in my silence, Daddy spoke up.

"Good. I'm glad we talked this out." Daddy held out his hand. "Aiden will call his friend. In the meantime, let's go find some new rooms for you. Hopefully, it will throw your enthusiastic fans off the scent. We can go and pick up your t'ings later."

"Thank you for this," Hailee said. "We're sorry about all the trouble."

"Is no scene, child." Daddy opened the door and stepped aside to let them pass. "You're family now."

Eliza lifted her phone, gnawing on her lower lip as she walked out. Hailee made a half-hearted attempt to take the phone from her, but Eliza dodged out of her reach. I watched them head for the elevators. Even though I felt sorry that Eliza had to deal with those awful comments, I had to wonder—did she not expect the news to get out? She certainly didn't go out of her way to hide the relationship.

"Reyna," Aiden said, before I could follow them. "Can I talk to you for a second?"

I stopped without thinking. I should've pretended I hadn't heard him. Now I had no choice but to wait for him to draw nearer. He looked a little tired, but no worse for it. If nothing else, it made him seem more approachable than he'd been since he arrived.

He stuffed his hands into his pockets. "Did you . . . get home all right last night? After we talked, I didn't see you around."

I shrugged and shifted my feet, unsteady in his presence. So he wanted to be nice now? Must've had something to do with the way I'd sobbed in front of him the night before. Still couldn't believe I'd done that. It was probably why he was okay with me joining them in Speyside. He felt sorry for me.

The idea of him knowing I'd stood right there with everyone else—that I'd watched him play and then kiss Eliza—made me nauseated.

"Yeah, I left right after that. Sorry I missed your performance."

"So . . . you left?"

"Yes."

He rocked back on his heels. "Okay," he said, sounding strained, like he was struggling to get the words out. Or holding something back. "But it wasn't really—"

"Reyna!" William came charging over. "We need to talk about last night."

I was relieved to see him—a feeling that truly illustrated how desperate I was to get out of this conversation with Aiden.

William did a double take when he saw who I was talking to. "When you're free. Sorry to interrupt."

"We're done anyway," I said, then told Aiden, "You should try to catch up." I pointed to the other end of the lobby where Daddy and the others were just entering the elevator. "You don't want to lose them."

Aiden's gaze swung from William to me. His jaw worked like he wanted to say something more. Instead, he spun around and left without another word.

William cleared his throat. I braced myself for what was coming.

"So, about last night . . ." A smug note wormed its way into his voice. "I'd say the party was a success, wouldn't you? This is a good a time as any for you to officially concede defeat."

I watched Aiden catch up to the others, the numbness I'd nursed all morning suddenly pierced by hurt so sharp, so deep, it threatened to break through. I retreated into Daddy's office, William on my heels.

"Come on, Reyna. Last night's party was a hit. Admit it. Everyone had a great time."

Not everyone.

"Yes, fine." I turned my back to him, facing the window. I wished he'd leave, the sting of oncoming tears brutal and unyielding. But William just would not let it go.

"So I win? You're admitting it?"

"Yes."

"Seriously?"

"Yes."

"No taking it back? The gazebo is finally coming down?"

Yes, I tried to say again, but the word was shattered by a sob.

Yes, I'd lost. Yes, he could take my gazebo. He might as well take my whole hotel for that matter. What was the point of holding on? Years passed, the world spun, my mother's face faded by the day. Everything was so far removed from the future she'd wanted for us I couldn't even see it anymore.

William swore, and the door clicked shut. There was a bit of shuffling footsteps before he spoke again. "This isn't personal," he said softly, but his tone was firm. "I'm not taking the gazebo down to hurt you. I'm taking it down because it can't stay up."

I closed my eyes.

"Reyna, it's a gazebo," he said with a touch of incredulity.

"Do you know how long it's been there?" I asked him. "Decades. Long before you or I were born."

"Rotary phones and fax machines are old too. You don't see us trying to hold on to those."

"It's not about how old it is. It's that it's always been there. A constant. Anytime I needed somewhere to take a break, to be alone, when the hotel got to be too much, that was my place." A tear slipped down my cheek. I swiped it away quickly, feeling foolish. I didn't know why I bothered trying to explain it to him. "I don't know if you can understand that—"

"I don't," he said, then added, "but I get that it means a lot to you."

When I looked over, William stood by the door. His shoulders were hunched, his torso slightly twisted to the side. He seemed no less uncomfortable with my tears than I was.

"But you know it needs to come down, right?" he said, his expression soft. "You see that it's time?"

I did. I had for a while now.

That didn't make it any easier.

TWENTY-ONE

THREE YEARS EARLIER

There are few things more terrifying than watching my mother burst in to break up a party, her wrinkled nightgown stuffed into a pair of high-waisted jeans, hair wrapped in a satin scarf, her socked feet shoved into sandals, her eyes spitting hellfire at everyone in sight. Or so I'd been told, the story well-circulated among my classmates. Mummy's wrath became the stuff of legend long before the new year even started.

I hadn't seen it myself, only returning to the suite after the teenage tourists who'd crashed the slumber party had been kicked out, the ten girls who'd been invited corralled into the bedroom where they waited for their parents to pick them up. Slowly, the room emptied. After the last disgruntled parent left, so did we.

Mummy and I drove home at dawn, the day silent in the early hour. The roads were nearly empty, but Mummy took every turn with a sharp jerk of the wheel, far removed from her usual careful control. I couldn't tell if the change was due to anger or sleep exhaustion or both.

"Do you have any idea what you've done?" Her fingers flexed on the steering wheel. "All those parents, the guests—what they must think of us? Underage drinking and smoking and goodness knows what at my hotel, at my daughter's slumber party—a party where you weren't even there!"

I looked down at my lap. "I'm sorry."

"After you begged and begged, I trusted you to supervise your own sleepover. To be mature. To respect the hotel."

"I'm sorry," I said again, but it didn't seem to be helping. "I left Olivia in charge. I don't know how it got so out of control."

"Did *I* leave Olivia in charge? No. You were in charge. *You.*" Mummy took a sharp right, swiping the curb with her tires. "But no. You were off with Aiden. Again."

My fingers twitched against the strap of my seat belt. The way she said it made it sound much worse than it was. Aiden and I were only gone for a few hours. We never left the hotel grounds.

It was amazing how quickly a night could change. Only a few hours earlier, Aiden and I sat on the cliffs overlooking the sea. We counted the number of yachts floating in the dark, making up increasingly ridiculous stories about the people on them. It had been perfect, the night not too cold, not too warm; our kisses soft and scattered between whispers and laughter. Overall, a perfect birthday.

Until my phone rang and it all went to hell.

Even now, if I closed my eyes tight enough, shut the world out for a second, I could still feel his cheek against mine, hear the wordless melody he'd hummed under his breath.

The car dropped, jolting me back to the present. Mummy had run right through a pothole.

"I don't know what to do anymore," Mummy said. "It was bad enough when you dropped piano lessons without telling me. I had to find out from your music teacher you stopped going. All those times I thought you were practicing, you were with Aiden."

"He's not— I stopped going to piano lessons because *I* don't want to go. It has nothing to do with Aiden." I should've told her before, but I knew she'd be this angry.

"Do you know how lucky you are? When I was your age, I begged my mother for lessons, so I could play like my friends. I never had the chance. We couldn't afford it. Now I can send you, and you just want to throw it away?"

"Because I don't want to play the piano. I don't enjoy it, and I'm not good—"

"That is why you practice—"

"I want to focus on art." I raised my voice, cutting her off the way she'd done to me. She was right about all those missed piano lessons spent with Aiden, but I'd also been painting, experimenting with new mediums and techniques, while he'd been songwriting. There may have been the occasional break for kissing, but for the most part, we'd been working.

Lately, my art teacher and I had been discussing my future. She'd encouraged me to build up a portfolio and seek out university programs, many of the websites bookmarked on my laptop. A few I'd found were in Trinidad, but the vast majority were out of the country. In the meantime, I'd practiced in secret and entered contests, hoping to earn enough prizes or to paint something so beautiful Mummy would look at it and finally see this as a viable future for me.

"Painting is a fine hobby," she said. "So is the piano. You could focus on both if you'd spend less time with Aiden."

"Oh my God, why do you hate Aiden so much? He hasn't done anything."

"I do not hate him. I just think it's interesting how, whenever you disappear or do something reckless, he's right there with you." Her brows pinched together. "I still cannot believe you ran off tonight. Every time I think about it, I . . . I don't know how I'm supposed to trust you anymore."

"I'm sorry. It was a mistake." A bad one, true. But how was I supposed to know some of the guests would crash the party?

"You should've been there."

"I said I was sorry."

"That's not enough."

"I don't know what else you want!"

A silver car came shooting around the corner to our street. The driver took the turn way too wide, their headlights off. Mummy swerved at the last second, running onto the sidewalk. Mummy screamed and I lurched forward, my seat belt cutting into my torso. Mummy's arms stretched in front of me protectively. Behind us, the silver car squealed down the street, out of sight.

Our car filled with the sound of heavy breathing. I tried to calm down, but my entire body shook. Mummy didn't seem to be any better.

"Are you okay?" she asked.

I nodded.

She cut the engine. We sat in silence.

Mummy rested her forehead on the wheel. Her eyes closed; a glitter of tears caught in her dark lashes. "You're still so young. There's so much you have to learn about growing up. If something happens to me, I just need to know you're going to be okay."

"Nothing's going to happen to you, so don't say that." She shouldn't talk that way. Not after what we'd gone through. "Next time I will be there, I promise." And I meant it with a conviction drawn from the depths of my soul, if only to make her stop crying.

Mummy turned her face to me. I noticed how much older she looked, and I realized I only saw it now because she was letting me. There was something hollow in her eyes, like she'd folded in on herself.

"What?" I asked.

Mummy's lips parted and she started to explain.

The rest of the night drained away, something awful slithering into place. Our new reality dawned on me slowly, like the pale blue that was bleeding into the sky. Somewhere a rooster crowed and a new day started.

TWENTY-TWO

Again, I got stuck in the back seat. The streets into the northern side of Tobago cut a winding path through hills and valleys. I spent the one-hour drive torn between twitchy boredom and motion sickness, reevaluating every life decision that led me to this point.

First off, the morning hadn't started well.

When Darren arrived to pick us up in a borrowed van, Aiden introduced us to him. Even though Aiden rolled through the names, mine jammed in line with the others, Darren still leaped on it.

"Reyna?" He pointed at my face, then looked to Aiden for confirmation. "Reyna?"

Aiden pulled his arm down. "Just open the trunk so we can put the bags in."

Darren frowned, seemingly as baffled by Aiden's dismissal as he was by my presence. He followed Aiden to the back of the vehicle, shooting me one last look before popping the trunk.

It was too much to hope that his excitement had gone unnoticed. As we stood there, I could feel the weight of everyone's curiosity. I caught Eliza staring at me, but did it really matter if they found out now? Aiden and I were old news. All anyone had to do was check Twitter to see which couple was trending.

How did I even get here, sitting in an overly warm van that smelled of cheap air freshener, sunblock, and damp upholstery, wedged between the window and Fish, who kept fiddling with the radio app on his phone? He sat next to me, playing DJ Bacchanal music near constantly, even after I'd conceded that *yes, DJ Bacchanal is popular here. Can we please, please, change it to something else?* He would not stop.

"Your rampant narcissism is deeply disturbing," Aiden called back to him from the front passenger seat.

Fish shushed him. "You know you love it!" He waited for the beat to drop, then started dancing.

I sighed and turned to the window. The mood in the van was weird, everyone wrapped up in their own thoughts. Using my finger, I sketched a flower into the condensation on the window. Outside, it drizzled lightly. The coast skittered past, houses clinging to seaside cliffs, telephone and electrical wires lacing one pole to another like black webbing against the blue-gray sky. We caught snapshots of daily life—children playing, people heading to work, road-side shops, churches, bars, and health centers opening for the day.

Another song started to play over Fish's phone. Something

slower, moodier. The reception wasn't good, so I couldn't make out the words, but I recognized Leonardo's voice layered with a choir of backing vocals. The song couldn't be one of their hits or I would've heard it before.

"What song's this?" I asked him. "I like it."

"Wow." Fish lowered the volume. His body was angled away from me and toward Leonardo, who'd fallen asleep against his window. "A compliment from you. I guess anything is possible."

"Are you mad at me?" I asked him. "Is it because of what I said? When the steelpan player was playing 'Hyperbolic'?"

"No." Fish lowered the music even more. "Yes. A little."

"I didn't mean anything by it. It was just . . . a surprise." When he glared at me, I added, "I wasn't having a good night."

"And every other time you've blown me off? Those weren't good nights either?"

Well, the last few days hadn't exactly been easy. Still . . . "I'm sorry."

Fish turned the music off. His voice dropped to a whisper. "Every time I try to talk to you, you cut me off. Or ignore me. Or disappear. I can take the hint, okay. You don't owe me anything. I hoped we might be friends, if nothing else."

"I do want to be friends."

"That's what you say." Fish kept his eyes on his phone. "But then you make it impossible to get to know you."

Ah, crap. I wanted him to look at me, to see I was sorry. He wouldn't raise his head. It wasn't his fault he didn't know the full story. And as it stood, I still couldn't share all of it with him.

While I tried to think of something to say—something to make it better—Fish turned the app back on. He scanned the channels until he found one playing "Hyperbolic." Again. A chorus of groans erupted from the other passengers.

His commitment to driving the van crazy made me laugh. Who would've guessed Fish from DJ Bacchanal was a massive troll? And a sweetheart. He was more than the glossy charm and showmanship of his public image. The whole group was. How lucky was I to get to see that? To know that about them?

Would it be so bad to open up a little more?

While Fish continued to scour the radio app for more proof of DJ Bacchanal's popularity, I pulled out my own phone and scrolled back to some of my earliest photos. No one had seen these paintings in years, including me. Looking at them now, pride sparked in my chest. My older work usually made me cringe, but these I was still proud of.

I turned the phone onto its side. The screen flipped, the photo filling the screen. I tapped Fish on the shoulder. "Here." When he looked at me, I handed it over. My heartbeat quickened, fingers tingling with nervous energy. I told myself it didn't matter if he liked them, it was the gesture that mattered. I still hoped he did, though.

Fish turned the radio off and sat up. He took the phone from me. "This is yours?"

"Yeah." The first photo, my painting of a dew-laden red

hibiscus, the tiny droplets like diamonds rolling off the petals. "If you swipe forward, there are two more. I did them for a competition a few years ago."

"They're gorgeous," he said, swiping through the others—a frangipani tree adorned with hundreds of orange-black caterpillars, then an old teak tree conquered by encroaching orchids and vines.

"I thought you might be good, Reyna, but . . . wow. Is it only plants?"

"These are." I itched to take the phone back. I'd never felt comfortable showing my art or talking about it. "Sometimes I do portraits, but I prefer painting flora to anything else. *Preferred*, I mean."

"Well," he said, swiping back to the first photo and looking at it again. "At least you know flowers won't get up and move before you're done."

"Yeah, but there *is* movement though. The wind, the shifting light. Nature is constantly growing, dying, changing. There's so much life within and around it. It's a challenge to get on paper, but—" I stumbled, realizing I'd been rambling. Heat snaked up my chest and neck. "I mean, I like painting them. *Liked*."

"Clearly," Fish said, smiling. "So the mural on the wall of Aiden's room—that's yours too?" When I nodded, he called to the front of the van. "Aiden, did you know the mural in your room was Reyna's? She painted it."

"Yes," Aiden said.

Something about the dryness of his tone made me suspect he'd been listening. A quick glance at the others revealed they had been listening as well. Even Leonardo, who I'd thought was sleeping, faced us now.

"Can we see?" Hailee reached over the back of her chair.

"Sure," I said, and Fish handed her the phone.

"Nice," Hailee said after she and Eliza looked through the photos. "I'd buy them."

"Impressive," Eliza agreed distractedly.

"Did you want to see them?" Hailee asked, already handing the phone to Aiden. He took it, and I wanted to sink into the floor.

"They are good," Aiden said, after flipping through them. He gave the phone back to Hailee, who then passed it to Leonardo. Aiden's voice was almost clinical. "The mural is better, though. At least, it will be when she finishes it."

An invisible band tightened around my chest. How did he know?

"It's not done?" Fish asked. "I didn't even notice." He smiled at me. "If it matters, Reyna, I think it's great as is."

I offered him a smile in return. "It is done."

Aiden looked away from us. "No, it isn't."

"Yes, it is," I said through gritted teeth.

"Yeah, Aiden." Fish relayed my phone from Leonardo to me. "I think Reyna would know."

"Thank you," I said.

Darren said something to Aiden, too soft for us in the back to hear. I noticed the rigid set of Aiden's shoulders, a hint of frustration.

What was he playing at? The only way he'd know about the mural was if he'd moved the bed to take it all in. No one would do that unless they were interested. Only then he would've seen the amount of details hidden by the bed frame.

Did he care? Why else would he bother?

"So you sometimes do portraits?" Fish asked with a sly tilt to his tone.

I dragged my eyes from Aiden to look at him. "Are you about to make a *paint me like one of your French girls* joke?"

Fish frowned. "Well, not now."

Around noon, Darren pulled off the road and parked in a gravel-packed clearing. He cut the engine and jumped out. "We here!"

Darren and his mother lived in a two-story structure built to conform to the rise and fall of the sloping land. The walls were painted a soft yellow, the roof a leafy green. A spacious front porch jutted over the edge of the hill, rimmed by a crisscross-patterned banister, supported by ornate white columns. Rows of miniature palms sat on either side of the steps, their leaves yellowing and shaped like unfolding fans waving us inside. The windows, shutters, and doors were all thrown open, the facade of the house wide and welcoming.

"Home sweet-sweet home," Darren announced, as we climbed out of the vehicle.

"You sure Miss Bee okay with *all* of us here?" Aiden asked Darren.

"You joking?" Darren said. "She out she mind with excitement. Since this morning, she cooking up a storm for dinner tonight, which she never does when is just me." He patted Aiden on the back. "So, yes, is a good thing you come."

"Oh. Yuh welcome, then." Aiden smiled, but it was strained. He rubbed the back of his neck and squinted up at the house. "Is a long time since I see the place."

I smiled to myself. Somewhere around King's Bay, Aiden's new accent had started to fade. He looked more relaxed too, his laughter louder, his smiles quicker. He had told me a few stories about his days here: how he and Darren played around the house, practiced football in the yard, picked bags of plums to sell to tourists on the beach.

I saw why Aiden would want to spend so much time here when he was younger. The stunning view from the cliff reminded me of the old folktales Pearl used to tell. I could almost believe naughty douens lived in the dense thicket of trees descending the hillside, mermaids hiding behind the rocks that studded the open sea.

I breathed deeply as the wind picked up, the scent of salt filling my lungs. We had two days out here. As far I could remember, it would be longest I'd gone without setting foot on the grounds of the Plumeria. The thought made my skin buzz with fear and excitement.

The door of the house burst open. A woman ran past us in a blur of long limbs, green ruffles, and braids. A floral perfume permeated the air in her wake. She crushed Aiden into a hug, the tip of her head brushing the underside of his chin.

"It's good to see you, Miss Bee," Aiden said.

"My son!" she cried. "You've returned!" She pulled back to look him over. "Look nah—look how you done grow up so handsome. And successful." She slid a sly look toward Darren. "Maybe you should go off and leave me too? What yuh think?"

Darren laughed drily. "As you can see," he told Aiden. "Ma still *kicksin*, despite her advanced age."

"Advanced . . . ?" Miss Bee moved like she was about to lunge for her son.

Darren leaped backward. "I helping with the bags!" He snatched two suitcases and ran for the steps. "Come nah! All yuh stickin'. Is getting late. If all yuh want to get lunch, you need to move!"

Miss Bee watched her son escape into the house. "Buh wait nah, this boy . . ." She shook her head and turned back to Aiden. "Come, son, introduce me to yuh friends. These the boys from yuh group?"

"Yes. This is Leo and Fish. An' this is Hailee and Eliza and Reyna."

I braced myself for some reaction to my name, but I got none. Miss Bee didn't seem to recognize it. One by one, we were all enveloped in warm, floral-scented hugs.

"All right, everyone grab your t'ings and follow me inside." Miss Bee ushered us to the steps. "I got dem bedrooms ready. Is been so long since I had so many people come and stay."

I followed her toward the house, lugging my suitcase behind me. The wheels bumped and swerved on the grass. The more I thought about it, the more it bothered me that Miss Bee hadn't reacted to my name at all. Had things gone differently between Aiden and me, meeting this woman would've been tantamount to meeting one of his parents. Did that mean Aiden had never mentioned me? It would be weird if he hadn't.

No, not weird. Upsetting.

It was one thing to know I wasn't a part of his new life, but I'd thought our past meant something. At one point he'd been one of my best friends. My boyfriend. My first love. To think I didn't even warrant a mention—it stung.

"Do you want help?" Aiden asked as I hefted my suitcase to the steps of the house. He held out a hand. "I can take it up if you want."

"No, thank you," I said, stiffly. "You can go an help Eliza."

Aiden frowned, pointedly glancing around. We were the only two left on the grass, Eliza and her bags were already through the front door.

I sidestepped him, dragging my suitcase along. I didn't want his kindness. Or his pity. Or whatever he was feeling—I sure as hell didn't know now. And it seemed like I didn't know then either.

We had just enough time to set our things down before we took off again, to the restaurant Daddy had recommended. Nestled in the shadow of a hillside, the structure looked more like a house than a restaurant. We sat at a table in the back corner, and an elderly woman with a charming gap-toothed smile took our orders. The food took a while to prepare, but it was worth the wait. Without hesitation, I dug into the pile of steaming brown rice and red beans, stewed chicken, and thick slices of sugary plantain, everything topped with a healthy spoonful of the best callaloo I'd ever eaten.

We stayed there for almost two hours, tucked into the shady corner. While other customers came, ate, and left, we stayed and ordered more drinks. Fish got a little tipsy on his second bottle of beer and started telling stories about their world tour, some of the tales awe-inspiring, and others too ridiculous to be true.

"I swear," Fish's voice cut across the table. "By the end of the night, all we had was a flooded bathroom, two Olympic medalists, three bottles of Grey Goose, a pink Pomeranian, and half a bag of shredded lettuce."

"Stop." Eliza rolled her eyes. "Now you're pushing it."

"*Now* he's pushing it?" I asked. "I gave up on him after the Pomeranian showed up. And I still don't get what the lettuce was for."

I smiled across the table at Eliza. Fish's stories seemed to have temporarily lifted her bad mood. I'd caught her checking her phone only twice since we arrived, which was an improvement over the hundreds of times she'd looked at it on the drive up. I felt bad for her, but I didn't know how or if I should try to do something. Eliza and I weren't exactly friends. In fact, of all the connections I'd made within the group, ours was the most tenuous. I hoped the reason wasn't obvious to anyone else but me. Jealousy was not a good look on anyone.

Her disposition, so different from her usual cheerfulness, stood out. I was pretty sure Fish wouldn't be trying so hard—or rather trying *harder* than usual—to make us laugh if he wasn't responding to the dip in the atmosphere.

Fish threw up his hands. "What do I have to do to make you people believe me?"

Aiden eyed him over his glass of soft drink. "Stick to the truth?" In contrast to Eliza, his smile seemed plastered to his face. Perhaps it had something to do with being home, and catching up with Darren and Miss Bee, but his joy was almost tangible. Even now, as he tried to look apathetic, the corners of his lips ticked upward.

"Okay, then." Fish rested his elbows on the table and leaned forward. "Your turn then. Tell us a good story. A true story. Bonus points if you can think of anything interesting that didn't include me."

Aiden sat back, considering Fish across the table. "Now, I not about to deny I've had many—let's call them interesting—experiences, which were somehow—if not directly—your fault."

Fish raised his beer. "Cheers."

"But there were other times—"

Fish plopped the bottle down. "Lies! I'm the best thing that ever happened to you, and you know it."

"Excuse," Darren said. "Childhood best friend. Sitting right here."

Aiden chewed on a piece of ice, his jaw working as he thought. "Well, there was the time my friend and I stole my grandfather's boat and nearly got eaten alive."

I froze.

"Looking back, obviously not the smartest idea," he admitted, smiling. "We met up by the dock around two in the morning. It was full moon, a clear night. We took the boat out on our own and barely got twenty feet from the dock when we noticed these enormous shadows, black fins popping out of the water."

Someone gasped, and Aiden cracked a smile. He seemed to be enjoying himself, telling everyone about us, never mentioning me by name. What was the point of this? I stayed silent, shoving the food around my plate.

"So, there we were, surrounded," he said. "My grandfather's boat giving trouble, as always. My friend is freaking out. I'm freaking out. Of course, it starts to rain." He shifts forward, arms on the table. "But despite all of that, we make it to the shallows. Almost to the shore, when this wave comes out of nowhere. It hits the boat at just the right angle and knocks us both into the water."

Aiden caught my eye across the table. For a flicker of a moment, the shared memory sparked a silent connection.

I broke first, looking away.

"What happened?" Hailee asked.

"They died, obviously," Leonardo said.

Hailee swiped the rest of her boyfriend's drink, ignoring his half-hearted protest.

"It was dolphins," Aiden finished. "If it hadn't been so dark, I would've realized sooner."

"Seriously?" Fish asked. "Well, that was anticlimactic. I think I liked Leo's version better."

Aiden flicked a pigeon pea, and it hit Fish right between the eyes.

"Hey!" Fish swatted at his face.

Aiden laughed, and our eyes met again. This time I didn't look away. He gave me the smallest of smiles. I returned it.

An hour later, we returned to Miss Bee's. Darren parked the van, and we climbed out. The air carried with it the sweet scent of ripe mangoes. I lagged behind the others, taking a moment to enjoy the view again. When I turned back to the house, I spotted Aiden on the stairs. He watched me approach, his hands stuffed in his pants pockets. He clearly wanted to talk to me.

Logically, I knew it was probably nothing important, but something about the way he looked at me made my heart race.

Then Eliza came up behind him. She tapped his shoulder, and he turned to face her. I was close enough to hear her ask, "Can we talk?"

"Yeah. Sure," he answered. Whatever he'd needed to tell me would have to wait.

I passed them and entered the house, trying to shake off a feeling of disappointment.

TWENTY-THREE

TWO YEARS EARLIER

I caught up to Aiden on his way home from the beach. I didn't bother with greetings, launching myself right into his arms. I didn't care about the sweat-and-blood stains, or the scent of fish that seemed woven into his T-shirt. I didn't care—I just needed him.

My time these days was limited, and I'd taken way too long to find him. Soon Daddy would have to leave for the hotel and I'd need to be home with Mummy. Someone had to be with her all the time now.

"I missed you," I mumbled into his shoulder, clinging awkwardly as he shuffled us away from the roadside for some measure of privacy. It had been almost a week since I'd seen him. It made me angry, though it wasn't his fault.

He'd come to visit Mummy in the hospital once, a month earlier. The entire visit was painfully awkward, capped off by Mummy's not-too-subtle statement that she'd understand if Aiden was too busy to visit her in the future. Her message couldn't have been clearer. She did not want him there.

Aiden took it hard. I tried to explain it wasn't about him. True, Mummy never warmed to him, but she resented *anyone* seeing her like this. She'd have turned Daddy and me away too, if she could. She never said anything, of course, but there were little gestures, sharp words that slipped through. She had flat-out refused to stay in the hospital one second longer than necessary.

Now she was home again, Aiden wouldn't come by the house at all. Not out of resentment or spite, but because he seemed genuinely worried he'd upset her.

"What are you doing down here?" he asked.

I wanted to shake him. Why did he think I was here?

"To see you. Obviously. I've got maybe fifteen minutes." I pulled him in for a kiss. His lips were soft, his touch always electric. But his movements were strangely stilted. I pulled back. "What?"

Was he worried about getting fish guts on me? Like I'd care?

"I need to talk to you," he said. "Can you meet me later?"

"No, I don't think I can." Daddy wouldn't be home until late that night. By then I wouldn't be allowed to go out. "Why?" I dipped my head to meet his eyes when he ducked away. "Just tell me now."

He glanced at the road, then led me farther into the brush. There was a little trail there. It cut around the playground and led to our street. The grass was damp. The tang of overripe guava hung in the air. Aiden's fingers laced through mine, intimate but loose. He looked at me for a second, the way he sometimes looked at his lyrics. Like he was searching for the right words and the best way to put them.

"Do you remember that American guy Mom's dating?" he asked.

That wasn't what I was expecting. "Yeah."

Timothy was a stout, balding man with kind eyes and a magnificent jet-black beard. I'd never met him in person. Apparently, Timothy had fallen hard for Aiden's mom, wining and dining her, and taking her out every night. In all the photos Aiden showed me, they were beaming. They looked happy.

"They're getting married," he said.

That really, *really* wasn't what I expected.

I laughed, relieved. "That's good news. Aren't you happy? I thought you liked him."

"I do," he said, but he might as well have had a mouthful of rocks the way he garbled it. He stared at me for a moment, feet shifting impatiently. I got the impression he was waiting.

And then I understood.

"How . . . are they going to make it work? Is he moving?"

I don't know why I asked. I already knew.

"No, Reyna. He's not moving. We are."

TWENTY-FOUR

Morning in Speyside started early. Even before sunrise, roosters crowed, stray dogs barked. And between Hailee's snoring, Eliza's frequent trips to the bathroom, and the old water pipes rattling in the wall behind my head, I had gotten very little sleep. It was only when the sisters woke, dressed, and left the room that I could finally drift off.

By the time I woke up again, the sun was blazing high through the window. The screen on my phone read sixteen minutes past nine. I couldn't remember the last time I'd slept this late. I shuffled downstairs, every room I passed open and bright. Ceiling fans whirred, appliances hummed, curtains fluttered on the wind. Voices floated from the front porch, but I continued into the kitchen.

Miss Bee stood at the stove, her hands dusted with flour as she cooked sada roti on a heated tawah. She smiled when she saw me. "Good morning. It look like we all getting a late start today. Breakfast still making."

"You need help?"

"No, I good. I have all de help I need."

As far as I could see, we were the only ones in the room, but I took her word for it.

Miss Bee's kitchen was an open space that seamlessly flowed into a dining area and then the living room. Two sets of large louvered windows let in the light, their frames draped with thin, layered curtains which were drawn back to reveal the plum tree outside. Stacks of newspapers, thick binders, and a smattering of office supplies cluttered the dining table. A massive fridge hummed in the corner, its surface littered with magnets with random sayings like *Any time is Trinidad time* and *Every moldy bread has its stinky cheese*.

A wall and side table in the living room was adorned with a few framed photographs and newspaper articles of Aiden—everything from local music festivals right up to the recent Grammy Awards ceremony. I walked closer to get a better look.

"My star pupil," Miss Bee said over her shoulder.

"Yeah, he did well, didn't he?" I reached out to straighten one of the frames. Even with the photographs laid out before me, it was mind-bending to think of how much Aiden had done. Then again, I'd always thought he was amazing, it just took the rest of the world a little longer to catch up.

"He did," Miss Bee said, a smile in her voice. "But is no surprise. The very day his mother bring him for lessons, I already saw it—that love for music. I is always say: no matter how hard you work, no matter how hard you practice, if you en have that love for what you doing, you'll never make. Without that love, there'll always be a little piece of you holding back."

I crossed the living room, the opposite wall covered with colorful posters and charts with basic music instruction. I particularly liked the cartoon treble clef explaining note values through rhyme. A few instruments were tucked into the corner, including a piano, a steel pan, a few guitars, and wind instruments. This was where Aiden learned to play. Where it all started.

"He's lucky." I wandered over to the pan and traced the edge of it with my fingers. A pair of sticks rested inside. The letters of the notes were painted onto the inner surface of the drum. "To love the thing he's good at. And to get the chance to do it."

"An' lucky to get paid for it," Miss Bee said.

"That too." I picked up the sticks, testing the weight of them in my hands. They were heavier than I'd expected.

"Always knew he'd do big things." Miss Bee shuffled between the fridge and the stove. "All he needed was a little guidance."

"You bragging about yuh teaching skills again?" Aiden came through the back door, a bouquet of chive, celery, and chadon beni in one hand, kitchen scissors in the other. He had a smile as he walked in and it seemed to widen on noticing me there. "Morning."

"Morning," I said, my voice as tentative as the smile I returned.

Miss Bee set her knuckles on her hips, her palms closed so flour wouldn't get on her dress. "And why I shouldn't boast?" she demanded from Aiden. "One of my students is an international superstar. I very well make sure everyone from Crown Point to Charlottesville know."

"And I, for one, am very proud of you." Aiden kissed her cheek, then leaped away when she swatted at him. He set the bouquet on the counter.

Miss Bee eyed the stalks. "You leave any herbs in meh garden?"

Aiden grimaced. "Is too much?"

Miss Bee sighed.

While the pair continued to bicker, I played around with the pan. Because the notes were painted on, it only took a bit of experimentation before I could tap out a shaky rendition of "Mary Had a Little Lamb."

"You a musician too, Reyna?" Miss Bee asked.

Aiden shot her an odd look of confusion. "She plays the piano," he said, then returned to chopping the herbs he'd brought in. From where I stood, I could see his cuts were quick and clean. His hands, a source of fascination for me even before I understood attraction, seemed as deft with the knife as they were on the keys of a piano. His brow was furrowed in concentration, his lower lip snagged between his teeth. When he looked up and caught me staring, he started to smile again.

"Reyna, you want to play us something?" Miss Bee asked. "The piano right there."

"Not really," I said. "Please don't ask. I'm terrible."

"I sure yuh exaggerating," Miss Bee said.

"She's not," Aiden muttered. When Miss Bee glared at him, he added, "I just saying, the piano is not her instrument."

"Okay, what about the pan?" Miss Bee asked me. "You want to give it a try?"

"Sure," I said, laughing. "Why not? I like the idea it was the piano's fault I couldn't play it. It wasn't my instrument."

Aiden stopped chopping. "Let's not go that far."

"Only one way to find out," Miss Bee said. "But you have to hold the sticks right first." She held up a wooden spoon and tried to show me. When I tried to mimic the hold, she wasn't satisfied. "Aiden, I have flour on my hands, go show her."

"Oh, that's not . . . ," I started, but it didn't matter; Aiden had already set the knife down. He wiped his hands on the kitchen towel and walked over. My stomach tightened with nerves.

I need to stay calm. *Be cool.*

Two weeks ago, I thought Aiden would never talk to me again, much less smile at me or joke with me like he was doing now. So what if it was born from pity? There was nothing in the world— not even my pride—that could make me break this moment.

"I'm having flashbacks," he said, his voice low. "Do you remember the time I tried to teach you the guitar?" He stopped beside me. "Actually, maybe this isn't such a good idea."

"Or maybe it was the guitar's fault, too." I smiled at the memory. The one lesson involved two hours of arguing and very little guitar playing. Eventually, we called it quits and spent the rest of the afternoon kissing behind his house. Images of us together rose

to the front of my mind, and with it a rush of warmth and aware-
ness of how close he stood.

"Well, I guess we'll see," he said.

I handed over the pan sticks.

"First thing—hold them like this." He demonstrated. "Keep
your grip loose, but not so loose they go flying."

He handed the sticks back to me, and I tried again.

"No, like . . ." He started to reach for one of my hands, then
stopped. "Can I?"

"Yeah." I shifted closer to him. Sparks erupted along the length
of my side.

He took my hands and pressed his thumbs between the stick
and my palms, loosening my grip even further. The entire thing
was very clinical, very detached. But it didn't stop electricity from
shooting up my arms. I looked up to see if Aiden noticed, or felt
something too, but his eyes were down. I missed the warmth of his
hands the second he let go.

"Never cross your hands when you're playing," he said. "Use
the hand closest to the note. That's why when you go for the C—"

I hit the C with my left hand.

"Harder than that!" Miss Bee called from the kitchen. "Don't
be afraid to lick de pan. It cyah hit back!"

Aiden tried not to laugh, his dimples appearing for a second.
"Let me show you." He took the sticks from me and played a scale
a few times, starting slow, then getting faster with each round.

"Show-off," I said, trying to get a glimpse of the dimples again.
I was not disappointed.

He spun both sticks around his index fingers and handed them to me.

I gave him an unimpressed glare.

Very slowly, I copied the scale he'd played. He caught me using the wrong hand the first few times, but after a while I made it all the way through, from first note to last. I upped my pace until it flowed without hesitation or mistake.

"Maybe you have been playing the wrong instrument this whole time," he said.

I punctuated my victory by trying to spin the sticks around my fingers like he did. One of them flew right out of my hand and across the room, smacking against a picture frame. We were both silent for a second, watching the frame wobble until it stopped. We both burst into laughter.

Aiden went to retrieve the stick from where it fell next to the table. I checked the frame I'd hit. We were the only ones in the kitchen now. Judging from the empty stove and clean counter, we'd been the only ones in here for a while. Miss Bee must've taken the food out to the others on the front porch, cleaned up, and cleared out, without either of us noticing.

Thankfully, the frame hadn't cracked. The photo inside was one of Aiden onstage, a guitar in hand. I could date it from the style of his fade haircut alone. His footsteps drew near and stopped beside me.

"Look." I pointed to the photograph. "Baby you."

"Hardly." His arm brushed mine as he picked it up. "I don't even remember this."

"I do. The Crown Bago contest. You came in third."

"Oh, right. I won the money for my laptop. How the hell did I forget that?"

"A lot has happened since then." Maybe too much. I couldn't help the unhappiness that leaked into my words. I checked his face to see if he heard it.

His dark eyes were on the photograph. "I was afraid of that, you know. Coming back home, I worried the place would've changed too much. Or that I've changed too much. That I wouldn't love it as much as I did."

"And?" I asked, staring up at him. "Now that you're here?"

"It's changed," he said. "I've definitely changed." The angle of light in the room cast shadows of his lashes against his cheeks. They swept upward as his eyes lifted to meet mine. "But not as much as I'd thought."

"Is that bad?"

Very quietly, he said, "I'm not sure."

"Aye—come nah." Darren popped into the kitchen. "What taking so long?"

Aiden and I stepped back from each other. When did we get that close? While Aiden returned the photograph to its spot on the table, I rolled my ponytail into a knot, my body vibrating with the need for something to do.

Darren frowned. "All yuh coming to eat or what? I'd like to leave for the waterfalls sometime today, thanks." He folded his arms, then wouldn't move until we left the room with him.

• • •

The trek from the parking area to the waterfall took about fifteen minutes. We had to tread along a dirt path littered with stones and dead leaves; thick, lush forestry on either side. Ferns, cocoa, breadfruit, and banana plants sprouted among the bushes. In the larger trees, wild orchids and vines tangled around the branches.

A few vendors lined the side of the path, their handmade wares displayed. Tables were crammed with dolls, figurines, wind-chimes, key chains, jewelry, and instruments. Most were carved from wood, bamboo, or calabash.

While Hailee and Eliza browsed the souvenirs, the rest of us approached one of the food carts. Even after that morning's hefty breakfast, I couldn't resist ordering one doubles (slight pepper, sweet sauce, no chadon beni). Despite Aiden's warning, Fish ordered his with full pepper. After one bite, he wordlessly traded it for the plain one Aiden had bought for that exact reason.

We continued our walk, eating in silence. The doubles were perfect—the fried baras soft, the curry channa savory. Everything just spicy enough.

"Do you like our music?" Aiden said, walking beside me.

"What?" Where the hell did he come from? I covered my mouth so channa wouldn't spray everywhere. Somehow, we'd ended up in the back of the group together.

"I've been wondering," he said. "Do you like DJB music? I mean before Fish overplayed our songs to death, did you like them? Tell me the truth. You never held back before."

I chewed slowly, thinking of what to say. On one hand, I was elated Aiden wanted to talk to me about his music. On the other hand, if I told the truth, he might never talk to me again. On the third hand, he liked when I was honest. On the fourth hand, he was an artist in a slump. Criticism might not be the most helpful at the moment.

"You're stalling," he called me out.

I swallowed. There were a lot of hands and not enough time to consider them all. "I'm trying to think of a way not to offend you."

"That answers that, thanks."

I grabbed his hand before he took off. "What I heard of your first album, I liked. But the newer stuff on the radio—"

"Is terrible."

"That's not what I said. Don't put words in my mouth. They're not terrible. They're just . . . fine."

"Fine?" His brows pinched. "How so? Fine like the new singles were bad? Boring? Generic?"

"Generic," I decided. "'Sweet Wine Rhythm' was the exception though." That was the song I didn't recognize when Fish played it on the drive up to Speyside. I'd looked it up. "I really liked that one."

His brow cleared. "Leave it to you to pick the flop of the bunch," he said, but he sounded pleased about it. "That's the one single that didn't chart. I think it's because the label didn't really push it." He started walking again.

I fell into step beside him. "Why not?"

He thought for a moment. "Have you noticed how Caribbean-influenced music is really hot right now? Plenty of it is Tropical House and EDM. A lot of DJB music is like that. I think that's why we blew up so quick. It was good timing."

"Except 'Sweet Wine Rhythm.'"

"Exactly. It was inspired by soca music, which isn't as well-known. I knew it would be a risk, but I only made it worse when I insisted on bringing a Trinidadian like Dessa King on the track. The label wanted someone with more international appeal. When I pushed against them, the song went from a risk to straight liability. They decided it wasn't worth the money to promote it."

"I'm sorry," I said.

He shrugged. "I know it's a business," he said. Then after a few seconds added, "'Sweet Wine' was my favorite too. It was the most exciting thing I'd worked on in a while. I would make a whole album featuring soca artists if I could."

"So do it."

"It's not that easy."

"I don't see why." If he'd been able to push for "Sweet Wine Rhythm," why couldn't he push for an album? Why should he have to write music he wasn't interested in? In fact, that was probably why he was blocked. "Miss Bee said something to me this morning. She said, if you're doing something you don't love, it'll never be great because there will always be a piece of you holding back."

"So, you think I should go for it?" He stopped and turned to me. "I shouldn't hold back?" he asked, something more than his question hovering just out of reach.

I wanted to say *yes*, but I hedged at that second. "Maybe. I don't know."

Aiden looked disappointed.

TWENTY-FIVE

We knew we'd arrived before we saw it, from the volume of sound alone. The falls were higher than I remembered, cascading down the hillside. One tier tumbled into another, the water white and frothy, each layer edged by gray rock and lush greenery. A few visitors swam while others idled on the large rocks that circled the pool. On the far side, people scaled the rope-railed incline that led to the higher tiers.

Trees rustled, birds sang. The air buzzed with the hum of rushing water. I felt a spark of excitement. Even though I'd been mostly ambivalent about coming, now that we were here, I was actually eager to see the falls again.

While Darren explained the climb to the others, I shucked my slippers, drawn to the edge of the glimmering water. I kept my steps small, careful not to slip on the slick stones that lined the bed. Tiny fishes darted between the rocks, the water so clear I could see the pebbles and silt that lined the floor.

A memory hit me—Mummy posed on the rocks of that very pool while Daddy took photos on his new digital camera. I braced for the overwhelming swell of grief that usually followed memories like this. It did not come. The memory still held a somber edge, but there was a sweetness to it as well.

I glanced over my shoulder at the others. Aiden and Darren were trying to persuade everyone to make the climb. Aiden hadn't been keen to come either, but now that he was here, he seemed determined to do it right. As he spoke, he gestured heatedly. "The climb is a must," he was saying. "Otherwise, why did we come in the first place?"

He'd never been the type to get riled up, unless he was truly passionate about the topic. He was passionate about Tobago. And, as always, passionate looked good on him.

"So . . ." Fish stood beside me, precariously balanced on a single rock with both feet. "How are you feeling? Out here, surrounded by all this nature. Any stirrings of inspiration?"

"Nope." I dipped my foot into the pool. A sharp chill snapped at my toes. I yanked it out. "Ah—cold!"

Fish pouted.

I sighed. "What?" I'd shown him my paintings to satisfy his perplexing curiosity about me, not to feed it. I should've known it wouldn't be enough.

"I'm not asking for much, Reyna. Just a ten-foot portrait of myself. I'd even let you throw in a few trees in the background."

"No."

"Look at me." He pointed to his face. "Tell me this shouldn't be immortalized on canvas." When I started to leave, he followed. "Okay, okay. What if we made a bet instead? If I win, you'll paint me."

I snorted. There was no way. I'd already been burned by a bet once this week.

"And I suppose it doesn't have to be ten feet," he said. "Hell, it doesn't even have to be of me. Just something. Anything. As a souvenir." When I kept walking, he rushed to add, "I won't ask about your paintings for the rest of the vacation."

I stopped.

His smile brightened like I'd already agreed.

"Okay." I decided to hear him out. If I lost, I'd give him one of my old paintings and say it was new. He'd never know. "What are we betting on?"

Fish thought about it for a second, then said, "What about Eliza? It won't be easy, but I bet I can get her to stop looking at her phone for the rest of the morning."

"There's no way." I glanced back at the others. Eliza stood slightly apart, staring at her phone again.

"What do I get if I win?" I asked.

"You tell me. What do you want? Money? Jewelry? Cars? My undying devotion?"

"I don't want . . . wait. Cars? Like plural?"

He shrugged.

I thought about it for a moment. Finally, I came to a decision. "Okay. If Eliza won't stay off the phone, I want you to tell me why you called yourself Fish."

Fish's brows shot upward. "You remember when I said cars, right?"

"I do. But I want the real reason for your name. Not one of the fake reasons you tell everyone."

He scratched the back of his head. "That's . . . not what I expected."

Good. He kept asking about my art, even though I didn't want to talk about it. Well, here was something he clearly didn't want to talk about. It felt pretty fair to me.

"All right," he said, after a while. "I agree to your terms."

"Okay." Honestly, I didn't expect him to agree. Did he know something I didn't? "I guess we have a bet."

"Great," he said. "Shake on it?" We did, then the second we let go, he turned to the others and shouted, "Hey, Lizzie! I just made a bet with Reyna. If you stop looking at your phone for the rest of the morning, she has to paint something for me."

"Hey!" I tried to stop him. "That's cheating."

"That's nice, Fishcakes," Eliza called back. "But what's in it for me?"

"Remember that spa gift certificate I got in the Grammy swag bag?" Fish answered before I could seal my hand over his mouth.

"Done!"

"Eliza!" I'd been had.

"Sorry, Reyna," she said, tucking her phone away. She did not sound sorry at all.

• • •

I had lied to Fish. Not that I'd ever tell him, but it was impossible to be there, surrounded by the forest, in the shadow of the falls, and not feel the stirrings of some inspiration. I would've given anything for just a pencil and a pad, and a few quiet hours to sit and take it all in, get it all down. I never understood how most people seemed okay with just witnessing beauty without the urge to lose themselves in it, pick it apart, and replicate it.

It was such a lovely day too, the sky clear and bright. We made the climb to the upper tiers without any problem. Apart from us, there was only one other group of visitors, so we had most of the water to ourselves. While the others swam about, I took a spot directly under the falls. The water was freezing when I first waded in, but I gradually grew accustomed to it. For the moment, Fish was wisely giving me a little space to cool down.

I exhaled slowly, the sound of the rushing water filling my ears. I let it drum over my head, my eyes closed. My muscles relaxed, my thoughts emptied, and the rest of the world fell away. Sighing, I tilted forward so the water beat against my back, sloshed over my shoulders and chest. Through lowered lashes, I looked for the others, my eyes instantly drawn to Aiden.

I knew exactly where to find him. I knew the way I always did; a tiny, persistent piece of my brain wired to notice his location in relation to mine. Right then it activated, like a beacon. He was close, but nowhere near close enough.

Aiden idled a few feet away, alone. His back rested against a rock, his dark head tilted backward, face bared to the sun. His eyes were closed, mouth loose and soft as if awaiting a kiss. Drops of water trailed the strong lines of his jaw, down his neck and shoulders.

His eyes opened and locked with mine.

My breath caught, and the pit of my stomach tugged sharply. A wave of want rushed over and through me, so loud and consuming I couldn't tell where the roar of the falls ended and I began. I dropped my gaze quickly. Lifting my hands, I cupped them to collect the falling water. It filled and overflowed. I played around for a bit, watching the water slip through my fingers. Instinct urged me to look up, look at him, *look now*. But I held back.

When I finally peeked, Eliza had joined him. The weight of disappointment crushed me.

Why did I do this to myself? Aiden and I were actually talking to each other, possibly on the path to becoming something like friends. It was more than I'd hoped for. Why waste time wanting more?

I turned away, about to climb out when I noticed Fish slinking closer. He had guts, coming over here. I had to give that to him.

"You still mad?" he asked.

"I don't know. Do you expect me to fulfill the bet? Because that's not happening."

This seemed to give him pause. He stopped just out of arm's reach. He sank deeper into the water, until the surface brushed his shoulders. "What if we made a trade instead?"

"What do you mean?"

"You're a little fish in a big pond," he said. "That's what my mom used to say." He slicked back his hair. It was charcoal gray when wet. "That's where my nickname came from. She used to say, *Right now you're a little fish in a big pond, but you'll be the biggest fish in the sea one day.* She was really supportive of my career." He sniffed and flicked the water off his nose. "And by *supportive*, I mean she was a full-fledged stage mom. I haven't had any contact with her since I turned eighteen."

I sank into the water until we were eye level. It felt awkward to be standing over him. An overbearing mother was something I understood, but from the sound of it, my past was nothing compared to his. "But you still use her nickname for you?"

"It's my name," he said. "I can admit now she was far from perfect, but if it weren't for her, I wouldn't have DJ Bacchanal. Or this life." He lifted a shoulder, drifting backward slightly. "Fish is who I've always been. The only difference is now I decide who Fish gets to be."

"And who's that?"

"Right now?" He wiggled his fingers. "A prune. I think it's time for me to get out."

I held up my hands for him to see. "Me too."

"Ugh." He wrinkled his nose. "That's not even a prune. That's raisin."

"Is that worse?"

"What kind of question is that? Of course it's worse."

I stood and my wet skin chilled in the open air. We started wading toward the bank, our steps low and careful.

"You and Aiden were so lucky to grow up here." He slowed

down for me to catch up. "You've got the beaches and the water-falls. You can just go whenever you want."

"Not *whenever*," I said. "We do have lives. Responsibilities. School, jobs, chores."

"But you could. If I lived here, the second I had some free time, I'd head straight for the sea. Just thinking about it makes me want to move here, drop everything, and retire early."

"Oh, please. You would be so bored."

"I don't know. I think it could be fun. Especially if I had someone like you with me."

I looked up from the water in time to catch the flicker of long-ing cross his face. It clued me in to the fact that this wasn't just hypothesizing, there was something more here. And I could see it too—what he wanted. An alternate reality where we might be together. But as quickly as that window opened it shut, swallowed by all the reasons it wouldn't work. The most obvious being I loved someone else.

I should've cut this off sooner. Fish's interest wasn't exactly subtle, but his sincerity in that moment still tripped me up—metaphorically, then literally, as my foot slipped between two rocks.

A prickle of pain shot up my leg. Losing my balance, I cried out in alarm.

Fish grabbed one of my arms and caught me. "You okay? What's wrong? Did you twist it?"

"No. I scraped it." I pulled my foot from the water to have a look. There was a pink bruise on my inner heel, beads of blood welling along a small jagged line where the skin had broken. "Yeah, it's nothing."

"What happened?" Aiden said, approaching us. "You hurt?" He wrapped an arm under my free shoulder.

"Just a scrape." It really was nothing. It barely stung. I lifted my foot higher to show them and lost my balance.

Aiden held on, adjusting his grip to take my weight when it fell onto him. "Just hold on to me." To Fish he added, "I've got it." That was the only warning I got before his free arm hooked behind my knees. The next thing I knew I was being carried to the bank.

"Oh!" I wrapped my arms around his neck, surprised. On the outside, I froze, stunned and afraid he'd drop me. On the inside, my heart thundered like a jackhammer. "You didn't have to. I think I can walk on it."

"We're almost out," he said with a hint of laughter. "Don't worry, I won't drop you."

"Is everything okay?" Hailee called out.

"It's just a cut! She'll be okay!" Fish answered them, then to Aiden he asked, "Are you sure you've got her?"

"Yeah. Could you clear our stuff off that rock for me? I'll put her down there."

The entire situation felt surreal. And yet, the little details of the moment sharpened—the rhythm of his breathing, the jolt of his steps, the flex of his muscle under my fingers, the pressure of his fingers against my skin.

"I don't remember you being able to do this," I said softly.

He laughed, and I felt the vibrations. Droplets of water fell from his hair onto my arm, from his chest onto my stomach. All too soon he set me down on the towel Fish had laid out.

Aiden knelt in front of me. "Can I?" he asked, and when I nodded, he lifted my ankle to get a better look. "We should clean it with bottled water," he said.

"Right!" Fish hurried in the direction of our bags.

"So, how does it look?" It stung a little, but it wasn't bad. His hold on my ankle, though—that was driving me crazy. It straddled the line between electrifying and ticklish.

"I think you'll live," he said.

"Thank you, Doctor," I said, a little giddy. His thumb brushed against the inside of my foot, and I nearly jumped out of my skin. Over Aiden's head, I could see the others leaving the water, coming over. I waved them back. "I'm fine!"

Aiden looked up. Wet and shirtless. A wealth of skin untouchable, but within reach. Dizzy with want, I wasn't sure what I would've said or done if Fish didn't return then. If I hadn't caught Fish's furrowed brow as he took in the sight of us. I realized how we must look. It reminded me to pull away.

For ages afterward, I felt the ghost of Aiden's touch on my ankle. I couldn't shake it. His touch had breathed life into a dying ember. Someone—probably me—was about to get burned.

TWENTY-SIX

TWO YEARS EARLIER

The day before Aiden left, we argued.

It was far from the first time. Since he'd told me, we'd had the same fight a hundred times. Most of it blended together in my head, ending the same way. Until this one. This stood out, sharp in my memory as the worst. And the last.

"Do you even care how I feel?" I asked him.

"How you feel?" Aiden said incredulously. "I'm the one that's moving. I'm the one that has to leave."

I paced about the sand, kicking broken shells and washed up coral. The heat was a sweltering shroud, hot against my skin. I barely felt it, the entire scene dreamlike—all dissonance and denial. A distance between me and the moment; an even bigger distance between him and me.

"Oh? Because you're so sad about it?" I said drily. Spitefully.

He winced. At this point, I wanted more. I wanted to draw blood. Because even though his regret seemed real enough, he couldn't hide his excitement, no matter how hard he tried. No matter how much he knew it hurt me.

He tugged at his hair. "What do you want me to do?"

"Stay." I stopped to face him. "Stay here. You could live with your grandfather."

"I can't. You know I can't. Even if I wanted to, Mom would never—"

"If you wanted to?" I repeated; the words burned like poison on my tongue. "But you don't want to."

"Okay, yes!" He bit his lip, breathing heavily through his nose. "I want to go. I want to—Reyna, come on. It's a huge opportunity for me to work on my music." He took my face in his hands. "We can make it work. We'll talk and text. And in two years, you'll be going to university anyway. Maybe we can look for somewhere we both—"

"What?" I demanded.

I couldn't leave. Not now. Not in two years. I had the hotel. Any plans I had to go to university disappeared the second Mummy got sick. And who was he trying to fool? We both knew he wasn't coming back. Once he got used to his fancy new school and his new family, he'd never look back.

"If you loved me, you would stay," I said.

"If you loved me," he said, "you'd love me wherever I am."

We stared at each other. I silently willed him to see reason. But in his eyes, I only saw my own anger and hurt and determination reflected back.

He broke first, his shoulders falling. "Enough, Reyna. This is my last day. I don't want to leave like this."

"And how did you want to leave?" I asked.

Did he expect me to be happy? That I'd kiss him sweetly and wish him well? That I'd bite back this overwhelming feeling of betrayal and wait for him like he wanted?

I turned my back to him and marched toward my house. I heard him following me.

"Don't!" I shot over my shoulder. "I can't talk to you right now."

"Reyna, please!" He stopped, as he should have. "My flight is at ten tomorrow morning!" A threat of urgency squeezed his voice. "I'll be home all night. I want to see you."

I did not stop. I marched all the way home.

Most of that night, I stared at the ceiling. Shadows stretched across the walls while I wondered if Aiden was waiting up for me. I guessed not since my phone remained silent. I thought of calling him, but then I'd slip right back into a loop of hurt. The more I feared he'd forget me, the angrier I got. The angrier I got, the more I feared he'd forget me. These thoughts swirled in my head like water circling a drain. At some point, I fell asleep.

I woke up twenty minutes after nine the next morning. A terrible panic gripped me by the throat, yanking me up and out of bed. What had I done? Why didn't I set my alarm? I called Aiden's cell, but it went to voice mail. No one answered at Old Man Chandra's house.

I ran to Mummy's room. She sat on the edge of her bed. Her satin nightgown pooled over her lap, revealing the varicose veins that lined her pale legs. Her eyes were a little unfocused. Her head covered by a silk scarf. I didn't know if she was just getting up or settling down.

"I need to go to the airport." I raced into the room. "Aiden's flight is at ten. I've got to go now." The drive would take about twenty minutes. If we left now, we'd still have time to catch him.

God, I'd been stupid. I needed to see him. I needed to say goodbye. I needed to kiss him sweetly and wish him well. All my anger meant nothing in the face of him actually leaving. Who knew when I'd see him again.

Mummy's eyes flickered to the digital clock on the bedside table. "If his flight's at ten, then he's probably already boarded. There's no point in going to the airport now."

"But . . ." My throat started to thicken. It couldn't be true. I'd missed him? "No, there has to be something. We could buy a ticket to get on board—"

"That's not how it works, Reyna." She rubbed her tired eyes. "You won't get on the flight. It's closed off."

Well, how was I supposed to know that? I'd never been on a plane before. "Then I can take the next one. I could meet him in Trinidad. I could catch him before he gets on the flight to America."

"You are not flying for the first time by yourself," she said firmly.

"Daddy—"

"Your father has to stay here. He has to manage the hotel. And clearly, I can't—" She waved over herself, the move sharp. Her voice laced with bitterness. "I'm sorry. But right now, I need you here. With me."

My lips parted. All protests died on my tongue. As I looked at Mummy, really taking her in, my heart sank with shame. She'd always been a proud person. Had things gotten so bad she'd actually admit to needing help?

I sat on the bed beside her.

"I'm sorry." I choked on tears. "I just . . . I didn't get to say goodbye."

Mummy laced her fingers through mine, her skin smooth and clammy. She licked her lips. "I know I'm asking a lot from you—"

"No, you're right." I squeezed her hand. I blinked furiously, willing my tears away. "You're right. I need to be here."

She smiled with relief, which only made me feel guiltier. A part of me still wanted to chase after Aiden. A part of me always would. I knew then, the only way I'd survive was to cut that part out. Eliminate it before it lingered and festered. Mummy didn't deserve my resentment, not when she was right. Not when she needed me.

"You're going to be an amazing woman when you're older," she said.

"Don't say that." I rested my head against her sharp shoulder. I hated it when she said things like that. Like she wouldn't be around to see it.

"You will," she said fiercely. "And you'll have other boyfriends. Many, many boyfriends. And you'll find someone who can be here for you. Someone who can be *here*. Aiden's going to start a new life now. He'll move on and so will you." She hooked a finger under my chin and lifted my face to hers. "You just have to try, Reyna. Promise me you'll try."

In Mummy's tired eyes, I saw a spark of her signature determination. The same determination that ran a hotel. The determination that raised me for over fifteen years. The determination that beat this messed up disease once before.

This was my mother. She was still here.

Right then, I'd have given anything to keep her with me.

"I promise."

Later that day, I blocked Aiden on my phone. On every app, on every device. I knew if I heard from him, even the simplest greeting, I'd break all over again.

It wasn't until Mummy's funeral that I slipped and tried to call him. I just needed to talk, to cry, but his number was no longer in service. I unblocked him on Facebook, but only for a few minutes. The second I scrolled to a post of him in his new uniform, smiling with his new classmates, I knew Mummy was right. Aiden had moved on, so I had to do the same.

TWENTY-SEVEN

At first glance, Smalls Shack appeared to be exactly what the name suggested: a tiny hut on the beach. But for those who ventured past the wall of booming reggae and the dimly lit bar, the back of the shack opened out to a mirror-lined dance floor, and beyond that a fairy-lit deck.

The drive from Miss Bee's had only taken us ten minutes. Eliza hung back in the parking lot to take a phone call while the rest of us went inside. That night, the place had a good buzz going. Not too busy with an equal ratio of locals to foreigners. We arrived just in time to nab two recently vacated tables on the patio.

We pushed the tables together, our spot on the deck covered by the edge of the shack's thatched roof. A couple danced on the open floor, clinging to each other, drunkenly swaying out of time with the music. I sat in the corner, back to the banister. One of the branches of a bougainvillea bush poked through the railings, tangling in my ponytail. I pulled free, shifting my chair closer to Aiden.

"Hold on." Aiden reached over and gently pulled a leaf out of my hair.

"Thanks." I smiled at him as he settled back in his seat. He looked gorgeous tonight, dressed in a black shirt. I'd once told him black was my favorite color on him. Did he remember that?

"Where are the waiters?" Fish snatched up the laminated menu from the center of the table. "God, I'm starving." He glanced around, fingers impatiently tapping the table. He'd been in a bad mood since we left the waterfalls. I'd tried to talk to him, but he was avoiding me. Even now, he'd taken the seat farthest from me at the table.

"You order up at the bar," Darren told Fish. He jerked his thumb over his shoulder just as Eliza strutted onto the deck.

"Big news, everyone!" She braced her hands on the table. "My agent just heard from the producers of that movie I wanted to audition for." Her face split into a smile that had a terrifying edge to it. "They've decided to pass. Apparently, not only does the *stigma* of an *internet celebrity* diminish the caliber of their fine film, but they're worried that the *drama* associated with my current love life might overshadow the entire project."

Aiden rocked forward. "Is it because of the video? I knew this would get out of control. We should release a statement. If we tell them we're just friends—"

"Don't you get it? It doesn't matter what we say. I'm already getting all the hate. I—" Eliza covered her face, exhaling slowly.

"Are you okay?" Aiden asked softly. "You know I'm with you. However you want to handle this."

She dropped her hands and reached for her phone. "Yeah, just let me—give me a little time to sort things out. I'll fix this." She started tapping the screen even before she walked off. The rest of us dipped into an awkward silence.

Fish broke first. "At least she's taking it well."

I turned to glare at him. So did everyone else at the table.

Fish sunk into his chair. "It was just a joke."

"I'll go talk to her." Hailee got up. She stopped Aiden when he also started to stand. "Let me try this alone first," she said.

Leonardo caught Hailee's hand as she passed. "Let us know if you need backup." He kissed her palm. She let it linger on his cheek before she left.

"Wait, so . . ." Darren frowned. "Eliza's an actress?"

"Yes," Fish said. "Drama's her specialty."

"Fish," Aiden warned. "Not now."

"Okay." Fish pushed his chair back and stood. "Since I'm the only one that seems to be hungry, I'll go order at the bar."

"An' now, what's his problem?" Darren asked us when Fish left.

"I can make a guess," Leonardo muttered, but he did not elaborate.

A huge, noisy group filtered onto the deck. They wandered about the tables, eyeing our open chairs, then circling back like vultures. A graying older man hobbled out of the shack to welcome them, but the second he saw us, his attention shifted. He was about Daddy's age, with my father's round build and salt-and-pepper curls. But while Daddy moved with the loose energy (and the attention span) of a boy, this man's face pinched as if he felt his age with every step.

"Beanie?" the man asked. "I know that's you! Long time I en see you down here."

"Evening." Darren stood and greeted him with a pat on the arm. To us, he said, "All yuh, this is Smalls. This is his place."

"Eh-eh?" Smalls drew back. "So, you remember me then? How you en pass by the back to see me?"

"Well, excuse me nah." Darren lightened his voice. "But you can't see I brought some guests with me? I can't have them traipsing through the back, can I?"

"Guests, eh?" Smalls harrumphed and put on his glasses. He squinted at us, eyes settling on Aiden. "Wait nah—is you? Madhura's boy. Yes, look at his face! Is so long he en remember me."

Aiden ducked his head. "I remember. Nice to see you."

"But ent you's a big musician now? Boy, whatchu doing in a place like this?"

"How you mean?" Aiden said. "When I come back home, I had to stop at Smalls. This is the place."

"Boy, I en no cocoa. Don't try an sweeten me up," Smalls said, but his chest noticeably puffed. "All yuh getting t'rough?" Smalls asked, approaching Aiden's chair. "All yuh need anyt'ing? Drinks?"

Aiden stood. "I was just going to get some—"

"Yes. I'll fix yuh up." Smalls slung an arm around Aiden's shoulder. "First though, I have some people I want you to meet.

My daughter especially. She's be playing your song all the time . . ." His words faded into the music as he led Aiden inside.

Darren rolled his eyes. "Well, we not seeing him for a while." He pushed his chair out and followed them inside.

"Should I go help him?" I asked Leonardo. "Aiden, I mean." I stretched my neck out but couldn't see him or Smalls inside. I bit my lip, considering. Aiden had always been bad at telling people no. I'd imagine it would be even harder for him to do so with fans.

Leonardo didn't answer me. He only stared at me with a bewildered expression.

"What?" I asked.

"Is the secret out then?" he said. "You can't possibly be hiding it anymore. Not the way you're acting."

"What are you talking about?" I shrank into my chair. "We're not acting any way. In fact, I think we might actually be friends again." And wasn't that the strangest, most wonderful thing. Just saying it aloud made my chest flutter.

Leonardo's expression did not change. We sat in silence for a while, until I couldn't take the judgment in his glare any longer. I entered the shack.

The music had changed to a blend of groovy soca and reggaeton. The place had started to fill, more people dancing on the floor. I spotted Aiden sitting at a table near the back wall. He was surrounded by Smalls, a few older men, and a petite young woman about our age. The young woman had a hand on Aiden's arm, while Aiden had one hand hooked over the back of the chair, his torso twisted to the side as if ready to bolt at the first opportunity.

I hesitated, Leonardo's words in my head. I thought we were acting like friends, but he'd seen something else. And I had to admit, watching the girl touch Aiden's arm, my motivations to intervene were not purely friendly. But then Aiden saw me and waved. His eyes widened with a silent plea. That was enough to spur me forward, no plan in mind. Only when I got to the table, and they all turned to look at me, I realized I'd have to say something.

"Evening!" I smiled, my voice ridiculously high. I rested a hand on Aiden's free arm. "I need to borrow him, if you don't mind."

"An' who is this?" one of the men asked. He had a heart-shaped face that came together in a sharply pointed chin. He wore a nondescript sports jersey that hung loose on his tall, gangly frame. "The girlfriend?"

"No," I said, at the same time Aiden tried to give me a heart attack by answering, "Yes."

"Join us." The man with the heart-shaped face pulled out the chair next to Aiden. "Have a seat nah. Family?"

Aiden stood. "No, that's okay, thanks." He took my hand and tugged me from the table. "Knowing this one, she want to dance."

With my back to the group, I glared at him. He knew damn well *this one* did not want to dance. Now that I'd caught on to his little deception, the shock of him calling me his girlfriend twisted into irritation.

"We'll talk later," he called back to them, then leaned in closer to me. "Smalls is trying to set me up with his daughter. Play along."

"You're using me?"

"Yes."

At least he was honest about it.

His hold on my arm loosened, his fingers skimming past my inner wrist before locking with mine. Everywhere he touched my skin buzzed. "We need to dance, or it'll look like I was lying," he said.

"You *were* lying," I said, a little breathless.

Where was Eliza? Shouldn't she be doing this instead?

We wove through the thrumming, swaying dancers. They parted like reeds, then enfolded us. Aiden glanced at me over his shoulder. My stomach twisted with the good kind of nerves. I focused on the weight and the curl of his fingers through mine. We stopped in the middle of the floor and drew close. His thumb tapped against the back of my hand.

"You okay?" he asked, searching my face. "I was only joking, you know. We don't have to."

"No, I'm good," I said, and nearly melted when his hands settled on the center of my back. I couldn't move for a second, my knees like jelly.

Aiden started to sing, his voice a soft rumble beneath the music. I tipped my head back to see his face. I found his gaze intent, his lips mouthing the lyrics.

Focus on me . . .

The song changed, the beat slowed. I spun around, back against him. I let the rhythm roll over and through me, Aiden's hands settling on my waist as I wined. Never before had I been more aware of another person. My heart thundered, more powerful than the bass that reverberated in my chest. The strings of fairy lights blurred overhead. The other dancers, the music—everything but him faded into the background. In all our years of knowing each other, we'd never danced like this. It was familiar and strange and wonderful at the same time.

His lips brushed against my shoulder, too light, too brief, but I felt it and melted beneath the heat of his lips and his body and my eyes fell shut. My head tilted to the side in a silent invitation for more. He obliged, pressing his lips to the crook of my neck, beneath my ear. Breathless, I opened my eyes and caught sight of us in one of the mirrors.

My entire body locked up.

I pulled away from him, pressed my hand to my chest as the taste of something awful burned in the back of my throat. I was going to be sick.

"Reyna?" Aiden followed me off the dance floor, grasping for my hand. "Hey! Wait! What happened?"

"What do you mean *what happened*?" I shouted over the music. "Did you forget about Eliza? You know, your girlfriend?"

It was one thing for me to have feelings for him; it was another thing for him to act on his for me. He had Eliza—poor, unhappy Eliza who'd just been rejected for a movie role she desperately wanted. Now we'd betrayed her too? No one should have their heart broken twice in one night.

Aiden blinked. "Eliza isn't—" he started, then shook his head. "Come with me," he said. "Just let me explain. Please."

I nodded. As angry as I was, there was still a part of me that hoped there was an explanation. Not to mention, there was a tinier, more selfish part of me that still wanted to be near him.

He tried to take my hand, but I shook him off. His jaw flexed. I followed him around the bar, toward the entrance. He opened the door, and we stepped outside. The music muted as the door shut behind us. The patrons inside were still visible through the windows.

We could've gone into the parking lot for more privacy, but Aiden seemed unable to hold back any longer. "Eliza is not my girlfriend."

He couldn't be serious. Was this a joke?

Was he gaslighting me? Because I was fairly certain there was tons of proof to the contrary, some of which was still trending on Twitter. "Do you expect me to believe that?"

"I swear to you, Reyna. Eliza is not my girlfriend. She never was. We are just—we *were* just—friends who occasionally hooked up."

"Friends who *occasionally hooked up*?" I repeated his odd phrasing.

He grimaced. "I'm trying to be delicate."

"Delicate?" Now I really wanted to punch him. "You want to be *delicate*? Now? After I've had to watch you two all over each other—touching, dancing, kissing!"

"You watched the video?" He sounded like he was in pain.

"No, you asshole. I was there! I saw it with my own two eyes. Right in front my face. Do you have any idea what that felt like? Especially after you were so sweet to play that song for Mummy. I almost wished you hadn't played anything. At least if I'd still been mad at you I could've— Are you smiling?"

"Sorry," he said, still smiling.

I grasped the end of his shirt and tugged on it. "Is this funny to you?"

"No. Not at all. I just . . ." He tried to suppress his smile and failed again. "So, you were jealous?"

I tightened my grip. "I'm going to kill you."

"And I deserve it," he said, close enough now that his eyes started to cross a little. "Completely. No doubt about it. But before you do, can I kiss you first? It's all I've been thinking about since the waterfall. Consider it a last request if you have to."

"You're not funny." I didn't realize I was shaking until his steady hand covered mine. His palm was warm and soft, and he smelled so good. I ached to lean into him. But I didn't move, neither pushing him away nor moving closer.

"Eliza's not your girlfriend?" I needed him to confirm it.

"No, Rey. And I'm sorry for letting you think she was. I guess, I could've told you the truth . . . even though I don't know why or how I would've brought it up."

I had to give him that one. I couldn't think of a situation where I'd want to hear about his hookups either.

"I thought one of my friends might've told you," he said. "They all know."

"Well, they didn't." My hold on his shirt loosened.

He used it as a chance to lace our fingers together. "We aren't hooking up anymore though. Just so you know."

I let his words sink in. "So you and Eliza aren't together." It wasn't a question—I believed him. But after labeling my feelings as tabanca for this long, it took a while to let it go. He still wanted me. It didn't feel real.

"I think I'm finally getting through to her," he said like he was explaining our situation to someone else. My eyes snapped up to his, and he raised a brow. "Done processing?" he asked, with exaggerated casualness.

"Shut up," I said, reaching for him. It was either kiss him or laugh at his dorky humor. I chose the former. Besides, in that moment, giving in felt more like letting go. Then, just as my eyes started to close, I caught the face watching us through the window.

Eliza. Her expression twisted with hurt.

TWENTY-EIGHT

"Eliza." I jerked backward as she disappeared. Stepping away from Aiden, I poked at his shoulder to get him to turn around. I pointed to the window. "Eliza!"

He faced the shack. "What? I don't see her."

"Her face." I pressed my hands against my cheeks. "I thought you said it was just hooking up. You said she's not your girlfriend!"

"She isn't." He looked so confused. But he hadn't seen her face. Nothing about her expression said *just friends*. She'd had the look of heartbreak. I recognized it after so many days of feeling it myself.

"We have to talk to her." I shoved the door open and ran inside.

She wasn't near the bar, but I still stopped and checked to be certain. Aiden followed, trying to talk to me, the music too loud for me to hear him. I crossed the floor of the shack and emerged onto the patio. Leonardo and Fish were there, not at the same table as earlier, but a smaller one nearer the steps to the beach. Fish had a platter of fries in front of him.

When Leonardo saw us, he jumped to his feet. "What happened? Eliza just ran by. I think she was crying. Hailee went after her."

"She was crying?" Aiden sounded faint. He dragged a hand through his hair.

"It looked like it." Fish pushed his plate away.

"What happened?" Leonardo asked Aiden. "I thought you and Eliza weren't—"

"I don't know," Aiden said. "I thought she . . . We . . ."

"Don't do this now," I said. It didn't make sense to stand around and try to work things out. Plus, we'd started to draw attention. "Somebody text Hailee. Maybe she's got Eliza."

"Can't." Leonardo reached into his back pocket and pulled out two phones. "Hailee asked me to hold on to hers."

"Try Eliza then," I said.

"You think she'd answer?" Leonardo asked.

Not really.

"Just try, please." I turned to Fish. "Can you go find Darren? Soon as we've got Eliza, we'll go back to the house."

"Yeah, okay," Fish said softly. He pushed his chair back and headed for the bar without so much as a glance at any of us. I watched him go with a sinking feeling.

"Aiden, come with me," I said. "We'll check the beach. I think that's where she went." If I wanted to be alone, that's where I would've gone.

"Wait." Leonardo stood in front of us. "Maybe I should check the beach. You two might be the last people she wants to see right now."

"Which is why we need to talk to her as soon as possible," I said. "We need to explain. Apologize." I glanced at Aiden, who was still silent. He had to talk to Eliza even more than I did, but he didn't seem to be up to searching for her on his own. I touched his arm, offering my hand to him. "Aiden, come with me."

Aiden blinked, eyes clearing a little. He took my hand. I held on to him as we descended the steps onto the beach, but after a few minutes of walking on the sand, I had to let him go. The events of the night started pressing on me, suffocating me. I let my hair down, then redid my ponytail tighter.

"But she said it was fine," Aiden said.

I turned around. He'd stopped a few feet back. I went to meet him.

"We talked about it." He stared at some point in the distance. "I told her I didn't want to hook up anymore. She said it was fine. It wasn't even a big conversation. I guess she has been a little off, but I thought that was because of the video." Finally, he looked at me. "I swear, she didn't have a problem when I ended it."

I wrapped my arms around myself, the cold air bleeding through my T-shirt. "Did you tell her about us?"

"You think that's it?" He looked even more confused. "I didn't. But it's not like I knew for sure something would happen between us. Not after the way you broke up with me."

I glanced away from him, wishing it were darker out here. The light from Smalls and a few other establishments on the shore illuminated the beach. I didn't want him to see how his words hurt me.

What were we doing? Aiden and I couldn't get back together. Our little slip on the dance floor, the almost kiss, all of it was just a flashback. An act of muscle memory. All we'd done was fall into an old rhythm, lured by a familiar beat. It was a dance we knew by heart, but like all songs, it had to end.

"It'll be okay." I tried to keep my voice steady.

"You think?" He frowned. Even with everything else going on, I still felt the urge to press the furrow between his eyebrows with my fingers, smooth it out with my lips. "I didn't mean to hurt her. She's one of my best friends."

The vulnerability and sincerity in his voice made my chest clench. "I can tell." I tucked a loose curl behind my ear. "You'll see, I'm right. After you talk, you two will be fine. Then we'll all go on like tonight never happened."

I glanced around, only a handful of people were night bathing farther down the beach. Otherwise, we were alone. My hair was coming loose again in the wind. I pulled my ponytail out and tied it back even tighter.

"What do you mean?" Aiden asked, voice flat. "*We'll all go on like tonight never happened?* Like what never happened?"

I looked back at him. He'd gone very still, all the distance in his gaze gone. He was very present, all his focus on me.

"Aiden, we should be looking—"

"What never happened?"

I didn't like the look on his face. Why did he have to do this?

Why make it harder? Now that we weren't caught up in a moment, didn't he see nothing had changed between us?

"We should be looking for Eliza," I said stubbornly.

"We are looking for her," Aiden said. "Answer the question."

I started walking.

"Did you mean us?" he asked, on my heels. "Are we forgetting the dance? That we almost kissed?" Then he was in front of me. "What exactly do you want me to pretend never happened?"

I came to a halt. "It was a mistake. Some old feelings came up. That was all."

None of it was true, of course. Not on my part. It would've been so much easier if it were.

Aiden shrank backward as if I'd hit him. He rubbed the back of his neck. He moved like he was about to turn away, but then he faced me again. "We may not have planned for it to happen," he said, his voice soft at first, then rising with each word. "But it did. I can't just forget it. I'm not you. I can't cut off my feelings. Most people don't work like that."

"That's not fair," I said. He had no idea what I was feeling—the sheer weight of it was crushing me.

"But it's true. You shut down any time something gets too complicated. Just look at that mural in the villa—a perfect example. It could've been great, but you just stopped. What happened? You started, then realized it was too much work? Did it get too hard? Too messy?"

"You don't know what you're talking about."

"Of course I know. Because you did the same thing to me."

"That's not what happened," I said, but he wasn't listening.

"The second things didn't go your way, when it got too hard, you cut me right off—"

"I stopped because there wasn't any point!" I shouted.

He snapped his mouth shut, watching me with wide eyes.

"You don't understand. With the mural—there was no point." I folded my hands to keep them from trembling. "Daddy pushed me to paint it, just after Mummy . . . It was supposed to distract me, I think. And it worked." I laughed at the thought of my past self; it was an ugly sound. "I lost myself in it, you know, the way I always do. Did. But this time it was more. The mural started with a simpler image—the part on top that everyone can see—but at some point, it became more to me. You know that feeling, when you know what you're making is going to be good?"

"When it clicks." He nodded. "I know what you mean. It's the best feeling."

"I just knew this was the best thing I'd ever created. And I *knew*, this would be the one—the piece that would finally convince Mummy I should be doing this for the rest of my life." I looked away from him. "But then I remembered. No, it wouldn't. Nothing I ever made would convince her now. It no longer seemed worth it. What was the point anymore?"

"So you stopped painting," he said. His tone suggested he'd reached an understanding.

"I stopped painting."

"And that's why you stopped talking to me two years ago?" He stared at me, his eyes wide and burning with vulnerability. "Because I wasn't worth it?"

"No, Aiden." My throat ached with all that I held back. "You're worth everything, and you should be with someone who can give you that. But it's not me."

"So it's not me, it's you? Really?"

"You're going to leave. I can't go anywhere. We—" I inhaled sharply, struck by a flash of déjà vu. "We've had this exact conversation before," I said with a panic-stricken laugh. "We're even on a beach again. Oh my God, we're stuck in a loop."

"Not a loop," Aiden said, his voice so soft, it was almost lost to the wind. "You're stuck."

I flinched.

"When I came back here, I promised myself I wouldn't do this—get caught up in you. In *this*. Then I do, because being around you again makes me think *maybe*. But, Reyna, you're stuck."

My eyes burned. "Aiden—"

"I hope one day you find something or someone you love so much it makes you move. I'd just sort of hoped it could be me."

"Hey!" Leonardo shouted from the shack. He waved his hands over his head.

"They must've found her." My voice was watery. I wanted to say more. Nothing I came up with felt like enough.

Aiden started toward Smalls without a word. I trudged after

258

him, a few feet behind. I stared at the set of his shoulders, my body aching with loss. Was this the closure Olivia told me to get? Why did it feel like I was being ripped open instead?

That night, I waited up for Eliza.

Hailee was somewhere with Leonardo. Darren and Fish had returned to the bar. As for Eliza and Aiden, when we'd gotten home, they'd walked off together. I sat alone in the bedroom I shared with the sisters. Now that everyone was fully aware, or had some idea of the situation, it seemed important to distance myself from the group. I wanted to give them time to digest, and probably also spare them the trouble of shunning me themselves.

Not once since we went horseback riding had I felt so excluded. But here I was, alone. Ashamed of what I'd done to Eliza. Mortified by all the things I'd admitted to Aiden on the beach. Devastated by the way Aiden hadn't looked at me since we'd left Smalls for home. There had to be some way to take it back, make it all right with everyone. I just didn't know how.

Despite my resolve to wait up for Eliza, I fell asleep. When I woke up, the room was dark but for the moonlight that bled through the curtains. Eliza was back, as was Hailee. Neither appeared to be awake. Had Eliza returned, seen me sleeping, and thought I didn't care enough to apologize? Guilt seized my heart and twisted it.

I grabbed my phone from where I'd left it charging and crept to the bathroom. I settled on the toilet seat and called Olivia.

"Reyna? I've been trying to get you for days. Now you want to talk? Do you know what time it is?" She sounded tired, upset.

Oh, right. I'd forgotten I was mad at her. My body sagged forward. I didn't have any more fight left in me. "Yeah, sorry. I shouldn't have—"

"Are you crying?" she asked. There was the rustling of movement on her end of the line. "What happened? Is it Aiden?"

"No." I blinked furiously, sniffed sharply, trying to reel in my tears. Thinking I'd gotten a handle on it, I exhaled slowly, but it was marred by a hitch. "Yes."

Why bother trying to hide it? Like this wasn't the reason I'd called.

"What is it?" she asked.

I told her the truth. "I messed everything up."

TWENTY-NINE

When I woke up the next morning, Hailee and Eliza were nowhere to be seen. Their bed was made, the dressing table cleared, all traces of them wiped from the room. I checked the time on my phone. Ten minutes after eleven. We had planned to leave Miss Bee's around noon.

As I got to my feet, the sounds of the day filtered inside. I had just enough time to shower, dress, and repack my suitcase, before seeking out the others. On the landing, I ran into Eliza. She was on her way downstairs. All the things I'd planned to say spewed out of my mouth in a garbled mess.

Eliza rolled her eyes. "It's okay, Reyna." She hefted one bag over her shoulder, grabbed the other by the handle, and started lugging them down the steps. "Aiden and I talked last night. He explained everything."

I hurried after her, my bag in hand. "Yes, but—"

"We weren't together. You don't need to feel bad about it."

"But I do," I pressed. "Please, Eliza. Can I say something?"

To my surprise, she stopped and waited.

I exhaled slowly. "Okay." I set my bag down, balancing it against my leg so it didn't tumble down the rest of the stairs. "Even if you weren't together, I thought you were. Knowing how I felt about Aiden, I should've never put us in a position where something could happen. It wasn't respectful to you."

"You're right," she said. "It was a sucky thing to do. You're lucky I'm not in love with him, or it could've been a lot worse."

"Are you sure you're not?" I asked, then sensing I'd overstepped, rushed to add, "It's just, you looked so upset last night." And despite what she said, she still looked miserable this morning.

"I was upset because I lost the part in the movie." She picked up her bag and continued down the stairs. "And I'm mad because the internet hates me. I'm *not* mad because a boy doesn't like me. I'm mad because he let me act like everything was the same as usual, when he knew he was in love with someone else. It's embarrassing." She shot me a hard look over her shoulder. "You could've told me too, you know. I thought we were friends. Maybe even family now."

I didn't know I could feel worse, but I did. "We didn't want to ruin your vacation." It sounded so ridiculous now.

Angry voices exploded in the entryway.

"Well, good job there," Eliza said flatly.

We found the others in the entryway, Aiden and Fish facing each other, the rest of the group, and their luggage, waiting near the front door.

"We did this for you!" Fish was saying. "This whole trip. Everything. I mean, what the hell, Aiden? There's even a surprise party planned for your birthday." He shook his hands in the air. "Surprise!"

"I'm sorry." Aiden rubbed the back of his neck. Unlike the rest of us, he wasn't dressed to go anywhere, too casual in a faded T-shirt and shorts. His gaze shifted to Eliza and me, then fell to the floor. "I appreciate everything you all did. I'll try to be back to the hotel before the party then."

Wait. Aiden wasn't coming with us?

"You'll *try*?" Fish said. His incredulity matched my own. "You're screwing up all our plans. Don't you think you've messed up the trip enough already?"

The muscles of Aiden's jaw flexed. "That's exactly what I didn't want."

"If that were true, you'd have been honest with us from the beginning."

Aiden looked up, eyes flashing. "You want me to be honest? Really?" His tone flattened. His body stilled like the air before a storm. "Okay. You want honesty. How's this?" He shook his hands in an imitation of Fish. "I hate horseback riding!"

He dropped his hands. "I don't like most of the touristy stuff, but I'll do it for you. I like liming with you all, so I still have fun, but stop acting like this vacation is all about me. Like the rest of you aren't getting something out of it."

Fish narrowed his eyes. "If you weren't happy with our plans, you should've said something."

"When? At the airport, when you surprised me with a flight home? When we landed and you told me where we were staying? When you arranged to have my ex-girlfriend accompany us *everywhere* we go?"

A flush crawled up Fish's face. "So it's our fault?"

"No, this is my mess." Aiden's eyes met mine, then lingered long enough for Fish to turn to see what he was looking at. "But I've recently been reminded that making yourself unnecessarily miserable to keep the people you love happy is crap. And the problem's not just this vacation. I'm talking about our music too."

"What?" Leonardo asked, from his spot next to the open front door.

"I mean, I'm tired of only writing songs I know you guys will approve of. I know when it's 'Hyperbolic' version 4.0 you're both right there, pushing it. But when it's something I love, like 'Sweet Wine Rhythm,' neither of you have my back with the label. I know if I'd had your support, they would've given it a fair shot."

"It wasn't that I didn't like the song," Leonardo said. "It just didn't make sense for us to promote it. It wasn't personal."

"It felt personal to me," Aiden said.

Fish shook his head. "I'm sorry about the song, but you can't expect us to read your mind. How were we supposed to know that's what you wanted?"

"You're right, you couldn't," Aiden said. "So, I'm being honest with you now. I need some space. Give me a few days."

"Come on, Fish," Hailee said. "Let's go. If Aiden wants to stay with Miss Bee for a while, it's not a problem."

I would've spoken up, agreed with her, but I felt like I shouldn't. Not just because I was on the outside of the group, but because siding with Aiden might make the situation worse for him.

"Thank you, Hailee." Aiden looked at the floor again, all the anger from earlier gone. "I promise I'll be back before we have to leave," he said, before heading into the kitchen.

Fish stared after Aiden for a long moment, then turned, grabbed his things, and marched out the open front door.

"Well, this is a mess," Leonardo muttered. While he and Hailee gathered their luggage, Eliza approached me.

"Can you do something?" she asked. "Talk to him? Clearly, we need to work out some issues, but we can't do that if he's here."

"Me?" I didn't know why she thought I could convince Aiden of anything. If he'd talked to her about us last night, I assumed he'd told her everything. Especially the part where I'd told him our relationship was pointless. "Maybe you should talk to him."

"Please, Reyna," Eliza said.

I sighed. After last night, how could I say no to anything she asked of me? It wouldn't make up for everything, but I hoped it was a start. "Okay. I'll try."

In the kitchen, Aiden stood at one of the windows. The morning light softened the lines of his silhouette as he stared at the steelpan. He lifted his head and took me in. His hands twitched on the edge of the instrument, like he didn't know what to do with them. Finally, he shoved them into his pockets. "Forget something?"

I shook my head. "They're not mad, you know. Just hurt. You

can't fix things if you stay here. Come back to the hotel with us."

He scrubbed a hand over his face. "All I'm asking for is some time. Some space."

"The Aiden I knew wouldn't hide from his problems."

"No, that's more your style, isn't it?" He folded his arms. "Besides, why do you care? You dumped the Aiden you knew."

It took me a moment to speak. I exhaled slowly, bracing my hand against the doorframe. "I always cared, Aiden. I still do." I thought that was obvious.

"But it's not enough, is it?" he asked, with a bitterness to his tone. "Not now, not then."

"You were the one that left," I reminded him.

"I didn't have a choice!"

"Well, my mother died, Aiden." I clamped down a spike of irritation. "The hotel needed me. Daddy needed me. I still can't leave, and you can't stay. Not now, not then. What other choice is there?"

His eyes flashed. "And you always know best?"

"No. But I'll tell you, I don't regret it." I couldn't believe I was saying this, but now that the cards were on the table, there was nothing to stop me from laying it all out. "Think about all you've done, Aiden. The album, the awards, the fans, the fame. Think of everything you've done since you left. For all we know, I would've only held you back."

"No." His eyes widened. "No, you do not get to take credit. That was me and the guys. You—you were nowhere. You just disappeared. You wouldn't talk to me. You blocked me."

"But you're living your dream now." My resolve sounded weak to my own ears. "You're happy. You got everything you wanted."

"You think *this* is what I wanted? You think I want to be a bad friend? Or a songwriter who can't write what he wants? Do you know hooking up with Eliza was the closest I'd come to a relationship since you? My love life's a joke and most days—" He lifted his eyes to the ceiling. "Most days, I don't even know what I'm doing anymore."

"Aiden—"

"Go home, Reyna." He turned to the window. "Go back to the Plumeria. Back to the life your mother wanted for you. Wasn't that everything *you* wanted?"

I bit my lip to stop it from trembling. I took a step back, and then another, until I was moving, leaving. I grabbed my bag at the entrance and nearly collided with Miss Bee on the front porch.

"I hope you wasn't going without saying goodbye," she said, smiling.

I busied myself with my bag, my head low so she wouldn't see my face. "Thank you for letting us stay here." My fingers fumbled as my hands shook. "We had a great time. If you're ever up by the Plumeria, you should come and say hi."

My purse slipped to the floor, and she picked it up. I tried to take it back, but she held on, until I had no choice but to look up.

"He a little lost right now," she said. "Jus' give him a chance. He'll find his way home."

I exhaled, no longer trying to hide. "He is home."

"And yet every school break, I would offer for him to come and stay here. But every time he could not wait to get back to Shell Haven."

I blinked at her, surpised and overwhelmed. "He told you about me?"

Miss Bee smiled. She helped me hook the purse over my shoulder, kissed my cheek, and disappeared inside.

As I strode away from the house, I thought about string theory. Pam tried to explain it to me once. I was too young at the time— not that I'd necessarily understand it better now. But since that day, I'd sometimes picture the world around me—every person, animal, thing—made of invisible connections. In that moment, leaving Aiden at that house, the strings between us felt almost tangible, drawn taut. It hurt to walk away.

THIRTY

THIRTEEN YEARS EARLIER

"Tell me again," I begged.

"Again?" Mummy sighed and closed the book on her lap. I'd heard that one before. Something about witches and enchanted woods, and naughty children who were nearly eaten when they didn't listen to their parents. Tonight, I wanted a different type of story. One where the magic was real and the heroes were family.

"Again." I tugged my covers higher. "Please!"

Mummy set the book aside, and I knew I'd won.

"Many years ago," she began, "long before you were born, there was a terrible storm. It drowned cities, sank ships, raised seas. It destroyed fields. It leveled houses. No one had seen a noon sky so dark. It snarled and roared like there was a great beast trapped in the clouds. Somehow, the Kingdom of Plumeria survived, but your grandfather, the king, did not.

"His wife—your grandmother—was pregnant at the time. She

didn't know what to do. She was never meant to be queen. To rule alone.

"One day she went down to the beach to cry, casting her tears into the waves, when suddenly someone swam right up to her feet. He looked like a man, but she saw the ghost of a fin on his back and the sharpness of his teeth. He was a shark without doubt, but he was handsome and he was there.

"*Do not cry anymore*, he'd said, *I'll help you. Let me save you.* And he did, for a few years. But all too soon it became clear the man was hard and cruel. He loved money. He sniffed it out and devoured it without asking. He did not care about the Plumeria or the queen.

"So when the princess was old enough, she went to her mother. She said, *This shark is cruel and useless. Throw him back to the sea, and I will help you rule. We will build something magical, something better than he ever could. Trust me, and I promise we will be happy.*

"And were you?" I asked. My eyes struggled to stay open.

"We were happy," she said softly. She patted my hair and kissed my cheek. "Ever after. Sleep well, Princess."

THIRTY-ONE

The ride from Speyside had been painful. So tense and quiet even Fish's trolling with the radio would've been welcome. Darren dropped the others at the hotel first, then me at my house. It was just past one o'clock when I walked up the driveway, the afternoon sun blazing. Home sweet home. I felt like Dorothy after Oz, returning to normal, my safety seemingly guaranteed in the warm embrace of the familiar. It was a lie, of course. As if anything in my life was normal now.

Case in point: Aunty Helen sitting with Daddy on the front porch.

It wasn't surprising to find Daddy at home during work hours on a Monday. What threw me was Aunty Helen being there too. At my house. Looking far too comfortable on the rocking chair, her legs tucked to the side. Her small feet were adorned with pink toenail polish, and a silvery anklet peeked out from the skirts of her purple beach dress.

"Reyna!" Daddy beamed; his shirt was a pattern of green and yellow palm leaves. "We were waiting for you."

"Welcome back," Aunty Helen said, like she'd been here when I left. "Cute purse. I have one just like it in blue."

"Cool." I was never going to use this purse again.

"Put your bags away and come sit with us. You can tell us about your weekend. Did you go to that restaurant I recommended?" Daddy lifted a glass of passion fruit juice. It was a frozen slushy, just the way I liked it. "I made your favorite. There's a whole bottle in the freezer."

"No thanks." I rolled my suitcase toward the door, then stopped. "Actually, there is something. The Musgrove sisters and their friends don't need a guide anymore, so I'm going to start back at the hotel."

Perhaps it was cowardly to phrase it like it was the group that ended the arrangement. In truth, no one had officially ended anything, but considering everything that happened, I figured they wouldn't want me around anymore.

Daddy frowned. "I'm sorry to hear that. I know you was enjoying yourself."

"Yeah, well . . ." I shrugged.

"It should be fine for you to start back now . . ." Daddy glanced at Aunty Helen, who nodded her head. Daddy sat up higher. "I mean, of course you can start back whenever."

I narrowed my eyes, not appreciating the silent conversation happening under my nose. "I'll start this afternoon." Now that I was home, it was back to business. Back to normal.

Back to the life your mother wanted for you.

"I'm going to change and head over there now," I said.

Thirty minutes later, I'd finished dressing, and they were *still* on the front porch. I grabbed a banana from the kitchen and headed out.

"Reyna." Aunty Helen stopped me. "Before you go, we want to talk to you about something." Her knees bounced with restless energy. "Can you give us a minute?"

I exhaled slowly, summoning a smile from the depths of my being. "Yeah, sure."

She set her glass down. "Your father and I have been talking. We want to run my idea by you." She smiled at Daddy, who nodded encouragingly. "It's actually a really big idea. But a good one, we hope."

My heart plummeted. This was it.

They were about to confirm what I'd suspected since Aunty Helen popped into our lives without warning. I didn't want to hear it. It wasn't that I had a problem with Daddy finding love again, but did it have to be so soon? I wasn't ready.

"I turn sixty later this year," Aunty Helen said. "For a while, I've been knocking around the idea of retirement, and I think maybe it's time. I'd like to move back here to be with Pam and my family."

I nodded, not trusting my voice. This was more serious than I'd thought. She was already planning to be here long-term.

"But I know myself." She laughed. "I know I don't have it in me to slow down completely. I need something to do. A project

273

to keep me busy." She looked at Daddy. "Can you imagine? Me? Cooped up in a house all day?"

Daddy's lips twitched. "Neither you nor the house would last more than a day."

Aunty Helen smacked Daddy's shoulder and some of his drink sloshed onto the floor. Daddy cried out and shuffled his feet away from the spill. They both dissolved into laugher.

"So, what's this about?" I asked, irritated by their foolishness. Did they add a little something extra to those glasses of slushy? Who said maturity came with age? "Are you saying you'd like a job at the hotel?"

"No, no." Aunty Helen sat back. "I'm saying I'd like the hotel."

"For what?"

"I want to buy the Plumeria."

I gawked at the grinning pair. "Is this a joke?"

Daddy's smile slipped a little. "We been discussing it for a good while now, Pumpkin. Today she made an offer. A very generous one."

I folded my arms, trying to contain the hurt. "Then it's too bad we're not selling." I couldn't believe we were even discussing it.

Daddy's brows rose. "I think we should at least consider it." He set his drink down. "You almost eighteen now, you'll want to go off on your own soon. And I been wanting to go back to work for the paper. Is a good solution for us."

"Except I'm not going anywhere. So there's no problem." I glared at Aunty Helen. "Or at least we didn't have one until she got here."

"Reyna!" Daddy stood up. "Watch yuh tone."

"It's fine, Eli," Aunty Helen said softly. "Reyna, I assure you I'm very serious about taking on the hotel. After looking through the financials, touring the grounds, meeting the staff, I can see why so many people love the Plumeria. But I can also see there's a lot of unexplored potential. I think I can change that."

My first thought was, *When the hell did she do all that?* Then I realized, they'd had all the time they needed. "Is that why you wanted me away from the hotel?" I turned to Daddy. "It wasn't because you thought I was working too hard, or you wanted to distract me from thinking of Mummy. You wanted to sneak around with Aunty?"

"Reyna . . . ," he tried, but his guilty expression said enough.

I faced Aunty Helen. "I don't care how many times you've toured the grounds, you don't know the hotel. If you did, you never would've changed the rum punch order to Simona. At the Plumeria we try to support local businesses. We're a part of the community. You come in and all you'll ever care about is the bottom line. Well, I won't let that happen."

I drew back, satisfied by the look of shock on her face. I started for the steps. "I'm going. They need me at the hotel."

"Reyna!" Daddy followed me down the driveway. "Come back here. We need to talk about this."

I ignored him. Why was everyone so dead set on moving on? And why was I always the one getting left behind?

"Stop right there," he demanded.

I spun around. "It's Mummy's hotel! Or did you forget that?

How could you even think of throwing it away? Does it mean nothing to you? Does Mummy mean nothing to you?"

That brought him to a stop. "You know she does. But at some point, we need to move on."

"Right." I yanked the car door open. "That's why you want to sell off her hotel to your ex-wife. Doesn't this feel strange to you?" I asked him. "Having her in our house? Sitting in Mummy's rocking chair? Now you're giving her the hotel? Is she supposed to be some kind of replacement? Oh, no. She came first. So Mummy was technically the replacement."

My father flinched. All the anger drained from his expression. "I loved your mother. You know that."

"I don't believe you."

He didn't move as I slammed the door shut and threw the car into reverse. The image of his face stayed with me long after I'd driven away.

By the time I got to the Plumeria I was still angry. If anything, the time in the car had given me a chance to work myself up even more. How dare they? Did they think I'd just let them take the hotel away from me? After everything I'd done for it. Everything I'd given up for it. I couldn't even imagine how upset Mummy would be. I almost wished Daddy and Aunty Helen *were* dating instead.

I desperately needed to shout at someone. Luckily, I had just the person in mind.

I threw the door open and charged into William's office. "How long have you known? Weeks? Months? I thought you were too friendly with Aunty Helen at the party. I should've guessed you would be up to something."

William watched me over the rim of his glasses. Slowly, he sat back in his chair. "So they told you about the sale."

"Oh, they told me. And I'm here to tell you it's not happening. We're not selling. Not now. Not ever. Whether you like it or not, I'm always going to be here, William. Either deal with it or leave like the managers before you."

William watched me, silent for a few seconds. "Are you going to cry again?"

"No," I said, then winced at the watery-edge to my voice.

Oh my God. I wiped my eyes. Why did this keep happening? I'd cried more in the past week than I had in the last year.

"It doesn't matter," I said. "My point is—we are not selling the hotel. Especially not to Helen. I mean, what does she even know about running one?"

"Well, she did spend years advising businesses on their finances, but go on."

"Is that supposed to make me feel better? So, she might be good with the finances—so what? She'll just turn the Plumeria into another soulless hotel. What about the people who've worked here for decades? You really think she cares about them?"

"You really believe that?" he asked.

"I know that."

William stood, buttoning his blazer. "I want to show you something." He made his way around the desk and out of the office. "Come on."

"Where are you going?" I followed him across the lobby and onto the main lawn. My confusion twisted into contempt as I took in the folded tarp, the half-erected scaffolding, and the workmen gathered around the gazebo.

I snatched the sleeve of his blazer and forced him to halt. "This is what you wanted to show me?" He'd wasted no time, had he? He'd probably had the contractors on the phone the second I'd lost the bet. "You brought me out here to—what? Rub my face in this? Make me feel even worse? I told you how much the gazebo meant to me."

"Which is why we're moving it." William yanked his arm away. "We're taking it apart and saving what we can. It's going to be the same design, but we'll fill it in with stronger, better material, and reconstruct it on the western corner of the lawn." He readjusted his sleeve, eyeing me wearily. "We've checked—the ground is nice and solid there."

"Oh." All the fight drained out of me. "You're moving it? I didn't know that was an option."

"Neither did I."

I shifted my feet. "I guess . . . I should thank you."

"Oh no." He snorted. "Not me. I still don't get the appeal. I would've taken it down. But after we talked about it, I asked for some advice." He raised a brow. "It was actually Aunty Helen who came up with the idea."

"She did?" I dropped my eyes, no longer willing to meet the judgment in his gaze. "Really?"

"After I explained how much it meant to you, she consulted the contractors, and this is the solution they came up with."

Could it really be that simple? I'd get to keep the gazebo? It felt wrong for it to be that easy.

"It's a good idea," I said softly.

"It is." William nodded. "And now you know who to thank for it."

THIRTY-TWO

I visited the villa a few times over the following days. Every time I went, the place was empty, the group probably at the beach or some other activity they no longer needed a guide for. I could've tried harder to catch them, sought them out earlier or later in the day, but there was a little part of me that was relieved each time I knocked and no one answered.

I did have an idea for one thing that might help. I procrastinated on that, too, until I realized the group had five days left on the island. There was no fixing my relationship with Aiden, but it might be possible to repair some of the damage with his friends. Especially Hailee and Eliza, who would be a part of my life—and my family—for the foreseeable future.

The first step of my plan was both the easiest and the hardest. All I had to do was sit my butt down and sketch something out. According to the rules of my bet with Fish, I didn't even need to paint it. The problem was, every time I picked up a pencil, there seemed to be something more important to do. Finally, I just had to sit down and commit to doing it.

It was just after sundown, raindrops a gentle patter on the galvanized tin roof. This time, I decided to warm up first. I kept my thoughts and hand loose, sketching whatever came to mind, sticking to subjects that were familiar and easy—flowers, trees, leaves. A pair of familiar umber-colored eyes.

When it clicks. I know what you mean. It's the best feeling.

I slammed the pad shut and clambered off the bed. Heart racing, I left my room, all the while itching to get back to the last sketch. To finish it, then start something else. Any one of the pieces I'd just done, except for the last, I could've used to fulfill Fish's bet. But none felt like enough. I wanted to keep going and that was dangerous.

I shuffled off to the kitchen, the floor cool under my bare feet. Unfortunately, the kitchen wasn't empty; Aunty Helen sat at the counter, Daddy standing beside her.

Daddy looked weary—an expression I suspected mirrored my own. I couldn't remember the last time we'd fallen out like this. He never got that angry, never yelled. Somehow, I'd gotten the most easygoing man on the island to do both. The atmosphere was chilly in a way that had nothing to do with the rain. I didn't know what to expect. Another argument? A talk? An apology? Silence?

Without looking up, Daddy walked around me and disappeared into his bedroom.

So, it was going to be silence then.

I kept my head down, quiet as I went to fill the electric kettle. I'd planned to take a snack back to my room—a few biscuits or one of the ripe pomeracs Mrs. Clay brought over the day before—but after running into Daddy and Aunty Helen, the idea of eating anything made my stomach churn.

I set the water to boil and opened the pantry. I took out a box of mixed-fruit tea, all the while conscious of Aunty Helen's attention. I was still so mad at her for wanting to take the hotel away. Then again, there was the gazebo.

I steeled myself and turned to face her. "I should thank you. For your idea. To move the gazebo."

"You *should*?" Her lips twitched with wry amusement.

"Thank you," I said firmly, then returned to the kettle.

I slowly unwrapped the tea bag and shuffled my mug around the counter to look busy. There wasn't much to do besides watching the water boil.

"You know," she said suddenly. "I took Pam to Canada when she was two."

She spoke softly, almost like she was talking to herself. I kept my back to her but listened over the hum of the rain.

"Your father and I were separated even before she was born, so when my company offered me a job at a new branch in Alberta, I took it. And I took Pam with me. I don't regret leaving, but I do regret how I left. It wasn't fair to Eli." Her voice hitched, revealing a glimpse of some untethered emotion. "It's amazing the way your father refuses to hold a grudge. He's always had a big heart."

"Too big," I said bitterly.

"Too big," she agreed. "It makes him a good man, but not necessarily a good businessman. He does love the hotel, even if he doesn't know what to do with it."

I turned to face her. "And you think you do?"

She shifted forward, encouraged now that she had my full attention. "I know how to spot a good opportunity when I see one," she said. "The Plumeria has a good location, good architecture, and an excellent reputation. Your mom and her family built something wonderful. But the world is changing. A lot of what worked when your mom was alive doesn't work as well today and will become obsolete tomorrow."

"You think we'll get left behind," I said, with a sinking feeling. "You still don't understand. It's not about modernizing, globalizing."

"No, I understand," she said. "I know how important it was to your mother that the hotel stays in the hands of a local. And, Reyna, make no mistake, even with this Canadian accent, I am Tobagonian. I admit, I messed up with the rum punch. I'm still learning. But sell the hotel to me and I promise I will do everything I can to uphold your mother's ideals."

"Why?" I asked, skeptical. "Why would you do that for her?"

"Not for her. For you. For your father." Her gaze was steady. Determined. "You will always have a place at the Plumeria if you want one. It will always be your home. That will never change. I would never take that from you."

Daddy came around the corner. "All right, I ready."

I went back to preparing my tea. My thoughts swirled like the steaming liquid I stirred in my cup. The Plumeria belonged to Mummy. Now it was mine. That had always been the plan. But did any of it matter if I was holding it back?

"We going out for dinner," Daddy said. "So we won't be bothering you any longer. You have the whole house to yourself." His tone had a bite to it, like he expected me to come to some sort of realization that I was being childish. Like I was the one in the wrong. Instead, it only made me angry all over again.

I took my mug and retreated to my room. I listened for sounds of them leaving, but they were buried under the rain. Only when the beams of Daddy's car lights sailed across my wall, did I realize they'd gone.

I got up to turn off the lights, then crawled back into bed. I was sure the sound of the rain would lull me to sleep, but as the night wore on, the rain only got louder and harder. It sounded like thousands of hammers striking the roof, keeping me awake. There was a sudden sharp *click* and the air-conditioning cut off. The streetlights outside disappeared. My room plunged into total darkness.

I reached for my phone. The Wi-Fi was down, of course. So was my data service. The light of my phone faded, and I tapped it on again. It was my only defense against the dark.

Lightning cracked; thunder stomped on its heels. I left my bedroom and found an old citronella candle under the kitchen sink. I lit it and settled in the living room. After staring at the flame for several minutes, mesmerized by the soft glow, I retrieved my sketch pad from my room and tried to capture it.

Two storms stood out in my memory. The first was back when I was eleven, and I remembered it more for the aftermath than for the event itself. Everyone came to school the day after with stories of broken windows, uprooted trees, and roofs torn from houses. I'd listened to it all with terror and awe. Somehow, I'd slept right through it.

As for the second storm, I was much younger. It had rained for days. Electricity came and went. The rivers rose and overflowed. I awoke one night to a lake around my bed.

I remembered Mummy and Daddy came to get me. They scrambled and sloshed about the room, their nightclothes soaked, the water at their knees and rising furiously. *Grab her slippers!* Mummy had shouted, always practical—the rubber footwear our only protection against electrocution from sunken appliances, cords, and open outlets. I perched at the edge of the mattress and waited. As they stumbled about, I watched them with the naive excitement of a child. The night seemed more fantastical than frightening. I wanted to see if the bed would float away.

Daddy snatched me up before I found out. He carried me to the car. I must've slept through the drive, because the next thing I knew we were in a room at the Plumeria, the three of us lying together, safe.

When the road had reopened two days later, we returned home to find the door battered open, everything of value either destroyed or stolen. Mummy ran straight to her closet, where she'd forgotten Grandma's jewelry in the pocket of the coat tucked in the back.

They pulled everything out but couldn't find it. Mummy,

who'd been a rock until that point, crumbled.

I remembered Daddy held on to her for a long time afterward. He didn't let go until she was ready. *It's just t'ings*, he said over and over again. *You're here. We all right. That's all that matters.*

I set my pencil down. My hands were shaking. Tears blurred my vision.

How could I have doubted that Daddy loved her? Worse yet, how could I say it to his face? I'd lived with them for years, seen the evidence with my own eyes. I'd been unfairly cruel, and I'd basically sent him out into this rain for no reason. What if something happened to him?

The hours passed unbearably slowly. Ten o'clock. Eleven. Twelve. One. Two—

The door flew open and smacked against the wall. Wind blasted through the hall, bringing with it sodden leaves and rain. Daddy stomped in, soaked through and through. He closed the door with some difficulty, locking it.

He wiped the water from his face, spotted me in the living room, and stopped. "Pumpkin, what are you doing?"

I started to cry.

Daddy found more candles under the kitchen sink. I lit them and set them out while he dried off and changed. When he returned, he had on pajamas, a towel slung over his shoulder. We sat at the dinner table.

"I'm sorry." I hugged my legs, my chin hooked over my knee. "I shouldn't have been rude to you and Aunty Helen."

With a heavy exhale, he shifted forward, arms braced on the table. "You know I loved your mother. And I love you."

"I know," I said softly.

"Then why say it?"

"Because I felt like you'd moved on without me." My voice threatened to break. For so long, it was just the two of us, sharing our grief. We both had this massive hole in our lives only we understood. Then one day, all of a sudden, he seemed okay. And I wasn't.

"What are you talking about?" he asked. "I right here. I not going anywhere."

"Yes, you are! Everyone does. They fall in love, go after their dreams, travel, get married. Meanwhile, I'm just stuck here—"

"You're feeling *stuck* here? You told me you were happy."

"I am," I said quickly. My fingers wrung together as I tried to untangle my words. "I love working at the Plumeria. I love being there." And I did. I always would. I grew up on those grounds: playing on the lawns, studying in the office, fishing with Daddy, sharing sunsets at the lookout with Mummy. "It's my home."

"And it always will be." Daddy searched my face. "But, tell me, what you would do if it wasn't?"

I frowned, confused. "What?"

"What if the Plumeria didn't exist? What you would do?"

"I don't know . . ." My gaze strayed to the window. It was so dark outside. I hesitated for a minute, then admitted, "I would've applied to art schools. If I got into the same one as Olivia, I would've gone to London with her. We actually had it all planned out. We would've roomed together and—" I shook my head. "Never mind. It's stupid."

"What?" Daddy demanded. "Why it stupid?"

I shrank backward, confused by the anger in his voice. "It's not like I could've gone. It's like Mummy said—my life is here. My happiness is here."

Daddy squeezed his eyes shut, then covered them. When he lowered his hands, he seemed calmer. Sadder. He pointed to the wall behind me. "You remember when you painted that?"

The ibis painting, on the wall behind the couch. "Yes." I remembered the scene at the open house. Mummy's relief that I hadn't cheated. "It was pretty good for a ten-year-old."

"Is pretty good full stop," Daddy said. "And not only were you very talented at ten, but you were also defiant and angry, redoing your painting in front of all the parents and students. I remember watching you and thinking—buh whose child is this? Can't be my baby, Reyna." He dipped his head and laughed. "If you ever have children, I guarantee there will come a day when you realize they are their own person, with their own personality and desires that have nothing to do with you. And it will mess yuh up."

I wrinkled my nose at his slang.

He chuckled and leaned closer. "I want you to understand something. I loved your mother, but she was not perfect. When she got sick, she put a lot of pressure on you to take over the hotel, and it wasn't fair. She could only see all she was going to miss, and then she forgot you were your own person, with your own dreams.

I think it was her way of making sure she was still a part of your life after she gone."

"And now you and Helen want to take that away from her?"

Daddy blew out a breath. He didn't answer for a moment. The rain pattered away on the roof, filling the silence. Finally, he said, "I going to ask you a question. Don't answer immediately. I want you to really think about it. Search your heart, and only answer with the truth. Can you do that for me?"

I nodded, reluctant to play along. I knew where this was going.

"Okay, Reyna," he said. "Tell me the truth. Are you happy?"

The automatic *yes, of course* popped into my head. I opened my mouth to speak, then remembered not to answer immediately. I shut my mouth, let the words sit on my tongue like a sweet. But the longer they sat, the worse the lie tasted, more like a bitter pill than candy. When I finally tried to speak, I couldn't do it without a curl of my lips, a twist of reluctance on my face.

Daddy nodded, understanding. "We were lucky to have her in our lives as long as we did. Remember, she fought the same disease five years earlier. That's five years' worth of memories we might not have had. And you have her smile, you know? Her face. So much of you is her. That not going to change no matter where you go, or what you want to do."

"I do love the hotel," I said finally. Tears pricked my eyes. "I wasn't lying."

"But you don't want to spend the rest of your life working there."

I nodded.

"That's what I thought," he said. "The truth is, Reyna, I been thinking of selling the hotel for a while now, but I held on because I know how much you don't want to disappoint her. I see now you'll never feel right about going against your mother. So I'll make the decision for you."

I shook my head. "But . . . it was what she wanted."

"No, she would of wanted you to go and do what makes you happy. I know that for a fact." He shrugged. "If I wrong, she can come back and take it up with me she-self. And knowing her, she would very well try too."

A bubble of laughter burst from my lips. I still didn't know if I agreed with this sale. Mummy would've hated it. And yet, a part of me wanted it so badly.

"Even if we sold the hotel," I said after a while, "it's too late for me to apply to schools. What do I do with the rest of the year?"

Daddy smiled. "I guess that's up to you."

THIRTY-THREE

Eliza stood at the door to Daddy's office. "Going somewhere?"

I looked up from the box of junk in front of me. We weren't exactly sure when Aunty Helen would take over the hotel, but I thought I'd get a jump start on clearing out some of the personal items. If nothing else, the act would hopefully bring some closure, or be a distraction from my doubts about the sale. "I'm in no rush," Aunty had said earlier that morning. With the tone befitting a general, she added, "We must guarantee a peaceful transition of power."

When I left the house, she and Daddy were still laughing over it.

I'd ignored the rest of their early-morning banter, too weirded out by the fact that Aunty Helen had obviously spent the night. I'd been wrong about it being better if they were dating. So very wrong.

"Sort of," I said to Eliza, straightening up from the floor. "My father fired me."

"I . . . did not realize that was possible."

"Me neither."

"Well," she said, walking inside. The door clicked shut behind her. "That might make my visit a little awkward now. I wanted to ask for your help with something."

"What?"

"Can we sit first?"

"Sure," I said.

She took the seat across from me. I pulled the stack of empty boxes off the office chair and sat too. Something was different about Eliza that morning. I wasn't sure why exactly. She looked the way she always did—her hair loose, makeup immaculate. But there was definitely something different.

"You know, I'm jealous of you and Pam," she said suddenly.

I had to admit, "I did not know that." If she was jealous of my relationship with anyone, my half sister would not have been my first guess.

"I am. I admire how tight you are. Jake and I used to be close like that. But since he moved here, our relationship's been a little strained. We had a big argument before he left." Her lips stretched into a grimace. "Did he ever tell you he was supposed to take over our father's company?"

"He did mention that." I tried to figure out where she was going with this. Nothing came to mind. From the way she kept tapping the armrest and shifting in her seat, I got the impression she was anxious to talk this out. Either that or she needed to pee.

"I didn't get it," she said. "Why he would give up on his life like that? Pam too—the both of them. They could've been such a power couple, and they threw it away." She dragged a hand through her hair. "Before he left, Jake told me he didn't care what I or our family thought he should want, he knew what he wanted. He and Pam had made their choice, and we should respect it."

Eliza stretched her legs out, then crossed them. "When I came down here to visit, I admit I was expecting the worst. This new life had to be lame. Jake had to regret it." She tipped her head to the side. "So of course it turns out he's blissfully happy. He and Pam are still in love, and I still can't decide if their whole too-perfect-couple thing is adorable or gross."

I nodded, understanding. "I've accepted it's both."

"Yeah. Well, anyway, I've been thinking a lot about what he said back then, about knowing what you want. With everything going on with the viral video, I haven't been doing too well. I looked at what people were saying. Violated survival rule number one—I read the comments!"

She laughed at her own joke. "It's strange . . . when my relationship with Aiden was a rumor, some people used to ship us. Most didn't care. But the second it was supposedly true, not only was I not good enough for Aiden, I wasn't good enough to exist. Period."

"I'm sorry."

"Yeah, well." She waved dismissively. "I'm no newbie to internet hate. Those comments were awful, but they weren't the ones that got to me. It was actually the nice ones I got obsessed with—the ones that were supportive, cheering for me and Aiden. To deal with the hate, I started seeking those out, clinging to them." Her eyes skittered away from mine. "I started thinking, *Hey, maybe they're on to something. Maybe Aiden and I could be good together.* I mean, if so many people thought we fit—why not? At least, if we fell in love, it would make all the hate worth something."

She hooked her hair behind her ear, her eyes still on the floor. "Messy, I know. But that was the headspace I was in when Aiden told me he wanted to stop hooking up. Honestly, I didn't take it too seriously. I thought he'd change his mind later. But then I lost the role and I saw him with you, and I just felt worthless. And jealous. Like, I know Aiden and I aren't in love, but he never even considered it."

"I'm sorry," I said.

"Don't apologize for that. I know now I was in a bad headspace after reading all those comments. If Aiden and I had gotten together, I would've been doing it for all the wrong reasons. It wouldn't have been fair to him."

"Or to you."

"Or to me." Eliza smiled softly. "I'm happy to say I've stopped reading the comments—both the good and bad ones. Taking some time to try to figure out what the next steps for my career are. My agent sent me a script for the pilot of a series. It looks pretty good."

"I hope you get it."

"Me too," she said, sitting up. "Anyways, thanks for listening to me ramble. I thought it was important we clear the air. But that's not the only reason I'm here. The others and I realized Aiden was right about us not taking into account what he'd enjoy for his birthday. We still want to go ahead with the party, but since the plan for a fancy dinner in the restaurant is more our style than his, we want to ask if you'll help us change it to something he'd like. Because you know him so well. And, I mean . . ." She glanced at the stack of boxes on the ground. "It looks like you might have some free time on your hands."

"I'll help." I already had a few ideas in mind. "But maybe don't tell Aiden I did. We had a bad fight. I said some things . . ." I stared down at my hands, remembering the feel of Aiden's fingers laced through mine. "Whatever we had is done now."

Eliza gave me a flat look. "Trust me, if the guy was in love with you after two years, he's not getting over it in a few days."

"You didn't hear the things we said." I'd more or less told him loving him was pointless. How was anyone supposed to come back from that? Not to mention, Aiden and I still had the problem of long distance. And we lived drastically different lives now. Even if he did want to try again, where would I fit in? How would I deal with the scrutiny? The judgment? I saw what his fans did to Eliza, the way they eviscerated her online. Did I want to invite that kind of crazy into my life?

"Okay." Eliza got to her feet and walked to the door. "Do what you want. That's my new motto."

I laughed, and she smiled in return.

What did I want? It wasn't easy to answer. Not because I didn't know—I'd always known—but even with this certainty, it was still terrifying. I didn't want to be stuck anymore. Not with my art, not with my life. I wanted to move forward.

I wanted to figure out who I was, and I wanted Aiden with me when I did.

"Hey, Eliza!" I called out just before she closed the door.

She stuck her head back inside. "Yeah?"

"Actually," I said. "There's something I could use some help with too."

Hailee stopped by the room first. This was early in the morning, while I'd been carefully blending orange and red with a flat brush, adding details to the immortelle flowers already painted.

"I knew red was your color," she said.

"What do you mean?" I asked. My outfit was an old white T-shirt and jeans.

She pointed to my face, and I realized I'd gotten magenta on my cheek.

I would've liked to say it was easy painting again. But it wasn't. Each stroke felt like pulling teeth. Was I ever actually good at this? Or if I was, maybe I'd waited too long? I didn't use it so I lost it. Any talent I'd had all gone. Where was the spark—the *click*?

As the hours passed, it did get easier, but the total immersion I longed for was out of reach. I was going to have to work for it.

Eliza stopped by later, closer to noon. I'd paused the painting to outline the rest of the mural with chalk. While I worked, Eliza and I planned out the party. She took my advice well. For the most part.

"Come on," she said. "Just a few fireworks. As a treat."

"A treat for who exactly?"

"Aiden . . ."

I stared at her.

"Okay. Me." She sighed and scratched it off the list.

Leonardo stopped by in the afternoon, when the room had grown a lot hotter. The angle of sunlight through the window had shifted, and with it my mood. I'd given up on the chalk outlines, my hands lighter, my brush strokes quicker, submitting to the excitement and fear that I had absolutely no idea what I was doing. I might be making something beautiful, or I might be messing it all up.

"So what do you think?" Leonardo asked. "What kind of song do you think we'll be getting at the end of this vacation? A love song? Breakup anthem? Dance track?"

He'd lost me. "Dance track?"

"We need like six," he said gravely. "Minimum."

Unsure what to say, I told him, "Let me get back to you on that."

He walked away, seemingly unsatisfied with this answer.

Fish was last, coming to see me while I was clearing up. The mural wasn't finished, but progress had been made, and that was the point. Despite my rustiness, it didn't look half bad.

I stood with my back against the opposite wall and took a

picture. Satisfied with the angle, I sent it to Aiden's number. As the message marked itself delivered, it occurred to me he could've blocked me at any time. He never did.

"Are the fumes from the paint going to kill us in our sleep?" Fish asked from the doorway.

I smiled, pocketing the phone. "It's acrylic, so no. But I can leave the windows open, if you'd like."

"For lizards to come inside? No, thank you."

"Why? You took care of it so well last time."

He huffed, folding his arms. This was the first time he'd spoken to me since Speyside.

"I've got a gift for you," I said.

He eyed me for a long moment, then slowly came into the room. "Go on."

I retrieved my bag from the corner, pulled out a folder, and handed it to him. As always, letting someone see my work made my heart rate spike. "It was the first piece I've finished in two years," I said.

He opened the folder to reveal the sketch of himself at the waterfall. It was the moment he'd looked over his shoulder and I'd wondered *what if*. His fingers brushed the edges, his touch careful. "I wasn't crazy, right? There was something?"

I didn't want to lie to him, but I didn't want to leave hope. "There might've been, but we'll never know."

"But if I kill Aiden . . ."

I snorted. "No."

"If I find a time machine . . ."

"Also no," I said. "Actually, yes! *Please* find a time machine." I sobered slightly. "A couple of days ago, there was a situation where I hurt a friend of mine. I'm really sorry about it. But if I could go back in time, I would handle it better."

Fish closed the folder and tucked it under his arm. When he looked up, he was smiling. "Nah, you're good," he said. "You don't need it."

THIRTY-FOUR

"Are you sure he said I could come?" I asked Eliza. We were sharing one of the lounge chairs beside the pool. She was teaching me a card game called Spit, while the others played Marco Polo in the water. Well, actually Fish was in the water, Leonardo and Hailee were standing at the edge, darting around to the other side whenever Fish got close.

"He did." Eliza set the queen of spades on the king of hearts, then flipped a new card. "I told him you were helping to plan the party. Which he should know—shut up. I'm not feeding into your selfless nonsense. Plus, if this party blows up in our faces, I don't want to be the only one going down."

"Thanks?" I said. "But did he say those exact words—*I want Reyna to come to my party*? How did he sound when he said it?"

"Listen." Eliza dropped three more cards in rapid succession. "Just because I want to be okay with you and Aiden doesn't mean I'm completely there yet."

That was fair.

I noticed an opening for me to play one of my jacks, but Eliza laid down one of her own.

"Besides," she said. "I don't know how he sounded. It was a text."

I sighed. Well, that was more than I'd gotten out of Aiden. He never answered my message. Well, it was just a photo of the mural, no text. But there was very clearly a message implied. Did he not understand? I could see he'd received it. As we drew closer to his birthday, and the final day of the group's vacation, all hope dwindled.

That's why, when Eliza passed on his invitation, I'd been so surprised.

I dropped my nine of diamonds on top of the bigger pile. What if he only invited me as a thank-you for helping with the party?

It was silly, obviously. If Aiden didn't want me there, he wouldn't have said anything at all. But now I had this tiny doubt. "You shouldn't have told him I helped."

"If it makes you feel better, he told me you could invite some-one named Olivia as well."

No, that didn't make me feel better at all. It sounded like he just wanted a bigger party.

Eliza dropped her last cards and slapped the smaller pile. "Ha!" She scraped the cards toward her. "Come on, you need to be faster than that. Do you need me to explain the rules again?"

"No, I got it."

Something in my tone must have alerted her to my misery

because she looked up. "Oh, for crying—" She rolled her eyes. "Do you really need to be so melodramatic. Yes, he wants you there. Just look nice, show up, and stop overthinking it."

I nodded, gathering the rest of my cards. Then it hit me. "What am I going to wear?"

Eliza stared at me for a long moment. Then, without a word, she set her hand down, stood, walked over to the pool, and jumped in.

"Who's being melodramatic now?" I called out, but she didn't hear me. Her splash had caused Fish to open his eyes, alerting him to Leonardo and Hailee's deception. After that, there was no talking to any of them.

By the night of the party, I still hadn't totally made up my mind about what to wear. Actually, I wasn't too sure about going at all. I knew I needed to, though. Aiden and the others would be leaving tomorrow. If there'd be any reconciliation it had to be tonight. To make sure I didn't chicken out at the last moment, I invited Olivia over. Instead of offering advice or helping with my makeup like a good friend, she spent the evening eating all our snacks, lying on my bed, and calling me ridiculous.

She was so rude, and I was going to miss her so much when she left.

"You look fine." She tossed a cheese ball into the air and caught it in her mouth. "Not that it makes a difference. If that boy half as into you as he was back in the day, he won't care what you wearing."

Well, I hoped that wasn't entirely true. If possible, I'd prefer he be into me *and* the outfit I'd put a lot of thought into.

I ran my hands down the knee-length skirt of my sundress. With its thick straps and a deep neckline, I thought it looked mature without being too daring. Not to mention, the vermillion color reminded me of the mural. If he hadn't understood my message before, I hoped to really drive it in tonight.

"You sure it's not too much?" I asked.

"Not at all. If you had told me you just rolled out of bed and tossed it on, I'd believe you."

"What?"

I caught her dry look in the mirror. Oh. "So, we've reached the unnecessarily sarcastic part of the evening."

"Believe me, it's necessary." She tossed another cheese ball into her mouth. "At least when you vex at me, you stop doubting yourself for a few seconds."

A knock on the door startled us. Aunty Helen's head popped inside. "Hey, girls! Reyna, you look fantastic. That dress is killer."

"Thank you," I said, fighting the reflexive impulse to burn the entire outfit. "That's what I was going for." Since Daddy agreed to the sale of the hotel, and it became apparent Aunty Helen was sticking around for the time being, I'd been making an effort to be nicer. Not to mention I'd recently developed a soft spot for second-chance romances.

Aunty Helen smiled. "There's slushy in the freezer if you want. Your father and I are heading out for that dinner with the Benjamins. Wish your friend a happy birthday for us."

"I'll tell him," I said.

After she left, Olivia quietly asked, "She living here now?"

"I'm trying not to think about it." After a glance at the mirror, I snatched my eyeliner off the dressing table, the tube a little dusty from disuse. "Here. Help me with this."

Olivia recoiled. "Eh-eh. You know I have a thing about touching eyeballs."

I threw my hands up. "Why are you here? You don't have any advice on my clothes, can't help with my makeup. You're not even coming to the party for moral support."

"It's not my fault I have work tonight. I'm not even supposed to be here now. If Grace ever asks, you had car trouble and I had to pick you up."

"You're always working lately."

"Yes, and now you know how I felt all these years with you at the hotel."

I returned to the mirror. "That is different. You're leaving in a few weeks. After that, who knows when I'll see you again. And even with Skype, you definitely won't have time for me when your new life starts." Holding my breath, I carefully apply the eyeliner. It had been so long since I'd worn makeup like this, but the old tricks were coming back to me. The hairs on the back of my neck rose, and I grew conscious of a sudden tension in the room. A quick glance at Olivia's reflection confirmed she was glaring at me. "What?"

"Nothing." She slid to the edge of the bed. The empty bag of cheese balls crackled as she crushed it in her fist. "I'm just wondering if we're finally going to talk about it."

In the background, the front door of the house slammed shut. Daddy and Aunty had left.

"What?" I asked, but I knew exactly what she meant.

"London. I know you still mad at me for leaving. I wish you'd just tell me how you really feeling."

I lowered the liner, sure if I kept going while this conversation proceeded, I'd likely poke an eye out. "What's the point of that?" Couldn't she see I'd been trying to be supportive? Why give voice to my worst thoughts? Nothing good would come of saying them aloud. She'd hate me for having them, then I'd hate me even more.

"I don't know," she said. "Maybe you should let it out so I won't have to deal with this passive-aggressive crap for the rest of my life."

I turned to face her. "What do you want me to say? That I'm jealous? I'm mad that I'm not going? I'm mad you are going? That I hate seeing you happy when you're leaving me behind?"

"If that is how you feel."

I returned to the mirror and uncapped the eyeliner to try again. My hands shook too much, so I had to stop. Did she have to do this now? Or ever? Didn't I have enough to worry about tonight?

"Well, for the record, I'm mad at you," Olivia said. Her voice was so soft I nearly missed it. Then her words resonated. I must've heard her wrong.

"Me?"

"You're the one who abandoned our plans," she said.

"I was supposed to be working. You know that."

"Yeah, if only your father had fired you sooner."

"That's not fair."

"No, what's not fair is that *we* were supposed to go to London together. We were supposed to mash up the town, learning from some of the best instructors in the world. Instead, I'm heading to a whole new country, where I don't know anyone, on my own. And it's all because of you."

"That's not—"

"You disappointed me, Reyna."

I snapped my mouth shut so hard my teeth clicked.

"We could've had a great time, and it makes me so sad when I think about all the things we were supposed to do."

"I'm sorry—"

"No, don't. Stop apologizing. I'm trying to make a point here." Her dark eyes met mine in the mirror. Slowly, she got to her feet and stood beside me. "You made your choice. Even though I don't like it, it was yours to make. Maybe you'll end up in London next year. Maybe you won't. If there's one thing I know, it's that you're going to be fine, wherever you end up."

"Thanks," I said, moved by her confidence in me. "I'm sure you're going to be fine too."

"Well, I guess we're about to find out." Olivia exhaled loudly, and a hint of something like anxiety flashed across her face.

"I'm sorry," I said.

She threw me a dry look. "What did I just say about apologizing?"

"Not about that." I'd been so focused on my problems, riddled with angst over the fact that Olivia was leaving me, it didn't occur to me Olivia was leaving *everyone*. "I haven't been a very good friend lately."

Olivia smiled at me. "Never too late to make up for it."

I really hoped that was true. The long distance would make things more difficult, but that only meant I'd have to try harder. If she needed me, I wanted to be there for her, one way or another. "Well, there is a pack of cheese sticks in the pantry," I said. "Daddy's hiding it behind the cereal boxes."

"Now we're talking." Olivia's smile turned blinding. "This is why we're friends. You just get me."

THIRTY-FIVE

For the record, a blindfold wasn't part of the plan. And yet, Aiden arrived at the party wearing one. It was our fault for sending the guys to collect him.

Fish held on to Aiden's arm, guiding him, while Leonardo hovered beside them. For every few steps they took, they seemed to pause for some debate. It explained why we'd been waiting so long. Eliza and I should've sent Hailee to supervise.

"Can I take it off now?" Aiden asked as they drew closer to our setup. He wore a sheer white shirt with the top buttons loose. The thin fabric billowed like a sail in the wind. "I'm tired of bumping into things. I know we're on the beach."

"Damn." Leonardo looked behind Aiden's back to speak to Fish. "I told you he'd know. We should've used the noise-canceling headphones."

"So I could bump into more things?" Aiden's voice pitched higher with alarm.

"You wouldn't bump into anything if you'd listen to my instructions," Fish said. "Now walk a little to the left—"

"Right!" Leonardo corrected him too late.

Aiden's sneakers came down on a chunk of coral. It cracked and he startled, nearly tripping.

Fish caught him. "I meant my left!"

"We have the same left!" Aiden pushed away from him, reached up, and yanked the blindfold off. "That's enough. I'm . . ." He trailed off, eyes widening as he took us in.

Hailee paused, halfway through lighting the candles on the birthday cake. Eliza had been using her hands to block the wind from outing them. Darren, who'd arrived early, had taken to tending the bonfire on the sand. Then there was me, doing my best to blend into the darkness, hiding behind a table of food. Since I'd arrived, I'd arranged and rearranged the layout, in a hopeless attempt to combat my rising nerves.

We'd ordered a selection of Aiden's favorites—sweet buns, currant rolls, bites of fried plantain dusted with brown sugar, and of course, crab cakes—everything specially ordered from the Plumeria's kitchen. The one exception, the birthday cake, I'd bought at the grocery store. I thought the taste of this particular generic brand was *meh*, but I remembered he loved it.

"Surprise!" Eliza busted out with an overly exuberant tone. She dropped it instantly. "Damn it, guys. You had one job."

"You said to get him here." Fish pointed to Aiden. "We got him here. Job done."

From the look Eliza gave him, it was safe to say she didn't agree.

"I said nothing about trying to kill him on the way."

Hailee smiled and continued to light the candles, using her free hand to block the wind. Darren left the fire and went to Aiden, the pair performing their usual bro-hug-back-punch. The rest of the beach was empty apart from us, but we'd chosen a spot blocked from the sight of the road just in case.

While I listened to them and tried to work up the nerve to go over to Aiden, I was caught off guard by a sudden twinge of sadness. It was hitting me—they were leaving tomorrow. Not just Aiden, but Fish, Leonardo, Hailee, and Eliza too. Admittedly, while they'd been here, some mistakes may have been made. We'd had a couple bad arguments, and a heartbreak or two. I'd miss them anyway.

Hailee called out, "Reyna, get over here quick!" She'd gotten the nineteen candles all lit.

I slunk out of my spot behind the table, meeting Aiden's eyes just long enough to make my heart flip. I joined the others around the cake, our backs to the direction of the wind. Within the first line of singing "Happy Birthday," the wide disparity of singing talent became apparent, the boys outdoing us girls. Even Darren jumped in with a surprisingly nice baritone.

As I watched Aiden on the other side of the cake, his smiling face illuminated by the candles, hair ruffled after pulling off the blindfold, I remembered the handful of birthdays we'd spent together. Could this be the last one?

He blew out the candles, and we cheered. The second he straightened his back, he looked at me, and my heart didn't just flip—it broke into a full gymnastics routine. I needed to talk to him. The last thing I needed was more regrets when it came to him; those I already carried were too heavy.

Armed with my new resolve, I tried to get him alone. This proved to be more difficult than expected. For my first attempt, I waited until Darren left him to check on the fire, then walked right up to him.

"You came," he said. Or asked. I couldn't tell.

Was that surprise in his voice? In his expression? Did he not think I would come? Or did he not want me to? Why did he even invite me?

"Um." I'd been silent for too long. I started speaking without thinking. "Yes. I did. Olivia had to work. She wanted me to tell you happy birthday and sorry. Sorry she couldn't make it. Not sorry about your birthday."

Oh no. None of that was in the script. Why was making words so hard?

It was almost a relief when Pam and Jake interrupted.

"We're here!" Pam shouted, shuffling down one of the sand dunes, Jake and Kesha a few steps behind her. "Did it start? Did you already cut the cake?"

My second chance took a little more engineering. It was an hour later, after Jake and Pam had split to put Kesha to sleep. They'd basically shown up, eaten their fill, then run off with two huge plates of even more food. The rest of us were all sitting around the fire, letting the conversation come and go in waves, the silent stretches comfortable rather than intimidating.

"Aiden, man, you should've brought your guitar." Fish stretched his feet out. His toes wiggled in the air. "What's a bonfire without a guitar? That would've made it perfect."

Aiden groaned in response. "No, Fish. This isn't a campfire. This is a *beach lime*."

Darren swatted at something in front of his face. "Complete with the requisite mosquitoes."

Aiden shared a smile with his childhood friend. He sat with his legs crisscrossed on one of the blankets. He'd taken off his shoes, and from where I sat, two people between us, I could see the pale underside of his foot.

Eliza sat next to him on a folding chair. She'd retied the turquoise sarong she wore so it fit her like a tube dress. "Hey," she said to Aiden. "Did you finish that song? The one you were working on while here?"

Aiden's smile froze. "Yeah, I did. I finished it at Miss Bee's."

"You did!" She smacked him in the shoulder. "Congrats! When are we going to hear it?"

Aiden's eyes slid toward Leonardo and Fish, then dropped to the blanket. The chilly night grew a little colder, the silence no longer comfortable. "I'm not sure. It's not really DJB type of music. We might have to give it to another artist."

Fish shook his head. "Any music made by DJB is DJB music."

"You say that now, but you haven't heard it yet," Aiden said.

"Don't need to." Leonardo shifted forward. "You were right. We were being ungrateful. You're the one who wrote most of our hits. Flop or not, you deserve our support, because we wouldn't be here at all without you. If you want the song on the album, we trust you."

"Yeah." Fish lifted the bottle of beer in his hands. "We've got your back with the label. We know there's no DJB music without you, and they know there's no DJB without all of us. We're not a bunch of naive high school kids anymore. We have leverage now."

Aiden brought his own bottle to his lips, trying to hide the start of a smile. "I still think you should hear the song before you make any promises."

"Who says we haven't?" Fish asked.

Aiden lowered the bottle and watched him. "You—" He pointed a finger at Fish. "*Again?* Why do I even bother with a password?"

Fish shrugged. "It would save us time if you didn't."

While they bickered, I went to the food table to grab a currant roll. When I returned, Fish had launched into another of his fantastical stories—something about an ice cream van and crop circles—and I noticed there was space on the blanket next to Aiden. Fighting against a wave of nerves, I made a quick decision. Instead of retaking my chair next to Hailee, I took the spot next to him.

His shoulders stiffened when I sat. After a few seconds, he offered me a tentative smile. Talk about mixed messages. He'd invited me to the party, then barely talked to me. Since I'd arrived, he'd hardly looked in my direction. A week ago, he'd been ready to give us another chance. Had his feelings changed already?

My palms started to sweat. "So, um. Did you see the mural? It's in your room, so you probably did. I worked on it."

"I saw it." Aiden stared at his bottle of beer. "It looks good so far."

It looks good? That's it?

"And Fish showed me the sketch you did for him." Aiden picked at the label on the bottle. "It's stunning. You nailed him. Fish is talking about having it framed."

"Thank you." I watched his expression closely. Something about his tone sounded off. "I'm glad he likes it."

Aiden took a long pull from the bottle. The fire snapped and crackled in front of us. "You know . . ." He wiped his mouth with the back of his arm and set the empty bottle down on the blanket. "I meant what I said before. I'm glad you're working on your art again. You never should've stopped. Whatever inspired you to move on doesn't matter. I'm happy for you," he said, then softly added, "or I'll try to be."

Before I could even begin to untangle any of this, Aiden grabbed his bottle and then got to his feet. "Need another drink," he muttered before walking toward the cooler.

I watched his back with a growing sense of confusion. Did he want me here or not?

Enough was enough. I was just about to get up and follow him, when I realized Hailee had called my name. From the sound of it, she'd been trying to get my attention for a while.

"What?" I answered, a little harsher than necessary.

Hailee's eyes widened. "I asked when you planned to visit us."

"You'll have to stay with us, of course." Eliza winked at me.

"It'll be our turn to show you around. We will not go easy on you, so prepare yourself."

Fish snapped his fingers. "I'll need dates. As soon as you get them. I need to start planning. There's this club in West Hollywood I love that we've got to hit."

"I hope it's not Nightscape." Leonardo sipped from the bottle of ginger ale he and Hailee were sharing. "We're not allowed back there anymore."

Fish's lips twisted into a grimace. "I swear, accidentally spill a drink on a Kardashian one time and you get treated like an outcast. I apologized to Kylie. I don't see what the problem was."

"It was Khloé," Aiden returned. "And you called her Kylie. That was the problem." He frowned. "And why are you talking about clubbing? After the incident with the python that we'll never speak of, you aren't allowed into one for the foreseeable future. Unless it's for a gig."

"Hey! You're not my dad." Fish pouted. "Besides, where else am I supposed to meet someone? I've been depriving some lucky person from loving all of this—" He circled his face. "For far too long."

"Truly tragic," I said, smiling. Then, more seriously, I added, "I'm sure you'll find someone." Despite his carefree tone, I knew he meant it.

He gave me a warm smile. "See? Did you hear how fast she was on that? I want the rest of you to take notes. That's a real friend right there."

"That's not fair," Leonardo said. "I call you tragic all the time."

Fish gasped in offense, and I started laughing. I had to set my plate on my lap so I wouldn't spill anything. Once I sobered, I became very conscious of Aiden's attention on me. The wrinkle between his brow made a reappearance.

"What?" I asked.

His frown deepened. "But I thought you—"

"Reyna, answer the question!" Eliza demanded, causing me to jump. "Are you coming to visit us? I mean, it's not like you have anything else to do now that you're fired."

"I've been jobless for two minutes. Give me a chance."

Aiden twisted to fully face me, spilling some beer on the blanket. "You're not working at the hotel anymore?"

"Daddy is selling the Plumeria. It's not finalized yet, but for the time being, we agreed I'd stop working there."

"In other words, she got fired," Eliza said too cheerfully.

"That's rough," Darren said. "If you're looking for a job, let me know. I could try an' hook you up with somet'ing."

"Thanks," I said. "I might take you up on that."

"Wait—" Aiden seemed confused. I didn't realize he didn't know. The news of the sale had been such a monumental step in my life, I'd forgotten not everyone had caught up. "You're selling the hotel? What about your plans? Your . . ." He struggled to find words. "Everything?"

"Plans change."

"And it's that easy?"

"You know it's not," I said softly.

There would never come a day when I'd walk the grounds of

the Plumeria without the weight of guilt. But these last few days made me realize how lucky I was to have people who loved me and wanted me to be happy. I wouldn't let them down.

I wouldn't let myself down anymore.

"Well, I'm jealous," Eliza said, waving her can of grape soft drink. "You get a chance to start over. Figure out who you are, et cetera, et cetera. Do you know what you want to do yet?"

"I know I'd like to give painting another chance." I glanced at Aiden, relieved to see I had his full attention. If I was going to do this, he'd better be listening. "Maybe it's been too long. And maybe I won't be as good as I used to be, but I want to try. Because I missed it, even when it wasn't a part of my life. Now that I might have a second chance, I don't want to waste it."

THIRTY-SIX

Aiden disappeared from the party.

I couldn't believe it. The night had been winding down anyway, Fish blasting music from his phone, the sound carrying as far as it could in the open air. While I'd been helping Hailee bury her feet in the sand, I noticed Aiden walking toward the cars with Darren. I'd thought he was just seeing his old friend off. The next thing I knew, Leonardo announced that Aiden had called it a night.

"He sent me a text." Leonardo flashed the screen of his phone too quickly. "Said he loved the party, but he's exhausted. He'll make it up to us with breakfast in the morning."

"Better be waffles." Fish lowered the volume of the music.

Eliza pocketed her own phone. "Omelets."

Did they get texts from Aiden too? Why were they so okay with him ditching them?

"Why don't you head on home, Reyna," Hailee said. "We'll take care of cleaning up."

"Seriously?" They should've been angrier at Aiden for leaving the party. If it were me, I would've been livid. Hell, I was livid. He'd robbed me of the chance to talk to him.

"It's okay." Hailee squeezed my shoulder on her way to the food table. "It's his birthday. He gets to make special requests."

"To go to sleep early?"

Hailee laughed nervously. "Yes, he's very tired."

"What's going on?" I asked, certain I'd missed something.

"Just go home, Reyna," Hailee said gently. "Thank you for helping us out today. Come say goodbye to us in the morning?"

"Of course." Okay, there was definitely something up with her, but Aiden's rejection started setting in. Going home sounded like a good idea.

Aiden must've known what I'd wanted to say—what I'd been trying to say all night—and decided he didn't want to hear it. I hadn't been particularly subtle. In fact, I might've laid it on too thick. Maybe I'd scared him off. Regardless, I would have to confront him in the morning. This time I couldn't let him get on the plane before I said goodbye.

The drive back to Shell Haven took no time. The streets were quiet at one in the morning. I hoped Daddy waited up for me, but I doubted it. Sometimes he went to bed and forgot not to put the chains on the door. Since he never heard his phone while sleeping, there was always a chance he'd lock me out of the house. The last time it happened, I'd had to stay with Pam and Jake for the night.

It was only once I'd parked that I noticed Aiden.

He was sitting on my steps with a guitar, his presence revealed by the beams of my headlights. I turned off the ignition and stepped out of the car in a daze. I floated over to him, not entirely convinced this wasn't a dream.

"You took your time," he said.

"I didn't know you'd be here, did I?" Was this why his friends were acting so weird? I tried to sound irritated, but it all came out breathless. "Why are you here?"

"Come sit with me." He shifted the guitar onto his lap. "I wanted to play the finished song for you. See what you think."

I sat beside him and set my purse in my lap.

Aiden strummed the guitar, drew a breath, and began to sing.

Dragged to the coastline
Mouth full of sand, said I felt fine
Caught me singing 'bout love my whole life
Now I only want to have a good time

Then like the rush of a symphony
The water came in, crashed over me
Dragged me out to the sea
Had me begging, baby please

Pulled me out into the water so deep
Sharks circling beneath my feet

Been singing about love my whole life
Now I'm just trying to survive

Then like the rush of a symphony
The water came in, crashed over me
Dragged me out to the sea
Had me begging, baby please

Washed up on your shore like I did before
Should have expected you alone
I can't ignore, wanting you more,
Your heart a place I call home

Then like the rush of a symphony
The water came in, crashed over me
Dragged me out to the sea
Baby, baby, please
Life brought me back to you
Back to me

Silence filled the space where the music had penetrated the night. The thundering of my heart seemed far too loud. Sitting this close, he might've heard it.

"Well?" He set the guitar aside and faced me. "What you think?"

"Depends. Is it about me?"

He rolled his eyes. "Yes, it's about you." Quietly, he added,

"Most of the love songs are, even when I don't want them to be. I think that's why it got so hard to write sometimes."

"I'm sorry."

He tipped his head to the side. "You want me writing about someone else?"

"I'm not sorry."

He reached for a paper bag set on the step beside him. "Then there's this." He handed it to me. "In case the song doesn't work. My plan B."

"It's your birthday. You should be the one getting gifts." I took the bag from him but didn't open it. "The party was my present for you, by the way. Like you heard, I don't have a job anymore."

"Yes, I got that. Please open it."

I pulled out a pack of toffees. "You're not serious. You—" I flipped the box over, my jaw on the floor. "How? Where—?"

"Priority shipping. It was very expensive." His eyes kept skittering to and away from my face, like he couldn't bring himself to look, but he couldn't entirely look away. "I ordered them after the night of the rum punch party. After we talked in the gazebo, I realized what an asshole I was being. Everything you'd been through with your mom—I should've been there for you more. I should've been more understanding."

"No, you had to leave." I set the box on my lap. "I knew that, and I still acted like a fool. I'm sorry for trying to guilt you into staying, then blocking you. It was stupid."

"It was. But then, we were both young and stupid. We're still young and stupid. And God, Reyna, there's nothing I want more than to give us a second chance."

"You do?" My mouth ran ahead of my common sense. This was what I wanted, but I needed to know now rather than after I got my hopes up. "Are you sure? Even though you're all . . ." I waved my hands in his general direction. Because he continued to look confused, I clarified, "Famous, rich, hot."

Aiden let out a bark of laughter. "You think I'm hot?"

"My point is, you could date anyone now."

"Not *anyone*," he said. "Where's this coming from? Aren't you the same girl who straight-up told me she was better than me when we met?"

"She got hurt. A lot of it was self-inflicted, but still." After a second, I added, "And that's not what I said when we met."

"It's how I remember it."

I rolled my eyes and picked at the edge of the toffee box. "Why were you so distant tonight? I started to think you'd changed your mind about us."

"Ah." He pulled his knees closer. "You noticed that."

"It was hard not to. You hardly looked at me."

"Reyna, you're gorgeous on any given day. But when you dress up, you're on a whole other level. Tonight it was hard, looking at you, knowing you were into someone else."

"What?"

He grimaced. "I thought you were into Fish."

"Why? Did he say something?"

"No, but he didn't have to. I saw how close you two had gotten. And then you did that sketch of him." He looked so miserable; my heart twisted.

I reached for his hand. "Fish and I are friends."

"That's what he said. But that sketch . . . I know it was for your bet, but I could tell there was something more to it. There's a relationship between you two that I don't quite get. Besides, if drawing him inspired you to work on your art again, that had to mean something. If you truly had feelings for him, I was going to try to be okay with it. If he's what it took to make you happy . . ." He lifted his head. "But then you said all those things tonight . . ."

"So you caught that?" My lips hurt, I was smiling so hard. "Good. I was worried I'd been too subtle."

"Like a sack of bricks."

"Which is apparently what it takes to get through to you." I reached for him. "I continued the mural for you. As part of a romantic gesture. I was trying to show you that it wasn't pointless. You weren't pointless. I'd been afraid to be happy after Mummy died, because I thought it cheapened her life or my relationship with her. But I know none of that is true, and I don't want to be afraid anymore. I don't want to be stuck anymore. I want to move."

His brows inched toward his hairline. "The mural was supposed to say all that?"

"Obviously."

"Maybe leave the romantic gestures to me in the future."

"Well, I'd say no. But since that song, I've been waiting for you to kiss me—"

He kissed me. The angle felt awkward until he cupped my cheek, drawing me closer. Every nerve sparked; every cell of my body flickered to life. I melted into him, my hands clutching his shoulders, his arms. My mind swam, drunk on his taste, his warmth, his smell. Familiar and new, easy and exciting.

The lights of the porch flickered on and off. We pulled apart, laughing. I spotted a shadow moving behind the curtains. Daddy must've been watching.

Mortified, I buried my face against Aiden's shoulder. "I am so sorry."

Aiden laughed. "It was my idea to do this here." He tucked my hair behind my ear, his touch lingering against my cheek before settling on my back. For a long time, we just held each other. When the lights started to flicker again, he asked, "I should go?"

"In a minute."

"I'm sorry I have to leave tomorrow," he said.

"I know. It's okay."

He'd be back. Or I'd go to him. We'd figure out how to make it work.

With one arm around his neck, I rested the other against his chest. I marveled at the rise and fall of his breaths, and the beat of his heart beneath my palm. I felt no lingering questions of tabanca, only the beat of a heart that was as much mine as mine was his.

EPILOGUE

ONE YEAR LATER

Pam told me that working with kids would be rewarding. So far I'd been rewarded with two tops and one skirt I could no longer wear, each one ruined by paint, marker, and glitter respectively. Not to mention the total destruction of a pair of Converse that led me to avoid using superglue for any further projects.

"Miss Reyna!" Five-year-old Kriss ran over to me, waving a paper over his head.

I failed to stop him before he grabbed onto my shirt to get my attention. Of the thirty-three children who attended the after-school program, he was one of the youngest. Even though we were meant to rotate the participants in smaller groups, each child attending a different activity every afternoon, Kriss tried to sneak into my group when he'd been assigned to another. I let him stay more often than not. Even at his age, I recognized in him the need for making art.

I only wished he'd remember to wash his hands after using the paints. Since my last session with the children was over, I'd changed into a fresh set of clothing for an important meeting. Now I'd have to go with a small cobalt-blue handprint on the back of my shirt. At least this one was watercolor and should wash out.

Kriss held the paper out. "This is for you!"

"For me?" I smiled and took the painting from him. "Oh? Is this me?" I asked, the red hair on the painted woman a dead giveaway. About a month ago, I'd gotten my hair braided, weaving in cherry-red extensions.

"Do I get to keep this?" I asked Kriss. I would add it to the massive binder I'd almost filled already. The children usually took their arts and crafts home to their parents, but sometimes they made something for me.

Kriss nodded, his body twisting back and forth. "Do you have to go?"

My heart squeezed. I'd only volunteered to pass the time. Who knew I'd get so attached to my little artists? "Yes, but I'll come and visit when I'm back."

"I hope so." Nicholas entered the workroom. He wore sports clothes, a little sweaty after playing cricket with his group that afternoon. With his full beard, he was almost unrecognizable from the guy who'd given me his card at Grace's a year ago. "Your mother's outside, Kriss," he said. "Wash your hands first before you go and meet her."

"Okay!" He gave me a hug. More cobalt blue on my jeans. "Bye, Miss Reyna."

Oh jeez. My heart squeezed again. I was actually going to miss these kids.

For the first few weeks after the sale of the hotel, I'd hung around the Plumeria to help Aunty Helen learn the ropes. But once she'd settled in, I'd had more time to volunteer and study for the SATs. After killing the exam, I'd applied and then got accepted into NYU.

Neither Olivia nor Aiden was particularly happy with my decision. Olivia wanted me in London, Aiden in California, so I'd picked somewhere in the middle. No, really, I picked it because I wanted to go there. Neither my best friend nor my boyfriend liked it, but they'd both pushed for a less-selfless Reyna, and this was her decision.

"When's your flight?" Nicholas asked.

"Tomorrow night." Eight hours long. "It's actually my first international flight." Luckily, I'd gotten an escort to accompany me.

"Well, stay safe and keep in touch."

I hugged him. "Thanks for everything."

"Thank you for joining us." He patted my back. "And thank your boyfriend for the donation."

I pulled back, laughing. "Another one?"

Nicholas shrugged as we walked out of the Community Center. "I'm not complaining."

Speaking of the boyfriend. I checked my phone and noticed a

missed message. Sent ten minutes earlier.

They told me they wanted a love song

All I could think about was you

I messaged back, I don't see a problem. His reply came instantly, like he'd been waiting.

Your heart in the beat of the drums

The rhythm of your breath in the tune

I bit back a smile, climbing into the car. As I drove to the Plumeria, I ignored my phone when it chimed again. Only after I'd parked, I checked it. No lyrics this time; only a picture of a familiar view from the western end of the main lawn.

In the lobby, I passed Aunty Helen and Pearl, who were stepping out of Aunty's office.

"Don't worry," I said as I passed them. "I'm not here to check up on the hotel. Just visiting a guest."

Aunty Helen shook her head. "I thought you might be. Invite him to join us for dinner tonight."

"I'll ask him!"

"Reyna, love." Pearl's voice made me pause. "Stop by my office before you go. I packed up some tea and sweets for you to take with you. You might find jub jubs in New York, but they won't be good like mine."

"Thank you!" I jogged back to give her a kiss on her cheek. "I'll pass by later. There's a young man waiting for me in the gazebo."

"Lucky you." She waved me off. "Go on then."

As I hurried around the pool and down the steps to the main lawn, I got another message.

Sing this line and split time

We fixed the bridge after the break

And there he was. Sitting in the corner of the gazebo, mouthing words and strumming a guitar, like he'd never left. As I approached, he looked up. A notepad and his phone rested on the bench next to him.

"Sitting alone?" I asked. "I certainly hope you're a guest of the hotel, sir. Or this might be a little creepy."

"You calling me creepy?" His brows rose. "Seems like a weird way to say hello to a stranger."

I approached him slowly, not stopping until I stood right over him. "Good thing you're not a stranger then."

He tipped his head back. "Lucky me."

For a few seconds, I stayed there, staring into his eyes, drinking him in. He looked good with a little stubble on his cheeks. And he'd cut his hair again, taking more off the sides. I wanted to run my fingertips through it, but I resisted. Aiden didn't move either, the both of us locked in an unspoken contest to see who could hold out longest. We let the moment grow taut, the thread that connected us humming with life and promise. I gave in first, lowering my lips. His quirked in victory just before we melted.

We kissed for a few seconds, only stoking the fire. I didn't let it generate enough heat to satisfy after months of separation, pulling away before he could deepen it. He made a noise of disappointment when I slipped out of his reach. But we had time now. I wanted to savor every second of it.

DJB had successfully convinced their label to let them record their third album in New York. We could have three months. Maybe even longer.

I hopped onto the bench next to him, leaning my back against one of the posts, making myself comfortable. "Go on," I told him. "I want to hear the rest of it."

Aiden, who knew I wouldn't budge until he agreed, started playing his next hit.

Like candy to my ear
You're the only song I want to hear
My first love, our second bloom

SOCA PLAYLIST

Soca music was created in Trinidad and Tobago in the 1970s, and was meant to capture the SOul of CAlypso—music that is joyful and uplifting—everything I wanted this book to be. Making a soca playlist for it was a must. A few of these songs are referenced in the pages, while others are just here to get the vibes right!

A quick warning for the uninitiated: listening to soca music inevitably leads to energetic dancing. Before we start, please take stock of your surroundings to prevent damages to yourself, your property, or the people around you.

"Differentology" by Bunji Garlin
We're starting off with a hype song. I can easily picture Reyna listening to this while getting ready for work. *Yeah, we ready, ready . . .*

"Hot-Hot-Hot" by Arrow
Throwback! Of all the soca songs on this list, this is probably the best known worldwide. It's one of Reyna's mother's favorites.

"Iron Love" by Nailah Blackman
Fun fact: Nailah is the granddaughter of Ras Shorty I, who created soca music in the 1970s. He did it by combining traditional calypso (which was Afro-Caribbean centric) with Indian rhythm instruments, thus merging the sounds of the two largest ethnic groups of Trinidad and Tobago. Nailah, an innovative artist in her own right, does a lot of genre mixing, incorporating dancehall and electro house in her soca music. This song is all about love for the steelpan, the national instrument of T&T. I imagine she's just the type of artist Aiden and DJ Bacchanal would love to collaborate with.

"Dear Promoter" by Voice & Kes
This pick is for the vibes. It also happens to be the most recent soca hit on this list.

"All Aboard" by Atlantik

I saw a comment on YouTube that said something like, *If you're at a Caribbean event and you don't hear this song, are you really at a Caribbean event?* It's so true. Every time Reyna and company are at a restaurant or bar, you can be sure this song has played in the background at least once.

"One More Time" by Machel Montano
More vibes!

"All My Love" [Remix] by Major Lazer (feat. Ariana Grande and Machel Montano)

I love this collaboration. A lot of DJ Bacchanal's music would sound something like this—a blend of EDM, dancehall, and soca.

"Savannah Grass" by Kes

A fantastic song. It's uplifting and joyful, with just the right amount of nostalgia mixed in. It perfectly captures the feeling I want readers to leave this book with. Plus, it's just a great song, period.

ACKNOWLEDGMENTS

The fact that I'm writing acknowledgments for my debut novel is mind-blowing. I would never have gotten to this point without the help of many wonderful people.

To my agent, Wendi Gu, who's been my guide through this mad world of publishing. Thank you for taking a chance on my voice. Your support has meant the world to me.

To my editor, Donna Bray, who understood the emotional core of the book right away. I'll be forever grateful for your brilliance and insights into the story. And for the fact that we both love *Persuasion*.

A huge thank-you to everyone at Balzer + Bray and Harper-Collins who worked on the book: Jessie Gang, Alison Donalty, Shona McCarthy, Jill Amack, Sabrina Abballe, Shannon Cox, Patty Rosati, Mitchell Thorpe, Tiara Kittrell, Alessandra Balzer, and my cover artist, Kingsley Nebechi. Thank you for bringing this book to life and getting it into the hands of readers. I couldn't have asked for a better team.

To my foreign rights agent, Stefanie Diaz. Thank you for your support and unwavering confidence in this book.

To my mentors, Lizzy Dent and Michelle Hazen, and my critique partners, Rebecca, Akuila, Iasmina, and Laura. Your wisdom and feedback not only made me a better writer but also gave me the courage to keep going.

To the Pitch Wars class of 2017 and the 21ders debut group. My writing journey has not been easy, but it's been a million times better with all of you in it.

To Brenda Drake and the organizers of the Pitch Wars competition, who work tirelessly and have helped so many—including me—make their dreams come true.

To Miss Boochoon, who showed me a new way to look at classics. Your confidence in my writing has meant more than I can say.

And, finally, to my family. My mom, grandmother, sisters, and brother. My uncles, aunts, and cousins. I'm not going to list out names because I don't want my second novel to be this acknowledgments section. I'm beyond grateful to have all of you in my life.

Thank you, thank you, thank you.